I0671022

LOST YEARS

EMMA GORDON

THE OLD BOOKSTORE PUBLISHING COMPANY

THE OLD BOOKSTORE PUBLISHING COMPANY
Published by The Old Bookstore

The Old Bookstore

No part of this publication may be reproduced, stored in a retrieval system, or transmitted in any form or by any means, electronic, mechanical, photocopying, recording, scanning, or otherwise except as permitted under Section 107 or 108 of the 1976 United States Copyright Act, without written permission from the author.

Limit of Liability/Disclaimer Warranty: While the publisher and author have used their best efforts in preparing this book, they make no representations or warranties with respect to the accuracy or completeness of the contents of this book.

The Library of Congress Cataloging-in-Publication Data

Gordon, Emma.
Lost Years / Emma Gordon.
ISBN: 0692584382
ISBN-13: 978-0692584385

1. Women_Naples_Fiction 2. Time-shift_Fiction 3. Golf_Olympics_Fiction
4. Purpose_Love_Fiction 5. Rio de Janeiro_Fiction

Library of Congress Control Number: 2015920164
The Old Bookstore, Naples, FL

This is a work of fiction. Names, characters, places and incidences either are the product of the author's imagination or are used fictitiously. Any resemblance to actual persons (living or dead), businesses, companies, events or locations is entirely coincidental.

Copyright © 2015 Emma Gordon
All rights reserved.
ISBN: 0692584382
ISBN-13: 978-0692584385
Library of Congress Control Number: 2015920164
The Old Bookstore, Naples, FL

For Curley Marie

To God all things are fair, good and just, but men suppose some things are unjust, some just.

Heraclitus

PROLOGUE

The Bahamas – Third Sunday, January 2015

He sipped his morning coffee on the terrace while he watched her taking her early morning stroll over the golf course. He loved her. Would she ever know how much?

Ivy's form blended into the color of the waving fog, carried over from the calm tropical sea as the first sun rays glittered on the freshly cut dew-covered grass.

In only a few hours, the luxury ocean resort would become the main attraction for golf lovers around the world as the LPGA celebrated the first winner of the season. And Ivy was determined to stand on this podium, starting off as strong as she had finished last year.

Last year, she had won the Rolex Player of the Year award and the money list title. It was only her first year on the tour. She was a rookie who had won it all. The headlines were bursting with hope and encouragement for her to go for the triple crown this year.

Jason Briggs, Jr., knew only too well how intriguing and fascinating the world of golf could be. His gaze followed Ivy's silhouette, which vanished in the distance. This year, the Vare Trophy for the lowest score was her primary focus—he knew that.

His own professional career hadn't taken him that far, but still he'd made it to the Hall of Fame before he opened his own golf academy. Tonight, he would ask her to marry him. His hand unconsciously reached to touch the jewelry box in his pocket.

He didn't know he wouldn't live to see the sun go down.

Soon, the terrace was filled with vibrant bustling activity as more golfers, sponsors, the press and lots of spectators arrived. The sun was slowly warming the chilly January morning, and everybody bustled to get whatever they needed to fuel their bodies before the final round started.

Nobody could have known what would happen in only a few hours to bring horror upon their elite world of bliss.

Nobody could have known.

A man sat with his daughter at a table in the shade, too irritated to enjoy his breakfast that morning. He too had watched Ivy walking the golf course, examining the slopes, studying the grass, and preparing for her fist big win.

That will never happen, he thought with a wicked smile and brought his attention back to his daughter, Julie. He was proud of her—she had given everything in her bones, muscles and mind to come so far in ladies professional golf, and he had been by her side.

But to what expense? He'd lost everything, including his wife, to the goal of winning. But for him, it was well worth it. At least it was, until last year, when all of a sudden Ivy Brooks emerged as a supernatural golf talent and shattered all his high hopes for Julie.

But all this was about to change. Henrik Ferguson had everything meticulously worked out.

ONE

Rio de Janeiro, Brazil – Sunday after Thanksgiving, 2015

After taking a final look at the note, Julie quickly stored it away in her dresser drawer. Marilyn was already knocking on the door.

It was time to leave. Yes, she was expected downstairs in the ballroom of the Grand Palace Hotel where this season's closing gala was in full swing.

Tonight was her night. Julie Ferguson, the superstar—the number-one world champion in ladies professional golf. This was a role she learned to play almost as well as golf itself over the last couple of years.

She held her back in pain as she carefully got up from her 18th century Louis XVI-style chair. Everything has its price, she thought. After a hard ten months on the tour, it was no wonder that she felt a little pain here and there. It will pass soon, she told herself with a sigh.

The penthouse suite was truly amazing, mirroring French

Versailles-style décor with a marble bath and private rooftop pool. The view of Rio and the bay was the best. From her terrace, she could see the Olympic stadium, the beach, the famous Sugarloaf Mountain and the majestic statue of Christ the Redeemer.

One day, she would take time to visit at least some of those major attractions. One day, she would live a normal life with a loving, supporting husband, beautiful well-cared-for children and a happy beloved dog. They would all run along the beach, laughing joyfully . . .

The knock came again, stronger, and a voice demanded, "Julie, are you ready?"

"Marilyn, I'm almost done. Wait, I'll get the door." Julie opened the door and Marilyn Wood, her guardian angel, coach, personal trainer and, most importantly, her dearest friend walked in, turned and inspected her closely.

"Julie, your hair looks sensational! I'd say money well spent to have Sergio personally do the styling. But you're kinda looking a little pasty here—why so glum on this beautiful night?"

"Thank you very much for the confidence booster! Marilyn, please . . ."

"No problem, darling, you're very welcome! Come on, sit down. Let me fix your makeup, and then we're gonna carefully maneuver your luxury body into this stunning evening gown. It's all silk, and I really love the deep V-shaped back and the pleats around the neckline. It's absolutely fantastic!"

"Won't I be a bit overdressed?"

"No way! It's very stylish, elegant and . . . hmm, well, kinda sexy. And you were right, this warm vanilla white is truly your color. Believe me, little princess, you'll look drop-dead gorgeous.

Let's get going!"

Marilyn went into the bathroom to grab the supplies she needed to transform a still childish-looking super athlete into a shining evening star. Once a professional golfer herself, she knew all about the magic spells to make a woman look like a joyful champion after a tortuous season.

Stepping into the superb gown, Julie looked into the antique dresser mirror. Marilyn was right. Her long golden-blonde curled hair was very hard to manage on the tour, but today, it looked absolutely gorgeous. Strands were parted to one side and blended slowly down into beautifully textured waves.

And with a more ladylike makeup application, she would once again belong to the elite world of glamor and stardom. Not sure how much longer, though, she thought, as she once again felt the stabbing pain in her lower back when she slipped into her rhinestone peep-toe heels.

"Wow, look at you, darling!" Marilyn came back carrying powders, blushes and eyeliners.

"Hey, the dress is super cool! I feel like I'm going to the prom I've never had."

"Julie, stop brooding. You're a rockstar, and you've earned all of it. You've worked the season with inhuman discipline, focus and perseverance. Now it's time to get rewarded with a big check and a nice diamond sparkled Rolex."

Marilyn made a sweet smile and winked at her. "Take all you can get, darling. Remember, get rich first and old later!" As the two burst into laughter, Marilyn struggled to apply eyeliner and mascara smoothly to Julie's face.

She was so proud of her princess. Over the last three years,

Julie had held the player of the year position of the LPGA tour twice and made the money list. And this year, she made it again. However, last year, Ivy Brooks, the youngster on the tour, surprisingly finished number one before Julie.

This year, at the season-opening event, Ivy had fallen victim to a tragic event. During the second round, she had finished a sensational hole-in-one, and as she walked to the next tee, a madman suddenly emerged from the crowd and hit her with a knife in the back. Then, in a second swing, he struck down her boyfriend, who had jumped between the two. He had paid with his life. The brutal attack was witnessed by hundreds of shocked spectators from the open-air suite overlooking the 18th green and was captured live on the Golf Channel.

Marilyn carefully wiped away some mascara residue that had fallen onto Julie's cheeks.

"By the way," she said, "Ivy may be there tonight. I saw her on the list."

She took a final look at Julie's beautiful face.

"Ivy? Are you sure?"

"Yes, darling."

"How is she? Do you know anything?" Suddenly, Julie was wide awake. What a horrible tragedy it had been to bring herself back to number one. Otherwise, that would have been out of reach, since Ivy truly was a supernatural talent.

"I've heard she finished physical therapy and works with a psychologist. However, she's not been seen on the course yet. So don't you worry. Now hurry up, we're getting late. Everybody is waiting for you to take your seat. They won't start the ceremony without you, darling."

"Am I done?"

"Absolutely! You're looking fabulous!" Marilyn was proud of herself. Julie was a completely different person. She looked so young and beautiful, ready to conquer the world.

"I just wish your mother could see you like this. She would be very proud of you, darling. And of course, your dad."

Marilyn packed up the cosmetics and pushed Julie toward the door. "C'mon, darling, take your clutch and give me your biggest smile!"

"Marilyn, I *am* smiling! I always do—for you and the press."

Julie moved enthusiastically and with almost no pain this time. She was truly grateful to have such an unselfish guardian angel who was completely devoted to her, and she confidently followed Marilyn down to the great ballroom.

Now, she was eager to get into the world. Deep inside, she was very proud of her achievements and looked forward to the awards ceremony. If only Mom could be here now, she thought.

Julie's mind suddenly went back to the note.

What did it say? *Your father will be here tonight.*

TWO

Naples, Florida – Sunday before Thanksgiving, 2005

H on, do you want me to put the steaks on, or should I wait? It's so beautiful outside. I love that clear blue sky. It's been awhile since we've last seen it."

Laura opened the terrace doors of their ocean estate. "Jim, could you please wait another thirty minutes? I think I'll go for a quick run first. And tonight, we'll see a magnificent sunset over the ocean—maybe even with some dolphins flipping in the air!"

"Okay then, have fun!" James Winchester finished marinating the two oversized New York Strips and placed them carefully onto an ornate silver tray. He looked up, but Laura was already out the door.

"See, Curley, your mom loves the beach as much as you do. And after eight months in the middle of nowhere, she's now crazy about the ocean. Let her go, she'll be back soon. And see, we've got all kinds of goodies here, don't we?" With the barbecue tongs he tapped on the tray and smiled across at Curley Marie, their

Golden Retriever lady. She was not sure why Laura had left without her. She figured she'd better stay close to the lanai door so as not to miss her return.

The Winchesters had arrived earlier in the morning at the Royal Palm Plantation Country Club, an upscale private ocean-front community in Naples, Florida. For the past seven years, they had spent the holiday season in their vacation home on the Gulf of Mexico. And every year, James looked forward to this special time.

It was time filled with rounds of golf during the pleasant tropical winter, partying at the club with his buddies who saw each other only for a few months, and long afternoon walks with Laura and Curley on the beach.

They loved watching the sunsets over the crystal blue ocean, sometimes with a green flash, and closing the day with a delicious meal catered in from one of the finest restaurants in the country. Instantaneously, he felt young again, almost like back in the days when he was a little boy out in the fields without a care in the world.

He put the silver tray with the steaks next to the outdoor gas grill and covered them with cheesecloth. Every move was closely traced by two hungry Retriever eyes.

Most of their neighbors were snowbirds and came down only during the winter months. That was not much different from the Roaring Twenties, as it occurred to him, a time when a person's wealth and success was mainly measured by what he possessed.

It was during those times that Barron Collier invested millions of dollars to develop Naples as a winter resort and created what today is called the Florida Lifestyle. Along with it came the booms and busts of real estate—in 1926, right at the peak of Florida's land boom, a devastating hurricane blew across the southern tip of the peninsula and was the harbinger of the Great Depression.

James went back to his master suite to finish unpacking. He nodded his head as he remembered that he too almost lost the shirt off his back in the dotcom bubble burst.

Fortunately, now, he and Laura were financially back on track and well secured. They owned one of the largest ranches in the United States, and Laura was doing extremely well with her hedge fund. She was quite right to have reinvested immediately when the stock market hit bottom and showed the first signs of recovery back in March 2003.

James loved their beautiful Naples home. The architectural style was Spanish Mediterranean throughout. It was constructed with every conceivable upgrade of design, luxury materials and the latest technology gadgets.

A smart home touch screen interface controlled all electric essentials, like in- and outdoor lights, multimedia and alarm systems, pool and spa area lighting, window treatments, shutters, heating and gas fireplaces.

He completed a quick walk-through and took delight in seeing that the caretaker had done an excellent job getting the house ready for the winter season.

He went to the garage to check on the cars and his beloved motorbike collection—he hadn't had the chance to do so since they had arrived by plane from Montana. It had been so convenient that the homeowners association opened the private airstrip last year. Now they could fly in on the Cessna. This added another level of convenience for planning short trips to Key West,

Cancun or The Bahamas.

James pushed the door handle, but the door to the garage was locked. He couldn't find the remote, so he decided to check back in the morning. It was already getting late, and he was getting seriously hungry. He checked his watch. Laura should be back any minute now.

Laura ran on the beach against the backdrop of a spectacular sundown. The glorious red fireball slipped softly into the dark-blue horizon and merged so gently with its reflection that it almost became one with the Gulf of Mexico.

Laura unzipped her hoodie and quickly took out her iPhone. This was the perfect shot! She would email the picture to her mom back home in snow-covered Montana.

Laura wished she could have convinced her mom to join them on their trip to Naples, but her mother had a mind of her own and would rather die than ever leave the ranch.

The ranch held a special place in Laura's heart also. It was her home, her roots, and she felt even more so since she had started professional horse breeding herself. Her parents always had horses on the ranch—working horses and ponies, sure—but recently, she had completely fallen in love with Thoroughbreds.

It started out as a hobby to get her mind off the financial markets. Being a very successful proprietary trader, she managed a huge hedge fund with big returns for more than twelve years.

She would never give that up. Looking over the ocean and daydreaming, Laura reflected on it all. A couple of years back, she had been called out to help deliver a foal one night. Unfortunately, the mare had been sick, and she died during delivery.

Under the circumstances, it was a tough battle to bring out the foal alive. Laura was hooked from the moment she met eyes with that little fellow. That look! Within a second she knew she wanted to start breeding herself.

Then, this August, in Saratoga Springs, she sold *Pieces of Eight*, a yearling, for over $120,000. Her best sale ever. Emotionally, it was very tough to let go of this Bay Filly she had watched grow up into an amazing long-legged high-potential racehorse.

Up to this point, Laura and James had bred horses and sold them as yearlings. However, for quite some time, Laura played with the idea of adding to their current training facilities and converting a certain area of the ranch to a more professional race track.

James wasn't so thrilled about it. He didn't say as much, but she knew.

Laura waited for the perfect moment to take the shot. The sky was so smooth right after the sunset, and then, all of a sudden, it came to life with the most amazing colors. Laura took a couple of shots and sent them off to her mom. She felt really good about being back in the sun for a relaxing holiday season.

Meanwhile, it was getting dark, and she felt really hungry —and James' home cooking was more than delicious.

Laura quickly stored her phone away and made a mental note to send her mother a more detailed email later with new pictures of the house and of James and Curley.

She watched the moon rise over the bay and decided to take

the next boardwalk, which would lead back to the community walking trail. Royal Palm Plantation was a private oceanfront community with only about one hundred estate homes spread around fresh-water lagoons, manicured golf courses and salt-water estuaries. It was nestled between the Gordon River and the Gulf of Mexico.

On her way home, Laura came close to the new airstrip as she felt unusually cool air coming in from the ocean. It looked as if the sea breeze had collided with the warmer inland air and was creating a weather front.

A thunderstorm? This time of year? That was rather unusual. Officially, they were still in hurricane season until late November, but it was rare that a storm approached the Gulf that late. Perhaps just a short rain shower, Laura reasoned and decided to take a shortcut across the golf course. Safe enough, since nobody would play this late in the day.

She was halfway across the green as a tremendous rumble of thunder shook the air. Surprisingly, the front had come much closer and formed a humongous dark cloud.

She increased her speed to a jog and took the direct route toward their home, across the greens and fairways. She hoped nobody would recognize her, since this was a little against the etiquette. But getting soaked was certainly not on her to-do list for tonight either.

She kept running along a meandering sand bunker, when all of a sudden, the gigantic cloud broke open right above her and a furious fire bolt struck down to the earth. Zap! A blinding red and yellow zigzag arrowed through the dark night sky, and an immense static discharge forced her down.

Laura screamed when she fell to her knees, rolled into a ball and instinctively covered her head with her arms. She experienced an intense bright light all around her. The air was electrified by a tremendous unseen power. And then, another deep, growling surge of thunder.

"Oh my God! What was that?" she cried. She shivered throughout her whole body. She was cold, dizzy. She had no memory of how she had gotten down there. A panic attack?

Still holding her hands over her forehead, she found herself unable to move. She couldn't see or hear anything but felt that she was heavily shaking. She had never been so afraid in her whole life.

Seconds later, the rain broke—cold as ice and very heavy.

James looked at his watch for the third time, and his concern grew to worry. Curley was anxious as well, he could tell. It was eerily dark now, and towering clouds were forming over the ocean.

Cumulonimbus clouds formed that were likely to bring thunder, rain and lightening. Being a pilot, James was familiar with the so-called Cbs because they can cause severe turbulence and other safety hazards.

A short while ago, he had watched the beautiful sunset from the main terrace. In the distance, he thought he had even spotted Laura taking some pictures.

But she should have been back by now.

The storm was approaching fast. He saw lightning bolts

striking through the polarized atmosphere, followed by deep, growling thunder. James closed the terrace doors and turned on the lights.

Darkness settled in quickly after the sunset. He was nervous and a little annoyed, since he would have loved to grill and eat outside on their first night back in paradise.

Checking his watch again, he grabbed his coat and said, "Curley, I'm going to pick up mom, all right. Why don't you join me?" He snipped slightly with his fingers and Curley was up and beside him in no time.

James walked down the hallway towards the garage. Curley heeled right behind him. In the mudroom he took the short leather leash and opened the key storage box. He took out the keys for the garage and to the Cayenne, opened the door, and stood for a moment in awe.

Forgotten were the lightning, thunder and rain, and his eyes lit up when he saw that all of the cars and bikes had been detailed to the finest. They literally sparkled at him, clean and shiny. So did the workbenches, shelves and electronic equipment. He was not disappointed.

The Cayenne was parked closest to the garage door. He opened the back for Curley and told her, "Okay, hop in!" He got behind the wheel and switched on the indoor lights so Laura would be able to see it was him inside the black SUV. The garage door rolled open, and he backed slowly out into the driveway.

James had just handled the *Tiptronic* as a lightning bolt hit the car straight down. Out of reflex he stepped on the brake and curled up to protect himself from the strike. Curley started barking.

That was close, he thought. As a pilot, James was pretty much relaxed with the weather conditions, but this was hefty and had come totally unexpected. He looked in the backseat to calm the Golden Retriever.

"Curley, are you all right? It's okay now, we're fine!"

He reached over, softly touched her head and scratched her left ear.

"It's okay, baby, we're save in the car—and dry!" He could hear balls of ice drumming onto the metal roof of the Cayenne.

"Let's go and pick up Laura now!" James headed down the driveway onto the main community street as the storm really let loose.

The tropical storm poured down in layers of an impenetrable wall. Laura was about ten minutes away from home. She'd left the golf course and took shelter in a breezeway between the garage and guest house of a vacant home nearby.

All was dark. The rain was drawn around her like a curtain, and small hailstones hopped on the small rooftop.

She felt a little chilly and damp. She had decided it was better to wait for James to pick her up than to run home on a flooded road in a torrential downpour.

She'd already texted James the address and was sitting on the edge of a huge flowerpot filled with red geraniums, blue lobelias and a nice palm tree in the middle. From there, Laura had a good view overlooking the community road, and she waited for James to approach.

Although he hadn't answered her text yet, she was sure he was already on his way. This was a routine, back home and here—especially here, in this tropical climate where sudden showers were not uncommon. She loved going for a run, and he loved being her hero once in a while.

Soon, they would be sitting comfortably in their loveseats beside the pool. A roaring fireplace would keep her warm while they enjoyed perfectly grilled steaks and a bouquet-rich red wine.

Her mind continued wandering—she was looking forward to meeting her friends, to re-joining them for amusing rounds of golf, and of course shopping at The Village or taking the boat out for a dolphin watch cruise or a pirates treasure hunt in the Ten Thousand Islands. She smiled. Life was good. But it hadn't always been that way.

Her mother, a born Hallbrook, solely owned and managed Hallbrook ranch after her father had died, and her sister had moved to New York to fulfill her dream of becoming a famous criminal defense lawyer.

The ranch, back then mostly cattle, determined her childhood completely. She remembered a few happy moments, but the hard times when money was tight dominated her memory.

They were always pinching pennies and cutting corners. She hardly ever had anything of plenty throughout her teenage years. One good year was followed by half a decade of bad years.

The yields from better years could not be properly invested in long-term growth. Instead, the money was used to catch up on overdue repairs and deficiencies, and the rest was saved at low interest rates. It was scared money.

It wasn't her mother's fault. Laura knew that. Her dad was

diagnosed with a severe form of diabetes type one in his early thirties and couldn't do farm labor anymore. He was bound to his bed and passed away only five years later. His death was sudden and unexpected, a shock for all of them.

At the time, Laura was nineteen and had started Harvard Medical School on a full scholarship.

Eventually, she had to quit Harvard and return home to support her mother full time. Her beloved father was gone, and her dream of becoming a doctor—a neurosurgeon—was shattered. So was she—something in her had died after that. Laura didn't like to be reminded of that time.

She checked her watch—ten minutes since she texted James. She checked her iPhone—no message. A little unusual, but perhaps he had the steaks on the grill and needed to take care of them before picking her up.

Laura laughed and her mind wandered back to her early twenties.

That's when she met James Winchester. James' family owned Holly Grain, one of the largest ranches in the United States, and it bordered to the south of Hallbrook ranch. They were much more diversified with a mix of cattle and grains like corn and soybeans.

As junior farm manager, James traded commodities to hedge against lower market prices. To her that seemed very sophisticated. They first met at one of their famous barbecues, and shortly after, they fell in love—and got married.

Slowly, Laura drifted back to the present. She was very cold. Her bones were itching and her bruised left knee began changing color. The icy rain relentlessly kept on pouring.

"James—please hurry!" she hissed into the storm.

After one round on the community road, James noticed that he had forgotten his phone. Laura had certainly called or texted him.

"Curley, I've to get back and pick up my cell phone. I left it in the office. You stay put, will you? Good girl!" James stopped the car and entered through the front door.

Inside, he picked the phone off the charger and jumped back into the car.

"Hmm, strange. There is no message."

He started the engine and called Laura. It rang three times—she didn't pick up. He waited.

"Ah, now!"

"The number you have dialed is currently not available. Please try again later."

This wasn't Laura's voice mail. It was a recorded message from the phone company. Could it be that the extreme thunderbolt knocked off the service in this area? James slowly drove down the brick layered road toward the golf course. They were passing mostly vacant and dark mansions, but there was no trace of Laura.

He was soaked from the heavy rain and tired from rushing around. His concern grew, and he also was getting a little angry. Why did she have to go? They had just arrived after a long and intense day.

He quickly checked on Curley in the rear mirror. She was asleep. Everything was dark outside. The wipers were flying across the windshield.

He stopped the car and texted her a short message. He hoped that she would text him back where she had taken shelter, as she normally did.

The rain was getting more and more intense. He lifted his head. Was that a hailstone hitting his car? A hailstorm was very unusual, but this severe storm was already extraordinary.

The Cayenne rolled along the winding road through the dark night. The vintage-style streetlights gave only little light to the walkways and golf cart crossings. Protection of wildlife, especially nesting and hatching sea turtles, was a hot topic.

Through the wall of rain, he saw another car approaching. It signaled him to stop. The security guard.

Had he found her?

The security vehicle stopped, lights flashing. James slowed down and came to a halt next to him.

"Ah, Mr. Winchester! Welcome back, sir!" The security guard rolled down his window just enough to talk.

"Thank you, Gerard. Not the best weather tonight." Normally, James hated to roll down a wet window, but tonight it didn't matter. He needed to get Laura back, soon, and unhurt.

"No, but they had it in the six o'clock news. Severe weather warning for tonight. This hurricane season is one of the worst we've seen down here. Wilma hit us hard. They had just finished cleaning up, and now this. Tornado watch is on until 10:00 p.m. It's the first cold front this winter. And it came in strong and fast. But the worst is over, I think."

"Good. Gerard, my wife was out running. Did you happen to see her?"

James was angry with himself. He remembered that air traffic control issued a bad weather advisory with a tropical storm watch for later this evening. He had totally forgotten about it. He should have warned her not to stay out for too long.

"No, sir, sorry, but I haven't."

"All right. Are you staying on Gulf Shore Drive?" James checked his watch again. Laura had been gone for over an hour now.

"Yes, doing my usual hourly round. I'll look out for her."

"Yes, please."

"Anything else I can do for you, Mr. Winchester?"

"No, thanks. I just started looking. Perhaps she is waiting at the Golf Club."

"All right then. I'll keep my eyes open. You have my number, right?"

"Yes. Have a nice evening!"

James didn't want to spend more time talking. He was sure Laura was waiting for him—but where?

It had been half an hour or so since she'd last texted James. Still no answer. And not one car had driven by. The rain was lighter now, drizzling.

James probably was caught up in his office, studying books he hadn't seen for ten months. He might not even have noticed the rain and how late it had gotten.

She checked her iPhone again. Now it flashed. The display showed 12:00 midnight in blinking red. There was no dial tone. The lightning bolt? Did it damage the phone, or was the whole area cut off? No, she spotted a streetlight beaming in the distance. Could it be that she had been struck by lightning?

She felt okay—apart from a slight headache. And of course she was soaked and very cold. But other than some bruises and scratches on her left knee, she was not seriously hurt.

Headlights! There he is, she thought as a car slowly approached, brights on. It stopped directly in front of her. It wasn't James.

It was a pink Cadillac, and a blonde woman was driving. Laura walked up and knocked on the windshield. In the high beams she couldn't see much of the driver's face—or anything else—and to her surprise, the car sped up again and left her behind in the dark.

Probably it was better to go home now than to spend more time waiting for James. So, she stretched her stiff legs and continued in a slow jog along the main road.

The rain had stopped completely as she made her way home. The air smelled fresh and clean. Finally, she turned into the driveway and passed the lit water spilling over the fountain.

All outdoor lights and lanterns were on. Her home and her garden looked so beautiful with all those freshly planted flower pots ready to greet the season.

Natural beauty with canopies of moss-laden oak trees, palms, and lush tropical scrubs. The first couple of days back in their vacation home always felt like paradise.

It was paradise, wasn't it? Laura thought as she opened the iron gate to enter through the garage side door. Oh! The door was closed. Perhaps she locked it as she left. Never mind, she walked around to the garage door and opened the code key pad.

She keyed in the combination and hit *ENTER*—but nothing! The automatic door stoically stayed closed. Wrong code? She tried to remember. She had it stored in her iPhone, but that wasn't working right now.

She didn't want to disturb James, who was probably caught up in his den, the only room with lights on while the rest of the house laid in the dark. It was so typical of him to sit comfortably in his leather armchair reading and black out the real world for hours.

Soon, she would be inside and bring him right back into it. Smiling and in a better mood, she thought about sizzling steaks and red wine.

She tried the keypad again, but there was still no movement. Finally, she gave up, walked over to the front door and rang the bell. In the end, the urge for a hot steam shower, fresh clothes and a lumberjack dinner overcame her consideration of James. Now, he had his last change to rescue her from the cold.

Again, she rang the bell and knocked on the glass inlet. Lights went on in the foyer, and she heard footsteps. The door opened.

"What do you want? What are you doing, sneaking around my house at night?"

❧

"Your house?" Laura looked up. Who was that?

"James, are you here?" Laura was looking straight in the eye of an elderly man with gray shattered hair who was casually dressed in old-fashioned English-style clothes.

"There is no James here. What are you talking about?"

He spoke very slow with a British accent and made no effort to hide his anger. Laura, in no mood for games, took one step further into the doorway.

"Listen carefully. This is my home. And I don't know what you are trying to achieve here. But I am cold, tired and very hungry."

Laura took a deep breath and tried to take another step inside.

"If you think this is funny, let me tell you, it's not! And now get out of my way and let me into my house and to my family, please."

Laura was determined and pushed him aside to get in, but the man stepped forward to block her.

"You stop right here, young lady." He grabbed her elbow and escorted her out.

"Let go of me immediately or I'll call the police! James? Curley? Where are you?"

Laura was furious. This had gone too far. First, no pickup in this horrible thunderstorm, and now this.

"The police? Good idea! Let me call security." He pushed the emergency alarm button to call the gate guard directly. Laura only knew too well about the button—she was the one who had it installed.

"They should be here any minute. Talk to them. Leave us alone." And he slammed the heavy Cantera door almost on her nose.

Laura's was very angry, but now fear was creeping into the mix. What was happening here? It seemed unbelievable!

She was sitting on the Italian marble steps in front of her home as the community security van turned in. The car stopped, and an armed security guard stepped out. He walked towards the front door, looked at her and rang the doorbell.

"Gerard, is that you?"

"Ma'am, please . . ."

He stepped back as if he was afraid of her touching his proper uniform. Laura's shabby appearance must have been the reason. Probably not a multimillion-dollar look, she thought.

"Gerard, don't you recognize me?" Laura gave it another try with more stamina and determination in her voice.

"It's Mrs. Laura Winchester—11238 Gulf Shore Drive. Right here. This is my home—the Winchester residence!"

"Winchester? James Winchester?" He rang the bell again, since nobody answered the door.

"Yes, James Winchester, my husband." Laura rose from the marble steps, straightened her hoodie, and tried to manage her hair when the door opened.

"Good evening, Lord Cunningham. Did you call for security, sir?"

"Good evening, Gerard. As a matter of fact, yes, I did call in."

"How can I help you, sir? Are you safe now? Is Mrs. Cunningham all right, sir?"

"Yes, thank you, Gerard. We are well. However, would you please take care of this lady here? She was soliciting, sneaking around and tried to force her way into our home."

"What?" Laura interrupted sharply.

She laughed. "You are intruding in my home. I just left for a quick run and now this."

She turned to Gerard. "It's a joke right? Oh my—am I being tricked? This is all on video, right? And it will be played at the Thanksgiving dinner party at the club?"

"This is not a joke, lady," Lord Cunningham said. He was not amused. "Gerard, please take care of it."

"Yes, sir. Will do."

"All right then. Thank you." And the Lord closed the front

door and shut off the lights.

"Good night, sir," Gerard replied into the dark before he turned back to Laura.

"Gerard! What is going on here?" Laura sat down on the marble steps again, made herself comfortable and crossed her arms. "I am not going anywhere. Besides, where should I go?"

"Mrs. Winchester, I think I remember you now. But it's been a while." Gerard's face softened. Curiosity showed on his face, and this time, he gave her his full attention.

"Yes, we just came back today. It's been about ten months," Laura answered tiredly and slowly, but she was also relieved that he finally recognized her.

But he did look awful. Maybe he was a little under the weather. He must have lost weight, and his face looked old with blurry eyes. And most of his hair was gone.

"No, no, Mrs. Winchester, not ten months—more like ten years!" He looked puzzled. "You look so young—where have you been all those years? Is your husband back too?"

"Gerard, please, not again. Stop teasing me! Where have I been, you ask? Right here, running down the beach, crossing the golf course. I got almost hit by lightning before I came back home along Gulf Shore Drive."

Laura folded her hands over her face, closed her eyes and really hoped that when she opened them again, all would be fine. But it wasn't.

THREE

Nine o'clock, Sunday night. Darkness. Rain was drizzling, though the worst was over. Laura sat on a folding chair in the gate house at the main entry.

Gerard insisted that she came here so that he could check his records. Her head started burning, and she was confused. Things needed to get straightened out soon. What was really going on?

"Ma'am . . ." Gerard looked up from his computer screen.

"Mrs. Winchester!"

"Mrs. Winchester, sure, I am sorry. However, I can't find any Winchester residence in my system here."

"We just left from there, remember? You picked me up." This was getting nowhere, she felt very tired.

"Yes, ma'am. That's what you've been telling me. But here, look for yourself. My system does not show the name Winchester in Royal Palm Plantation. No resident and no registered guest."

"Then your system has a bug, or somebody tampered with it as part of this whole joke."

"That may be. I can't tell. But according to the rules, I can't allow you to stay here unless you are a resident or guest. Is there anybody who could pick you up?" Gerard's voice did change back to its official tone after he had double-checked that no Winchester was listed.

For more than twenty years, he was a reliable and trustworthy security guard for the super rich who resided here. This was his responsibility. And although he might have remembered her, he couldn't be sure.

The lady had no picture ID, and even if she were Mrs. Winchester, they didn't live here anymore. He had no choice other than to call the sheriff.

"Listen, Gerard. I'm tired, cold and hungry. My husband must be here somewhere, driving around, looking for me. And Curley, you know my Golden Retriever. She always comes straight to you to play fetch with her two tennis balls, remember? I don't know what happened. Maybe we'll figure it out in the morning. However, now, I need a hot shower, fresh cloths, and something to eat. Why don't you call the Lord and tell him that I live here or used to or whatever . . . Please ask him to offer me a guest bedroom for tonight. Then at least, I'm back in the house and things will clear up. I still hope that this is all a joke and will be resolved sooner than later. Can you do this, please?"

"I am afraid no, I can't bother Lord Cunningham again. This is the Cunningham residence, and they've lived here for at least five or six years. He is on the board."

"Oh . . ." Laura sounded exhausted, the headache was getting worse, and she felt like in the middle of a reality show. But what choices did she have? She felt like Scarlet O'Hara when she'd lost it all.

"Ma'am. Please try to understand. I am sorry for your situation, but if you have nobody to pick you up, I've to call the police. My next round is due, and I cannot leave you in here by yourself."

Gerard stood up, straightened his uniform to underline his responsibilities and called the Collier County Sheriff's Office.

A few minutes went by before a deputy arrived with a patrol car. Gerard quickly explained the situation and showed his discomfort with having the police officer standing visible in his gate house.

Laura rose from her chair and went outside. The rain had stopped. She took a deep breath.

"Mrs. Winchester, Mrs. Laura Winchester? Is this right?"

"Yes." Laura followed the officer to the back of the patrol car.

"I am Deputy Haynes. Here, please take this blanket. Do you want a bottle of water?"

"Yes, please. Thank you." It was good to be treated with some courtesy, but she still felt like a caught animal. She was confused because she did not know how to behave in front of the officer, strong and demanding or vulnerable, like a victim.

"Do you need me to call for medical attention?" He opened the left door to the back seat. The seats were made out of smooth red vinyl and smelled like disinfection spray.

Laura reluctantly got in, afraid he too would close the door. But he didn't. He stayed outside, close to her. He looked around and enjoyed the fresh sea breeze. Then he took a good look at Laura. He was still waiting for an answer.

"Oh, I've been better, but I'm all right. The blanket and water are what I needed most. Thank you again." Her head pounded and smoldered, but Laura wasn't exactly thrilled by the idea of an official medical exam.

She was uncomfortable and very stiff on her seat and tried not to touch anything. She had never been in a police vehicle before or had ever envisioned being caught up by one. She looked around.

The driver seat was protected by a steel protector panel, which could be locked as well. On the inside a red light lit the passenger's seat mounting unit with a laptop, video recorder and other electronic devices. All looked very state of the art, high tech and expensive.

"Okay," he said with a slight smile.

Peter Haynes had been with Colliers County Sheriff's Office for over twenty years. He worked mostly in Old Naples and the beach area—all upper-class society.

His handsome appearance and sensitive management style made him a respected, admired and often welcomed officer in those circles.

Since his wife died three years ago, he liked to work the Sunday night shift. Sunday night was special—a lot of melodrama, and if he could be of any help, then he would help. That was what kept him going.

And this lady he had just picked up in the most affluent private community at the beach was such a case in point. She needed help tonight. Who knows what had happened to her at home?

She was just awesome beautiful, he thought. Her look had the kind of effortless cool with her crystal-blue eyes being wide open, alert and much too clear to hide anything.

He really liked how she managed to sit in the back of his car with utmost grace and nonchalance, with her stylishly curled hair still wet and her clothes soaked and muddy.

He could tell from experience that she belonged rightly to the uppermost class. She had perfectly manicured nails as she picked up the water bottle. And her smooth, spotless hands, he noticed, carried the most sparkling diamond ring on the right and a sophisticated platinum wedding band on the left.

Haynes closed her door before he took his seat in the front and locked his as well. The night was clear, stars appeared and a cricket started its calling song.

"So, then, Mrs. Winchester, let's start, tell me your story."

The water was restoring her. She was feeling a little better despite being caged in like a criminal. Still cold and shivering, she tightened the blanket around her shoulders.

It seemed a long time since somebody took her seriously enough to address her as Mrs. Winchester. He did, continuously. Somehow she trusted him.

He started the recorder and took notes directly into his laptop, while she reported how they had arrived this morning in their little Cessna. Then they'd taken Curley for a walk on the beach.

Haynes looked up. Laura halted, "Yes! We know, dogs are not allowed on the beach in Collier County."

However, Curley got special treatment. She was so cute, and when spotted roaming freely on the beach, she won over the hearts of law enforcement and every state park ranger immediately. Haynes continued typing notes, only interrupted to check his dispatcher and his watch.

Laura told the officer about James and her taking a nap before preparing dinner and her decision to go for a run. Suddenly, Deputy Haynes got busy and started asking very specific questions about the inside of the home and about the time she started running. Then he inquired about the day they bought the house, the sales price and certain details in the deed not shown on public records.

He double-checked this information with the records on file. For a second, without Laura noticing, he looked puzzled and studied her one more time in his rearview mirror.

Laura finished her story with how she got caught by the storm, almost hit by lightning and surprised to find her house occupied by a total stranger—Lord Cunningham—what a phony!

She found the interview encouraging, and her hopes were restored that everything would be all right soon. She knew this was all a joke—it had to be. It was just one of those games.

∾

"Is there anybody in here—in the Royal Palm Plantation—who could identify you? A friend, or a neighbor?" Deputy Haynes looked through the front seat protector steel bars straight into Laura's crystal blue eyes.

"Identify me?" She slid a glance to him, surprised.

"But why? I thought you checked back in your computer." Laura was leaning forward to get a better look. On his screen was displayed public record information.

"Isn't it true what I've been telling you? The date when we bought the home? Or how the fireplace looks in the master suite?"

"Sorry if I gave you wrong implications, Mrs. Winchester. All information, as far as I could retrieve them, is deemed correct."

"Deemed correct?" Laura's regained hope of clearance and

being transported back to her home faded slightly. Frustration mixed with helplessness began to crawl up her throat. Tears welled up silently, not visible yet, and she had to swallow deeply to hold them back. She closed her eyes and tried to focus on a beautiful thought—red roses.

This headache was driving her nuts, yet she still tried to breathe slowly and evenly as Deputy Haynes twisted backwards, facing her directly. She kind of sensed what he was about to tell her, but she didn't want to hear it.

"Mrs. Winchester, please listen carefully, and I don't know if I can say it right, but please hear me out first. And then I promise to help you as much as I can—deal?"

Deputy Haynes knew that he probably couldn't be of much help tonight, but he promised himself to give it his best.

"Deal." Laura answered, not knowing what other alternative she might have.

"Okay then. First, good news is that the information I received from you tonight matches those on file. So do the pictures and the description of your clothing, provided you are really Mrs. Laura Winchester—"

"Hold on, I *am* Mrs. Laura Winchester," Laura interrupted.

"Let me finish, please. Deal, remember?"

"Yes, sorry. Please go ahead!" Laura took a sip from her water bottle.

"So, if you are Mrs. Laura Winchester, all information you gave me is confirmed through public records and the sheriff's office records on file," Haynes confirmed, flipping through pages.

"See, I told you, they are already looking for me. Probably at the beach or the golf course." Laura got some color back in her cheeks.

Deputy Haynes lifted his hand politely. "Please let me finish."

"Sorry." Laura leaned back.

"According to our records, a missing persons report was filed for Winchester, Mrs. Laura Winchester. Dated exactly to the day ten years ago." This time, Haynes did not look up.

"Ten years ago? What do you mean?"

"Yes, ten years ago! It was late Sunday night, the Sunday before Thanksgiving, as today. Mr. James Winchester reported his wife, Mrs. Laura Winchester, missing at 10:05 p.m." Deputy Haynes waited for a reaction, but Laura was speechless.

"Mr. James Winchester had searched for her for several hours during a stormy night. The reports says that Mrs. Laura Winchester was leaving the house in good health shortly before dinner for a quick run into the sunset at the beach. The weather was fine as she left. When a severe storm front approached, he set out to search for her. It started raining. First lightly then heavier. Followed by thunder and extreme lightening. He continued driving around for hours, then informed security and called 911. As soon as the weather cleared, they called in for the Aviation Unit and the Marine Bureau to help out with the search. The search went on for three days straight with helicopters and boats, using highly specified search and rescue units. The subject was not found."

Haynes looked back to check on her and was amazed. She looked almost identical to the photos he found on a file dated ten years ago.

What was going on here? An alien abduction? No, that was too far off. Haynes, stay professional, he commanded himself. But kidnapping wouldn't have kept her that young.

"I don't know what to say . . ." Laura was totally perplexed. She was not sure what to make of all of this.

Ten years ago? She leaned back, closed her eyes and pretended she wasn't there. This was her worst nightmare ever. Couldn't be over sooner.

She just needed another shock, and she would be awakened. Back in reality with James holding her tight and Curley licking her face. Anything would be better than this never-ending drama that was going on right here, in this dark red, gloomy, horrible police car.

Deputy Haynes looked out through the windshield of his car into the now clear sky. He took a deep breath of cold crisp air and said, "I think I remember that night. We had a weather forecast reporting a cold front coming in, but when it arrived, it was a dense tropical depression that looked like another hurricane, only four weeks after Hurricane Wilma. What a year, first Katrina into New Orleans and then Wilma hit Naples. Some suggested there were some kind of military weather projects going that caused these hurricanes, but who knows, right?"

He looked down onto his screen. "Yes, Sunday before Thanksgiving. I remember because my wife told me to stop by the Fresh Market to pick up a young fresh turkey. And I couldn't get one—it was too late. Well, that cost me some trouble, but anyhow, back then, I was with the mounted patrol searching the beaches with my horse, *Little Cowboy*."

"So, what happened after that?" Laura almost automatically said. Somehow, she was watching the whole play around her as if from a distant planet. So far, she didn't comprehend any of this.

"The search continued for three days—we couldn't find the subject, I mean you, of course. And then, they shifted the units, got more people involved and . . . oh, sorry, I can't tell you more."

"But, where is James? My god, what happened to him and Curley?" Laura was shaking heavily now.

"Listen . . . I don't know if this is in your best interest, but I have to report you in."

"Please, no! I'm not feeling good. I've a kind of headache and blurred vision. I've never had that before. I feel like I'm coming down with something real strong. Let me call the ranch—my mom—she'll tell you that I am Mrs. Laura Winchester, and then, if you don't mind, please drop me off at the Ritz."

Laura knew by now that this was a puzzle she couldn't solve tonight and needed to shift her attention to her own well-being. She'd been too long in the cold wet weather. She urgently needed a hot shower. And dry clothes.

Stretch out, relax and close your eyes, she thought, and everything will be all right. The nightmare will be over. Just the idea of spending the night at a county jail made her stomach turn.

"Can't do that, lady, sorry." Deputy Haynes seemed suddenly like a stranger to her.

What had changed him? Something in the reports? What else happened that night? "So, you're back to 'lady' then? Please, call my mother in Montana." She gave him the number, and she saw him typing it in. Was he going to call? She couldn't tell.

"Okay, back to the question: Is there anybody here in Naples or Collier County who could identify you right now? Family, a friend or a neighbor? Think, please. Otherwise I have to bring you in for tonight."

Deputy Haynes was trying to help as much as he could, knowing that he probably should have called the office immediately, since the picture on file of the missing Mrs. Laura Winchester was so similar to her.

The description of the clothes the subject wore when last seen by her husband were identical to what the lady in the back was wearing right now.

However, if the data on file were correct, then this was not a cold case. Not an open investigation either. It was closed two years ago, with Mrs. Laura Winchester being legally declared dead.

He couldn't tell her, who knew how she might react? He was concerned about her physical and mental health. Nevertheless, he had to make the official dispatch about his finding. It would trigger the re-opening of this case, he was sure about that.

Multiple agencies would be called in right away. In addition to the Collier County Sheriff's Office, certainly the FBI, the U.S. Attorney's Office, the Florida Department of Law Enforcement and the State Attorney's Office—not to mention the press.

So, in delaying it a little further, maybe after midnight, they would leave her alone at least for tonight. If he only knew were to let her stay, safe and secure.

Laura was in shock and shivering badly now. She tried to remember names of neighbors, friends. It'd been awhile for her, ten months, and for them, ten years. Think! Try to remember. She couldn't, sensing deep inside her that something had gone terribly wrong.

Then a vision of a person appeared, laughing and calling out her name, it was blurred and in black and white—Regina? No, it was Regine. A German name. Yes. That's why she remembered it. But what was her last name? Think. Was it Goodman? They played golf every Thursday morning. Coleman, it was Coleman. Now she remembered.

"Try Regine Coleman. They live here, at Dolphin Lane. The guard should know the exact address, their phone number. Call her, please. She certainly remembers me." Laura got some color back into her cheeks.

"Okay, Regine Coleman, Dolphin Lane." Deputy Haynes checked his records. "Hmm, I have a Bradley Coleman at 6185 Dolphin Lane. The property must be listed under his name only."

"Brad, yes, of course. He's her husband. I know him. He's a friend of James. And once, he wanted to know more about naked puts, so I gave him an introduction."

"Naked puts?"

"Stock options." Laura said shortly.

"So, should I call them?"

"Yes, please ask them if I can stay there for tonight. They might also know where James is."

FOUR

Laura! Is this you? Where have you been all those years? What did they do to you?" A very handsome gentleman in his early fifties, tanned and fit, opened the front door. He was dressed casually in a custom-tailored tweed jacket over a hand-woven cashmere jumper and silk scarves paired with blue jeans.

"Mr. Bradley Coleman?" Deputy Haynes took the lead.

"Yes, sir. What can I do for you?" Coleman spoke in a low-tone, soft but determined voice. His cool blue-green eyes were quickly scanning the faces of his late-night visitors.

"Good evening, Mr. Coleman. I am Deputy Haynes with the local sheriff's office. We spoke on the phone."

"Oh, yes. Good evening. Please come in." Brad Coleman widened the iron cast door with its stained glass inlets and guided them through an impressive marble stone hallway to the living room.

Filled with modern artwork, paintings, expensive antiques and a heavy leather sitting area, the spectacular room showed its master's taste.

The air carried the scent of ember firewood mixed in with a slight note of cigar tobacco, mellow and tangy. It all came from the rear where a fireplace provided coziness and warmth.

"Please, take a seat. Can I offer you anything, Deputy Haynes, Laura?" Coleman asked his guests in an old-school, gentleman-like fashion, as if the maid and butler had their night off. Which they probably had.

"No, thank you. I'm fine." Haynes sat down on the hand-nailed antique leather couch facing the huge wood burning fireplace.

As if awakened from a bad dream, Laura slowly felt more comfortable again, and took the seat next to the deputy.

"And you, Laura?"

"Thank you Brad, but not now." She all so slightly touched the soft leather of the armrest, which brought back memories from a life she lived only hours ago. All gone now. Where were James and Curley, her mom?

Coleman went to his antique Georgian wing chair next to the fireplace, where an aged single-malt whiskey and a smoking cigar were waiting for him on the side table.

"Excuse the cigar. I just lit it. A Sunday night indulgence I just can't let go of." Coleman smiled and squinted his eyes, not letting Laura out of his view.

He was fascinated by her looks. Not sure if hers was an unusual appearance after all this time. Her youth! Or her dressing so very casually in this running outfit with some hair streaks curling into her face.

At first he couldn't believe it. Laura was back, after all those years. Her sudden disappearance—nobody knew what had happened to her—and now she was sitting right here in his living room.

"All right. Mr. Coleman."

"Call me Brad, please."

"Brad then. First of all, I apologize for interrupting your Sunday night. We have come here to clarify an important question concerning the disappearance and now presumable return of Mrs. Laura Winchester."

"Presumable?" Laura turned to Haynes.

"Yes, as a matter of fact, I need to ensure that you are the person you claim to be, Mrs. Winchester. This is why I brought you here. I already called the office and gave my first report. If Mr. Coleman can identify you to his best knowledge, I got the green light to leave you here for tonight. However, first thing in the morning, the sheriff's office will send out more people to investigate. Most likely a medical examiner and the FBI. Probably the U.S. Attorney's office will join in on this investigation as soon as they get their unit ready."

Deputy Haynes flipped quickly through his notepad. He surely didn't grow up with these electronic devices, but he had gotten pretty good at using them.

"But where is James? Can't he come and pick me up? And why do we need to involve the FBI and the U.S. Attorney's office? I'm back, and I'm fine. Isn't this what counts most? Okay, do your DNA test or whatever it takes to prove that I am who I say I am, but isn't that it?"

Laura looked puzzled. She couldn't, wouldn't let go yet. Isn't the game over? She looked around, hoping that James would appear from one of the other rooms with Curley charging at her happily reunited. And where was Regine, her friend?

"Laura, James doesn't live here anymore. He'd sold the house and moved away, there was another woman, I think—anyway, we lost contact over the years."

Brad Coleman wasn't the most sensitive person when it came to people issues, he knew that, but one look at Laura confirmed that he had reached a new level tonight.

"You didn't know?" Abashed, he looked at Laura. Suddenly, she seemed so distant, paralyzed, detached from reality, with her whole body frozen and her face white as snow.

"Didn't you tell her?" Brad turned to the deputy.

"No, not yet." Haynes wasn't so sure if it was the brightest idea to bring Laura to a neighbor. It must have been difficult for Coleman, too, to be confronted with such a traumatic past event.

If he had taken her into the office, at least she would have been given some medical attention right away.

Coleman, although well known and respected in Naples for his philanthropic engagements, didn't seem too concerned about Laura's well-being.

Obviously, he was more fascinated and thrilled by the story of her reappearance. Maybe he should have briefed Coleman in more detail on the phone. But it was too late now.

"Mr. Coleman, Brad, can you identify this person as Mrs. Laura Winchester? Please answer with a simple yes or no for the protocol."

"Yes." Of course he could. This was the least he could do for her right now. However, Brad Coleman wasn't so sure what he could do to minimize the damage.

Back then, they really thought she was kidnapped that night, and that probably something went wrong, that she was killed and her body had been disposed deep in the Everglades or out in the Gulf of Mexico.

At least that's how James had put it. Soon after, he'd started dating a woman he knew from his Rotary Club, wanting to get on with his life. Nothing wrong with that, he thought, although it seemed as though he had rushed into something, but it is hard on some men to live alone for longer.

One thing Coleman was absolutely sure about: he would do all in his power to help Laura to re-establish her life, to bring her back to normal as much as normal could be.

Shivering. Cold. It was so cold around her, and her body was so stiff. What was happening? Was she awake or dreaming? She wasn't sure.

She vaguely remembered taking a long, hot shower and dressing in borrowed clothes, finally calming down and lying down in one of Brad's guest bedrooms, where she'd be staying for the night.

It was the middle of the night. All was quiet, with only the sound of the ocean waves breaking ashore filling the darkness. She still had a terrible migraine, but it helped her feel alive. There are no migraines in heaven, so I must be alive. The thought made her smile.

Laura pulled the down duvet up to her chin. It smelled good—the fragrance of fresh roses with morning dew while the sun was rising created a nice image, and it made her feel warmer and more comfortable.

Brad was a good host. He did what he could to give her some reassurance of her existence. After Deputy Haynes had left, Brad had had fixed sandwiches and brewed hot tea with a shot of rum. While she ate, he filled her in on the situation as he remembered it ten years ago.

Ten years ago! She still couldn't believe it.

About six hours ago, *her* time, she had left James and Curley to go for a short run—and came back ten years later? What had happened? She had no idea, and there was no memory of the time in between, only this pounding headache that seemed to surge every time she thought about the past.

One thing she recognized with amazement was that she looked the same. She hadn't aged at all. In the bathroom she'd given herself a full check-over. There were no signs of aging, no marks on her body, no wrinkles on her face or around the eyes. Nothing but the scratches on her knee from her fall during the storm.

This should have made her happy, yet this was only more evidence that something was terribly wrong. The scratches on her knee looked fresh, about six, seven hours, not ten years old.

This is ridiculous. A very bad joke. Close your eyes, slowly, count to ten, reopen them and all will be good, she thought, but she'd tried this—unsuccessfully—about a hundred times over the last hours.

Brad had changed. He looked older than she remembered, and it suited him well, as it gave him even more charisma and presence. And he'd told her that Regine, her friend, his wife, had died two years ago.

While eating her sandwich, she'd asked Brad to turn on the TV.

She needed proof. Needed to see the date, the time, some news.

And with the first report about the upcoming 2016 Olympic Summer Games in Rio de Janeiro and the delay on some construction sites, Laura was blown apart. She'd just visited Athens this summer with James on their yearly trip to Europe, and they had seen both the 1896 Panathenaic Stadium and the modern Olympic stadium from the 2004 Olympics.

On the TV was a report about the remodeling of the Naples Pier, the landmark of the city, and the special arts event held on Thanksgiving Day this year. Sure, it needed a fresh and cleaner look, she agreed.

Although she was still struggling to grasp the reality of her new situation, she needed to get some rest.

First thing in the morning, the medical examiner was scheduled to come in for a check up. He probably would take blood samples for a DNA test to confirm her identity. By then, the FBI and other agencies would have arrived, and of course the press.

She needed a very clear head, so if sleep wasn't an option, at least she should try to rest. She opted to use deepening meditation to relax her body and mind, to connect to her inner power source and to get some clarity, and maybe some answers about her new life.

Yes, that was what she was longing for—answers. Honest answers.

Where is James? Is he alive? How does he look ten years older? Is he remarried? And Curley? Ten years! She was six when I left the house. She'd be sixteen now—very senior for a Golden Retriever. She may not even be alive anymore. Tears welled up in

Laura's eyes. And what about my mom? She may be gone as well.

Too many open questions unsettled her, but she refused to focus on them. Instead, she tried to bring back happier memories. Like the summers at her ranch, when she was training and developing *Pieces of Eight* to her superior ability and her pride in herself in letting let go and selling her—of course into very well-selected hands.

Pieces of Eight? What had happened to her? How old would she be now?

"No! No, don't go this route," Laura said out loud to herself in a strong voice.

Go back to happier times. Playing with Curley at the beach. Throwing tennis balls into the ocean and compete with her swimming through the waves to get them. Flying with James in the Cessna over the ranches, the surrounding mountains and valleys into the open blue.

What fun they had had. What a great family they were—or had been.

With these thoughts in her mind, she finally found some rest and eventually fell into a deep sleep.

"Mrs. Winchester?" A soft knock at the door awoke her. "Laura! Are you awake?"

The sunlight beamed into her eyes—bright and warm. To warm for this heavy duvet which brought her such comfort last night. She folded it back slightly and sat up, supporting her back against the headboard with some of the pillows. "Yes, I'm awake.

Who is it?"

And while the door slowly opened, a bright, smiling familiar face appeared. "Mrs. Winchester—"

"Martha, is this you? Oh my God—what a joy to see you!" Laura was overwhelmed to see her former housekeeper walking in with a silver tray loaded with breakfast goodies. She looked definitely older, somewhat smaller, even fragile, and she had more grays in her hair, but her smile and her rainbow-colored eyes were as happy as ever.

"Laura!" Martha couldn't hold back on her tears of joy as she walked over and took her hands. "Mrs. Winchester, you haven't changed a bit! Look at you. Your hands are so small, so soft and you look so young. Your face—not one wrinkle—you look beautiful. Only the tears on your cheek tell me that you didn't sleep well last night, am I right?"

"Martha, please keep it as Laura. You always called me Laura. I haven't changed. What time is it? Do I need to get dressed?"

"It's almost nine o'clock. Mr. Coleman asked me to check on you. See if you are awake. I checked in a little earlier and you were still sleeping. But now it's time to get up. The police called earlier, and some officers will be here within the hour."

Martha placed the tray on a foldout table next to the bed. "I brought you some breakfast. The way you like it—hope you still do? Coffee with steamed skim milk, organic, I know. Some oatmeal with black cherry yogurt and some fresh blueberries. Let me know if you want some toast, butter and jam. Mr. Coleman has always fresh croissants in the morning, special delivery, some filled with chocolate. You want some of those?"

"This looks and smells very good. Thank you Martha, and it's all I want. Actually, I'm not sure, if I can eat, to be honest—I don't feel much like eating."

"Please try some. I'll leave you alone now and will be back soon with some more appropriate clothes for you. I found a nice suit from the late Mrs. Coleman that will be perfect for you—for today—once I have steamed it."

"Thank you so much, Martha."

"Eat your breakfast. I'll be right back with the suit, and we'll try it on. A couple of stitches are probably needed to fit a size six."

And with these words and an encouraging smile, Martha left.

Laura was aware that her new life was just to begin. How would it look? Who would be the major players in it?

All she knew was that, from now on, she was on her own. In a new world—ten years in the future—with her being unchanged, at least physically. This alone will make headlines.

She needed all her strength to deal with this situation, the authorities and the media.

❧

"Very good, Mrs. Winchester. Thank you for reviewing the events from last night and answering our questions in such detail."

FBI Special Agent Gardner, a tall, athletic man with sun-tanned skin and short, dark, slightly wet hair, looked up from his oversized tablet. He had probably gone for a lengthy swim in the ocean before he rushed through the shower to get here. His eyes were steel blue.

Dark hair, blue eyes. Interesting, Laura thought. It was almost entrancing to look straight into them. His partner, Special Agent Woodward, was stout and rather unattractive.

"You are very welcome." Seated on a leather chair in Brad's living room, Laura was wearing Regine's suit, an elegant dark brown French-tailored suit. She was directly facing the special agents as they went through all the necessities to get her re-instated.

"Let me quickly summarize." Special Agent Gardner flipped through the pages on his tablet. "You left the house around 5:20 p.m. Sunday night and went directly to the beach, taking the boardwalk behind your property at 11238 Gulf Shore Drive. Is this correct?"

"Correct." Laura nodded.

"At sunset, you took a couple of pictures, mailed them to your mother and continued your run. The approaching storm front took you by surprise, and you think you may even have been hit by a lightening bolt, since your phone wasn't working anymore. Correct?" He looked straight into Laura's eyes, piercing like laser beams searching for the truth.

"Yes, Agent Gardner. It was very intense. I even thought my heartbeat stopped for a second or so. I couldn't breathe." Laura added and sipped at her coffee. She was more relaxed now that she'd survived the medical exam. They had finished all check-ups and had taken blood and hair samples.

It had helped that the medical examiner was a very sensitive woman, working quickly without unnecessary comments.

"All right . . . couldn't breathe," Agent Gardner took more notes and handed his tablet over to Agent Woodward, who looked concerned and uneasy. He got up to make a phone call.

Gardner continued. "And after the lightning bolt hit you, you said you felt no difference in your body, no heat, no electricity? You didn't notice no difference in your environment?"

"No. I was just wet and cold. My left knee hurt. I was looking for James. He knew my route. Especially when I jogged at night, in the dark. And he always picked me up. It rained heavily, I was hurt and I looked for shelter close by the main road so that he could find me." Focusing back on the events again and again gave her the creeps. When will it stop? she thought, getting impatient.

"Nothing unusual there? Did another car approach you? Did you ask somebody to give you a ride home? Maybe you got sedated, kidnapped, and in shock you may have lost your memory?" He looked up again, focusing on her reaction. His eyes were scanning her face and met her eyes once more.

"No!" Laura rose, feeling trapped and uncomfortable, and she turned toward the window, looking out over the ocean.

"Sorry." Agent Gardner pushed on. "But I had to make sure. We still have no explanation for what happened to you that night. Where have you been over the last ten years? And why is it that you reappeared last night—exactly ten years later? And why at the same spot with the same clothes on, with no signs of aging?"

He hesitated, waited for his partner to return.

"Andrew, do you have a minute? I've got new information."

Agent Woodward came closer, holding his phone up. The dark suit with the stereotypical white, starched shirt didn't fit his short red hair.

"Would you excuse me, please?" Agent Gardner got up and talked for a few minutes in private with Agent Woodward. Then he turned back to Laura.

"Please, look at my knee. Here." Laura carefully opened the bandage and showed them the fresh bruises on her knee. "This is real. Besides, where should I've been? And why should I make up such a story? I lost everything. I've nothing to gain."

"Yes, I see," Agent Gardner confirmed, but somehow, he seemed distracted.

Laura shifted on her feet. "Listen, I don't know what happened. I don't even know if what I'm telling you is the truth or not. The only thing I do know is that I went out for a run. All was good. No fight with my husband. No drama. Nothing. I got into a thunderstorm—boom—and then it's ten years later!"

Laura got back to the couch, sat down and let out a huff of breath. "James couldn't find me because I was already gone. Beamed into the future. Is this real? You tell me!"

Pleading for some companionship, Laura leaned over to his partner. "But I need answers. I need to know. And please, give me my life back, passport, ID card, my name and a good story about what might have happened for the press, so I can try to move on."

"Mrs. Winchester, I do understand your situation. Don't get me wrong. We are here to help. But whoever held you kidnapped over the last ten years could have just waited for this moment. They dressed you in your old clothes, drove you down here and during the rain last night, they pushed you out of the car. That's how you got your fresh bruise."

Agent Gardner pushed further in the hope to find a more plausible explanation than an alien abduction or a ten-year time shift due to a thunderstorm. He looked for Agent Woodward's support, but he was on the phone again.

"That's ridiculous! Where should I've been?" Laura was

getting upset. She had hoped that this morning would bring some clarity. And that all the bureaucracy and paperwork would bring her identity back, at least after they got confirmation through DNA testing. But kidnapping? She had no recollection of anything like that.

And bad enough, nobody has yet bothered to answer any of her pressing questions. Like where is James, and her mom and Curley? When can she return to the ranch?

She needed a new driver's license and some money to buy a ticket to fly home. To organize her life. She had a lot of catching up to do. Shopping for new clothes, learn about new styles, learn new tech devices. And finally, what had happened to her hedge fund? Who had managed it, and is it still active?

"Mrs. Winchester, please stay calm." Agent Woodward put his BlackBerry down.

Laura stood up and walked towards the terrace. The sight over the ocean on this beautiful sunny morning gave her balance. Then she turned around and faced both agents. "Let's get over with it. Finish your report, let me sign a couple of papers and get me my IDs."

Laura gestured towards the papers and file folders on the coffee table before she turned back to the ocean view to hide her tears. "And quickly, please."

"Laura, what is going on here? Are you all right?" Brad Coleman was determined when he walked in. He had overheard parts of the heated discussion from his office, and he didn't like what he saw.

In order to get calmer before he would address the agents directly, he moved to the sidebar where coffee and tea were waiting in silver-plated warming carafes. Deliberately, he took his time to prep a coffee for himself with hot steamed milk before sitting down on one of the leather chairs across the agents.

"Gentlemen, please!" Brad, well rested and fit in his elegant suit, took a sip of his coffee. "I think I know where you are going. You are reopening a cold case, investigating a crime. The kidnapping of Mrs. Laura Winchester, the wealthy hedge fund manager. It made headlines back then, and it will make headlines today."

He placed his coffee cup on the antique side table next to his leather chair. "I remember it only too well. You investigated, and everybody who was residing here was at some point a person of public interest. In the end, however, only James was left as your main suspect."

"James, a suspect? For what? Kidnapping me? That's absurd." Laura stepped in. "Only after his name was cleared," Brad continued disregarding her comment, "and this was many months later, did you resume searching. In the public eye, James Winchester's name was never really cleared. So he moved on, and much later, he started the legal procedures for declaring Mrs. Winchester dead, because he wanted to make his current relationship—at that time—legal. Am I right? James told me this before he left Naples."

"This is correct, Mr. Coleman." Agent Gardner looked up, confident and a little annoyed. He knew he couldn't let this slip again. It had almost cost him his job back then. And he was not willing to let this happen again.

"Trust me, we are only doing our job here. Trying to get to the truth. This step is necessary. So, may I ask you to let us finish our job here, please?"

"Sure, just focus on the finish."

"We will. I see your point. Just a few more items, and we'll be on our way."

"And Laura has a right to know. So, please answer all her questions and start the reinstatement process as soon as possible."

With these words, Brad Coleman rose. "My lawyers will contact you later today to ensure everything goes smoothly and quickly. They will handle all paperwork and represent her."

Brad Coleman left no doubt that he liked to be in control and that he didn't like to have his home swamped by police and federal agents for too long.

❧

A half hour later, after they'd finally left, he asked Laura to join him in his office. "Laura, please sit down." Brad pointed to the leather sofa next to his desk. "Would you like another coffee, or should I ask Martha to bring some juice? Fresh-squeezed ruby red grapefruit juice?"

"Oh yes, I would like a glass of juice, and tell me about James, please." Laura was exhausted after this morning's investigation marathon. "Is it true? Did he remarry?" She couldn't believe it. Her James married to another woman. Laura was shaking her head. "No way!"

She was sitting down in the leather seater facing the nineteenth-century oak desk while Brad opened the file drawer and scrolled through the folders.

"Ah, here it is!" He held up a manila folder full of papers, closed the drawer and sat down behind the desk. In the meantime, Martha brought in coffee for Brad and juice for Laura.

"Sir, is there anything else I can do for you?"

"Thank you, Martha, that will be all for now. And please, no phone calls or any other disturbances for another half hour."

"Very well, Mr. Coleman. I'll handle it. Don't you worry."

"Great. Thank you!" Brad closed the discussion with a smile before sending a small grin over to Laura. He waited until the door closed and he heard Martha walking back to the kitchen. Stirring his coffee he leaned back and opened the manila folder.

"She is so happy that we have company. Somebody to cook for and to take care of. So, Laura, please feel right at home here. Make yourself comfortable. James was a very good friend of mine, and he would have done the same for me or my late wife." Brad took a sip of his coffee. "And after all, it is Thanksgiving week, and I expect my family over—my sister Crystal with her husband and my two nieces. You will join us, of course, won't you?"

"Brad, I might and would love to. But I don't want to be in the way."

"Oh, you're not in the way," Brad assured. "This house is large enough. They'll only stay for two nights anyway. Come on—do me the favor and say yes."

Now, Laura was smiling for the first time. "I'm glad that I'm welcome. And yes, I'm happy to join you for Thanksgiving. It will probably take some time for me to get going again, and I don't know where I should go. Probably back to the ranch."

Laura stopped and scanned Brad's face, his brown well-trimmed hair had not a single detectable gray hair, and he was good at hiding with his poker face anyway. What was he so hesitant and secretive to tell her? she thought before she took a sip of her juice.

"Hmm, it's very good, and my first in ten months—or ten years, apparently!" Searching for the right words, she continued. "See, I learned this morning that I'm not only officially dead and penniless, but I also do not even own the clothes I'm wearing right now. Oops, I'm sorry, they are wonderful, I admired Regine's style, always did. I'm very sorry about your loss."

I sound tactless, confused and stupid, she thought, where is the old Laura, she strong one?

"Laura, please." Brad held up one hand.

"Let me finish." Laura said shortly. "I may have lost everything, but I still have my pride, my values. Sooner or later, I'll get my life back in order and then I'll pay you back all expenses plus interest. But for now, I want to thank you for your help."

"Laura, please, I . . ."

Brad paused again, trying to find the right words. He didn't want to promise anything out of spontaneous sympathy that he might later regret. Yes, he had had a crush on Laura. And from the second he'd opened the door and saw her standing there in front of his house, it was back. The sensation. The lust. A burning desire to hold her.

As he woke up this morning, he felt very happy within and was joyfully looking forward to having her in his home, despite the strange circumstances. For the first time since Regine died, he was jumping out of bed, greeting the new day with enthusiasm.

"Okay, here it is. This is what I was looking for. Some old newspaper clippings from the day you disappeared. About the search and more details about the investigation. Look through them. Here is a statement from James—years later as they started the procedure for declaration of death. James had to move on. It was awful to see him suffer so much. He had changed. He held himself solely responsible for your disappearance."

Laura took the clipping, looking at a picture of James. How much he had aged. His hair all gray. His eyes filled with tears.

The article read, "'After years of painful struggle concerning my wife's disappearance, I still refuse to accept anything other than finding a resolution to this nightmare,' said James Winchester in front of the county courthouse. 'I will forever love her. But this step is necessary. We all need to continue on.'"

She saw her mother close behind him, and next to him an attractive brunette. A tear ran down Laura's cheek. This was not something she could accept. Not yet. She knew it must be true, but for her it wasn't.

There was another clip. She pulled it out. It was about the ranch. The agents had told her this morning that her mom had died two years ago. James had sold the ranch soon after. She had just left her mom yesterday morning in good health. She had just left the ranch. It was still so fresh in her memory, how she touched her mom, kissed her a quick good-bye before hopping on the plane and waving to her as they took off into the crisp, sunny sky. And James, where was he now? Would he care?

This morning, she absolutely refused to talk to any psychiatrist. She would deal with all of it on her own. Once she knew how to survive the next couple of days, weeks and months.

James could help—of course. But the agents didn't know anything about his whereabouts, provided he was still alive. And nothing about Curley Marie either. The last trace of James was at her mother's funeral. After that, nothing. He gave power of attorney to the family attorney's office, and they handled the sale of the ranches. He had sold his too and dissolved the hedge fund.

She was still holding the clipping with James's picture in her hands. Brad spoke. "First of all, we need to get your identity—your name back. My lawyers will start this process immediately. And as I said, you can stay here for as long as you wish. I'd be glad if you would."

"Okay," Laura said and looked straight into his blue-green eyes. They seemed very confident. "I'll stay—at least this week. But I need to pay you back all expenses. Later."

"No problem. I wouldn't have expected anything anyway," Brad said smiling, relieved that she had accepted his offer and a little surprised with himself that he felt that way. It actually felt very good to help somebody, beyond just giving money to charity or financing a project and being invited for the opening gala to cheer up for the press, as he was accustomed to doing.

No, this was real. Lending a helping hand. Time. Effort. Food and shelter. Not just money. However, money was important. He looked at her. She needed stuff—of course, all ladies did. New clothes, cosmetics, a car, everything.

Brad opened the middle drawer and pulled out his checkbook. He opened it and started writing a check. He paused. To whom? Laura looked at him. He looked back. She noticed his unspoken question. To whom should he make out the check?

No identity, she thought, and before she knew if she should laugh or cry about it, her tears broke, and she started crying. He got up and walked over to her. He desired to hold her, to hug her, but didn't know how.

The Laura he knew had always been a very respectful, attractive and powerful woman who liked the formal distance. So he just sat down next to her and gently took her hand.

FIVE

Thanksgiving Day, Laura thought, jumping out of bed. For the first time in several days she awoke rested and refreshed after a dreamless night.

And without this terrible headache which had been dragging on since that time leap last Sunday.

It was very early—about five o'clock, still dark outside. She opened the french doors to her private terrace and inhaled the salty sea breeze. The sun would be up soon, presiding over another gorgeous day in paradise.

Today is Thanksgiving. Oh, how she always loved this time of year. And, although it felt unreal, Laura felt free, happy and ready to take on the world.

She decided to take a quick shower and then dress up in her brand-new running outfit and go for a run on the beach. She hadn't been running since that bewitched Sunday night. They still had no clue what had happened, and they may never find out.

Over the last few days, she had spent all of her time in countless interviews with the agencies, county, state and even federal offices and lawyers and dealt with the press. The story is out now! Her name will be cleared soon.

Brad and his attorneys did an amazing job, and with a little luck, she may get a temporary ID card, maybe even a passport, by tomorrow. Then she would be able to start her life again. Slowly, step by step.

As tragic as the experience had been, she decided she'd finally suffered enough. For three nights she had cried in sorrow and in anger; she couldn't believe or accept what had happened to her.

Just in this moment, though, standing here outside in the fresh morning breeze, she felt born again—almost truly joyful and happy. A new life waited. A second chance, with new opportunities and new challenges.

But what should she do? Where should she go once her name was cleared? How should she earn the money she needed to support herself? Should she try to find James? What if he did marry that brunette, had a new family, maybe a baby? How would she deal with her recurring nightmares, her unanswered questions about the past? And then this thing with her visions . . .

The visions were something she couldn't get off her mind. Last night at dinner she'd had one again. A sudden flash in her head, and a clear picture, a vision of what Brad wanted to say before he did it. It was all so clear—just like a movie reeling in her mind. As if she could read others' thoughts without any kind of magic. Being the logical, analytical person that she was, it felt pretty weird to her.

It had started earlier this week. Monday as she dealt with FBI agents and lawyers, she'd noticed it for the first time. The lightning strike that hit her on Sunday night had probably triggered that strange sensation.

She'd done a little research on it and found something called Remote Viewing, but she needed to investigate it more deeply. That's why she'd started a journal to note all of the occurrences with each date and time.

The good news was that the terrible migraine she'd had since Sunday night was completely gone. This was a very good sign, the first step to recovery, she thought, glancing through the bay window next to her little desk.

She needed time to think. And a long morning jog on the beach, in the early sun, watching birds and dolphins would help her with that.

Soon Laura was on her way, down the boardwalk and through sea oats-covered dunes straight down to the low-tide sea. She breathed deeply, running along the shoreline at a slow pace. The sun rose slowly over the mangrove and oak trees in front of the rooftops and terraces of a few secluded oceanfront estates.

She paused as she saw the first glimpse of her home—her former home. The Tuscan-style terrace overlooked the lagoon-style pool, the blue-white stripped beach cabana and yes, her white-turquoise Hobie Cat was still there, hidden in the mangrove scrub, probably not having been used for a long time. The colors had been washed out by the sea gust and rain, and the mast was broken.

She pushed herself to keep her pace. Don't stop, she thought, don't think. This was part of a former live. The past. Today was what she had. Keep on running—faster, she repeated like a mantra as she passed the too-well-known beach with the gated boardwalk and its sign that read *Private Property—No Trespassing!*

Back at Dolphin Lane, Brad Coleman stood outside with Larry, a handyman, and Martha, discussing flower arrangements and some changes in the seating group placements for proper installation of the Christmas decorations. Larry was setting them up today.

Brad expected his family to arrive around noon, and everything should look beautiful and in perfect shape by then. Without noticing it, he had stopped talking as he watched Laura coming back on the boardwalk to the house.

"Is this Laura?" Larry was asking, "Mrs. Winchester?"

"Yes, it's her," Brad confirmed and nodded while he was still looking out to the beach.

"Larry, why don't you get started by setting up the entry and the front as discussed." Brad pointed to the new string of lights and the storage boxes with the other decoration materials.

"Martha is going to serve breakfast here at the terrace soon. The weather is a little cooler today, and it will be perfect for being outdoors. Also, she has set up the dining room table for tonight's family feast."

"All right, sir. I'll get right on it." Larry took one of the boxes with him and walked up front while Martha got busy carrying fruit plates, juice carafes and other breakfast goodies out to the terrace.

"Oh, Mr. Coleman, I am so looking forward to seeing your sister again with the little one. And of course Ivy. Will she come? How is she? Has she recovered from her tragic accident?"

Martha clattered around with silver and plates. Today was the busiest day of the year for her. Everything had to be just perfect, as if late Mrs. Coleman were still commanding the Thanksgiving dinner preparations to perfection—a woman of character with German ancestry.

"Ivy?"

Brad turned around, surprised. Martha had just dropped a name that brought sadness and discomfort.

"I haven't talked to her since she returned from the clinic and rehab center in Vail." He glanced over the terrace, his eyes focused in the distance, toward the sea, as if he tried to find some answers out there.

Regine, Ivy and now Laura. Bitter fate, nothing he could do, nothing his influence or his money could bring back—the good old days, filled with laughter, big heart and even bigger dreams.

"But," Brad continued, "I spoke to Crystal last week, and all I know is that Ivy is coming today. She was supposed to go to Rio de Janeiro for the season's finals this weekend, but she skipped that tournament too. So we will be six for dinner."

The thought of the Thanksgiving family reunion made him smile and brought his attention back to Martha, who was putting red hibiscus flowers on Christmas napkins.

"Martha, this looks lovely. Regine couldn't have done it any better. I miss her, every day, but more so on days like this. You know how she loved to decorate, cook and prepare for the holiday season. Never mind—you must promise me, please, to take it a little easier today. I know you want everything to be perfect, and it will. However, preparing the Thanksgiving dinner and having guests staying overnight at once is more than you are used to."

"I will be fine."

"Yes, I know you will, and to ensure it, I have called in for help. Jeanette or Jacqueline, I can't remember. But she is serving at the club once in a while and was recommended by the operations manager. The club is closed today. She should be here shortly."

"Mr. Coleman! No, please, I can take care of it by myself." Martha was finally putting a full-bloom poinsettia as a centerpiece on the table.

"I know you can," Brad said warmly but firmly, "but I—"

He looked up to see Laura arriving through the mangrove trail, where she hopped up the stone steps to the terrace.

❧

"Good morning, everybody!"

"Good morning, Laura. I'll be right back with fresh coffee." Martha had her bright smile back on. And before she returned to the kitchen, she looked at Brad Coleman, nodding and silently saying thank you for the additional help. She knew—they both knew—that she needed it more than she would ever admit.

"Good morning, Laura! You look like a teenage girl in your new running gear. It suits you very well, and I assume you are feeling better today. Could you get some sleep?"

"Thank you, Brad. Yes, I feel better. I even got up for an early jog at the beach."

"Hungry? I thought we'd take our breakfast outside. Martha needs the space inside for dinner preparation. And the weather is so beautiful, still cool, a little breeze and low humidity. Isn't that what we longed for all summer?"

He pulled out a chair for Laura.

"Please, Brad!"

"What?" Laughing, he looked up to meet her eyes.

"Oh, it looks so inviting. All of it. However, I'm sweating and will be getting cold. Let me take a shower first. Give me ten minutes. I'll be right back." And Laura was gone. Fit and fast.

Brad looked after her and wondered how long it would take her to get fully accustomed to her new life. How long he could convince her to stay in his house?

He wasn't ready to admit it quite yet, but he was feeling considerably comfortable with her. He had to come up with an idea to keep her busy here, a project, a new challenge, and an idea was already taking shape in his mind. Over breakfast, before the family arrived, he would talk to her about it.

The phone was ringing—his secured private line had a special ring tone. Who could it be? He looked at his Patek Philippe Grand Complications, got up to his office and closed the doors behind him.

Laura was already relaxing at the table in the shade of a potted mango tree and was served fresh coffee as Brad reemerged.

"Coffee for you too, sir?" Martha asked.

"Yes please, thank you, Martha." Brad was in business mode, short spoken and over-correct. "Did Jeanette arrive?"

"Yes, actually, it is Jacqueline. We are getting started right away with dinner preparations. It can be ready as early as four o'clock." Martha poured steaming coffee in Brad's cup.

"Hmm, okay."

He sat down across from Laura, trying to smile. His mind drifted off, still on the conversation he just had. He'd expected a phone call from his office. His business affairs were foremost.

His foundation in support of distressed children, the Coleman Foundation, was planning a new project. A park project similar to the Disney theme parks combined with a summer or year-round camp.

But this phone call came from his lawyers to update him on the progress of Laura's papers. She should have gotten them in the morning. This was fast.

And then he mentioned something else, something about a weather control project gone wrong about ten years ago that would fit into Laura's story. The attorneys needed clearance and more funds to further investigate. But this Brad was not willing to approve, at least not just yet.

Before that, he needed to make a couple of phone calls himself, and the very first one required a high-security connection to Washington D.C. He checked his watch again—he had about fifteen minutes before he had to take that call. And he better had something substantial in his stomach before he took it.

"Let's plan to have dinner at six o'clock, then we have time to watch the sunset, here at the terrace, with a cocktail in our hands." Brad's mood lifted, slowly. He was looking forward to the party tonight.

"What a great idea!" Laura took one of the croissants. "What's the dress code? I found some new dresses at the Waterside Shops yesterday. I've a cocktail dress and a more formal dress. Both need a little stitching, but not much." She glanced over to Martha.

"I know you're very busy today, but if you could just help me with the dress once the turkey's in the oven?"

"Oh, I'd love to. We will get you dressed up for tonight." Martha winked.

"Thank you. And I'm really looking forward to meeting your sister and her family." She was in a very good mood. The run at the beach had brought back happy memories.

Memories about James and Curley. How they celebrated Thanksgiving here at the beach. And about her mom. She missed her, missed the chance of taking care of her and saying goodbye. But she knew she would need to deal with it later. There was nothing she could do about it now.

And James? Would she search for him? Sure, she would. She had to know. To find more answers.

Her eyes glanced over to the sea, searching for some dolphins in the distance. What a beautiful day. Running always stimulated her in a very positive way. The endorphins released into her body during the run did their job. She could count on that, and it kept her going for a run whenever she could.

In addition, she loved being surrounded by true nature, hearing her steps crashing through the dead shells at the beach or touching the soft tightly knit turf of the golf course. And here was the sight of all this lavish natural beauty around her. The ocean, the magnificent estate homes, a sea gull feeding, a pelican stealing bait.

Moments of truth—life as is—true magic.

She decided right then to grab hold of her life. Here she was, a beautiful young lady, healthy and intelligent. There must be a way that she could support herself. After all, did she not know how to trade? And the stock market was still there, with thousands of securities and derivatives moving up and down each day.

She just needed time to pull herself together, to refocus and to catch up. That's all. And some seed money to get her started, of course. With this, she looked over to Brad.

"Brad, I need to talk to you before your family arrives." Laura sat back in her chair facing the distant-looking gentleman, who obviously had had too much on his mind this morning.

"Wait, Laura. I know what you're going to say." He nervously checked his watch. He didn't have much time, but wanted to share his idea with her.

"You do? How?" Laura looked puzzled, not because he appeared to know what she wanted to say. She had had another very clear vision of him telling her that same sentence—he was going to offer her an initial fund to start trading again, and as a deal, he was asking her to teach him more about option hedging strategies for his own portfolio.

Boy, she thought, if I could do this while day trading the markets, I won't have to worry about my future at all.

"Laura, please listen to me first. I know it isn't easy for you as an independent woman to accept support from a stranger, a neighbor. Although I regard myself more as a friend." Brad halted as if waiting for an interruption, but there was none.

He continued. "I have thought about your situation, and I wanted to ask you if you would be interested in teaching me more about financial strategies like naked puts and . . ."

"Deal."

"What?"

"You got it. I agree. We make a deal with the trading."

Now, Brad looked puzzled. Women could be hard to understand, he thought—as mysterious as they sometimes are, this time he liked the outcome.

Laura tore a piece from her croissant, added some butter and apricot jam and enjoyed the delicious bite. After her morning jog, she deserved a little indulgence. Glancing back over to Brad, she smiled, not knowing where her new ability came from or how to use it, yet she also liked the payoff.

"Okay, then." Brad finished, buttering his toast.

"As soon as you have your ID, we are going to open an online broker account. Please let me know which one you selected and print out the wire instructions. The initial funds . . . how much do you think you will need to get started?"

"A million would do," Laura said as she fished for another piece of her croissant.

"And Brad, just to make sure we understand each other. I'm very, very grateful for what you do for me. However, the deal is that you lend me the seeding capital to get me started. But I want to pay you back. And in order for me to be productive and successful, I need my own space and no pressure. I've ten years to catch up on, and I don't know if I can start right away."

"Laura, take all the time you need. You know you are most welcome here. Make it your home as long as you wish."

He paused as Martha came out to refill their coffee cups. "Oh, Mr. Coleman, the phone call you're waiting for. Your contact's personal assistant called in and said they needed another half hour for your connection to be ready."

"Thank you, Martha, then I'll take another cup." He didn't like to be put on hold, but he enjoyed the cup of coffee and the private time with Laura.

Still, if it were for his business, he would know how to react, yet in the political world he was still a newcomer, and he needed to play by their rules—until his time had come. And it would come, he was sure about that.

He looked over at Laura, and liked what he saw. She did have quite an appetite this morning. It was good—she had barely eaten anything over the last couple of days.

"Thank you, Martha," Laura said with the refill of her cup. She folded her linen snowman napkin and devoted herself to her coffee and her new mission.

"I would need an office. Maybe I could use the other bedroom next to my suite. I mean, after your family is gone. There is no rush. I need to do thorough research on broker accounts and platforms, so I'll start on it right now. Oh, and I need a PC with four monitors. Tomorrow would be the best time to order the computer stuff."

She laughed and looked over to Brad. "Some things never change, right? The big shopping on Black Friday?"

"No, I suppose not."

"Okay, then. I'll start looking for the latest models. I can't wait to see what's available on tech gadgets these days. After ten years." She shook her head in disbelief but was really curious.

"Hmm, money transfer and clearance will take a couple of business days. That will give us time to convert the bedroom and I may need . . ." Laura stopped abruptly when she heard the doorbell ring.

"Are they here?"

Brad looked at his watch. "Too early!"

"Well, Brad, thank you so much for everything. Really, I mean it." Laura got up and added, "And a deal is a deal. I will show you how to make money with selling puts and calls."

"Laura, there is one more thing I wanted to say," He hesitated.

"Can't it wait? I really need to get going."

Laura was eager to get back to her room to do some research for a couple of hours before the party. She needed an online broker and new equipment, a PC, monitors, and more.

She wanted to have a trading account opened for her as soon as possible. She loved trading so much. And she wanted to pay all her debts back to Brad.

Actually, she liked him—always had. He was handsome, a good friend of James, a very wealthy businessman with political ambitions and a pretty fair golfer.

Nevertheless, she knew he probably had to use some old connections, turn some switches and use money as an igniting pilot to get her back to normal. She knew she could expect her passport by tomorrow and couldn't wait to see her name under a picture on a formal ID again.

It meant a lot to her. It meant freedom. A new start. A new chance.

"Sure, we can talk later." With Laura in his thoughts, Brad finished his breakfast in silence. She had so much energy. And she looked so happy this morning. As long as she was not leaving too soon, he would be okay. He felt more than just sympathy for her.

Only four weeks after her diagnosis, Regine had died of lung cancer. It came unexpectedly, and Brad had suffered from depression. He lived alone, seldom left the house and did most of his business on the Internet and over web conferences. Until one day, when Martha knocked at his door.

Wasn't that right after James Winchester sold his estate and moved on? Martha didn't know where to go—she didn't want to leave Royal Palm Plantation. She'd received a good financial package from James, but more than money, she needed a home.

He hesitated at first to welcome her—was he afraid of the change? Maybe he didn't want to feel pressure to get up in the morning or get shaved and dressed properly. It was only then that he realized how deep in depression he had fallen. A downward spiral had him in its grip.

With Martha's arrival, all this changed quickly. No doubt she turned his life around. She constantly engaged him in community activities, told him what was right and wrong out there. In the real world. And that it would need men like him, with his powers and courage, to fix it.

Every morning with breakfast came the Naples Daily News on his table, with one particular headline of interest highlighted by Martha. It was back then, about two years ago, that he started to pay more attention to local society needs. And it turned out that Martha was right.

So he started supporting charity and soon founded his own non-profit organization, The Coleman Foundation.

The Coleman Foundation's philanthropic priorities included enhancing the life of children in distressed families. They offered programs for children living in families facing abusive parents, financial stress or divorce, among other issues that would prevent a healthy upbringing.

"No child should be forgotten" was the motto of the foundation's work, which provided all kinds of support during times of temporary distresss in the children's families. The goal was to provide interim support during times of disorder. It started with getting children ready for school and preparing lunch boxes and other meals.

A home-cooked dinner sometimes works wonders to bring back joy and harmony into stressed families. Supervision of homework as well as playing time, going to the movies and filling fridges and pantries were all part of duties of the many volunteers at the Coleman Foundation.

Today, it was one of the largest private foundations in the nation, and it had opened doors for Brad's own political ambitions.

"Mr. Coleman, that was Larry at the door." Martha interrupted his musing, and with a slight smile, he thought to himself that right now, almost everything was perfect in his life. Martha came as a gift two years ago, and now here was Laura.

"Larry finished the front and is now ready to decorate the terrace, pool deck and backyard." Martha started cleaning up the table. Brad folded his napkin and got up.

"All right then. I am finished here. For the next two hours I will be in my office, and no interruptions, please." With that, he left the terrace.

❧

Four thousand miles away, at a hotel bar in Rio de Janeiro,

Brazil, a man was getting drunk. With a slight Eastern European accent, he ordered another whiskey, a Bourbon on the rocks.

Last one for tonight, he thought, as the barkeeper placed the glass on a fresh paper napkin and refilled the peanut jar.

He needed to calm his nerves. By Sunday night, his last installment plus bonus would be paid in full, and he would belong to the rich man's world. Finally! The red carpet golf gala would be his personal retirement celebration.

Nobody would bother him anymore with dirty jobs. No more killing. No more blood.

He would enjoy the rest of his life—a sweet life—right here in Brazil. He had his eyes on a hacienda up in the mountains, south of Rio.

Just two more days, he thought, as he picked up his Bourbon and took a long, last swallow.

SIX

Laughter, hugging and kissing abounded in the house as Crystal, Brad's younger sister, and her family arrived at the Dolphin Place.

Ivy, Crystal's oldest daughter, coined it the Dolphin Place when she was about five years old and saw a pod of dolphins playing out in the ocean from her bedroom window.

Having become a famous professional golfer, Ivy laughed about her dolphin story with her inviting high-pitched giggle. But not so today. Ivy's giggle had been silenced.

Brad looked over to her as she hugged Martha. He could see that she had lost weight since he last saw her, and a sadness overshadowed her natural beauty. She was still hurt, and inside her, a deep depression had eaten away at the once-joyful child.

If only he could help. Nothing more devastating could have happened to a nineteen-year-old top-ranking golfer with the world of professional golf devoted to her than having it all taken away in a blink of an eye.

Back in January this year, she had been attacked with a knife and injured on her way to the next tee at the season's opening tournament. But even worse, she had tragically lost her high-school sweetheart and fiancé, Jason, who jumped in between her and the offender and was deadly wounded in the assault. Only minutes later, he died in her arms.

"Brad, don't worry about her." A soft touch alerted him to the present. Crystal who'd seen his look, came over and gave him a kiss on his cheek.

"She'll recover. It takes time. But I know my girl—she's very strong."

"Crystal, it is so good to see you. This was a tough year for you, too. It is so sad. Ivy is such a talent, a natural. And so beautiful, full of life and joy. I remember last year when she was about to finish up the season as number one, and her excitement was so infectious. And now . . ."

"Yes, she didn't play this year, hasn't touched the clubs at all. And she lost her T1 ranking on the money list. However, money was never the main thing. As you said, she is a natural. And she loves the game."

"Anything I can do to help?"

"Hmm, what she needs most is encouragement, confidence and a new goal, I think. She's still so young, and we all agree that she could jump back to the top ranks if only she would find the love for the game again."

"I see."

"Jason's gone, and nobody can bring him back. But that's not the open wound . . ."

Crystal took his arm and walked him outside. She didn't want Ivy to overhear her next words. Outside, in the fresh air, she faced Brad directly. Her expression changed, and he could see how her wrinkles had deepened and her eyes looked tired and sad.

"Brad, I worry about her, to tell you the truth. The thing is that she—we all—think that injustice has been served."

"Injustice? I don't understand. I thought the police caught the guy right there, on the course, with the knife in his hands, blood all over. Hasn't he admitted to the crime?" Brad looked puzzled.

"Oh yes, he has. Only too openly. But see, this is part of the problem. He let on to be a devoted fan of Julie Ferguson, the former number one and previous child star, and couldn't bear the fact that Ivy was playing better than Julie. Allegedly, he was driven by sudden rage and claimed he committed the crime out of passion. Do you remember just a year ago, Thanksgiving, when Ivy was on her sensational rise to the top and finished the season as T1, and Julie had to step back for the first time in her career?"

"Yes, I remember very well. She drove balls from the terrace into the ocean to show me her straight 240 yards. She couldn't take her mind off golf—she was so passionate in her own world."

"Yes, she was amazing. Well, in court, the defense attorneys claimed convincingly that he was mentally ill at the time of the attack. The first trial closed three weeks ago, and he was released with no probation restrictions, and so he roams free. But Ivy is tormented and cannot deal with this preposterous injustice. Each day she retreats more and more into her own dark world."

"Crystal, I had no idea!" It was true. He had no idea because he didn't follow the story. He considered that maybe he should have used his power to get justice served for her.

"Nobody knows who provided the money to pay his top-notch defense lawyers, and there are other things that really don't add up. That's why we have to put the issue in our own hands now and push for a second trial."

"A second trial? You are going for a second trial?"

"Yes, we will."

"So, what are you planning? How can I help?"

"First, we need to present more evidence that this was not a spontaneous attack of a madman, but a thoroughly planned plot against my girl. This was not the act of a confused and mentally disturbed person. We need to find out who was really behind it.

"Do you really mean—"

"Do you think he smuggled a nine-inch boning knife through security to a professional golf tournament? No way! The weapon had to have been planted before."

Ivy opened the french doors, accompanied by her father, Roger.

"Here comes my girl! Come on, give me a big hug." Brad took her into his arms and held her very tight. He could feel how thin she had become.

"Uncle Brad, let go. You're squeezing me." Ivy stepped back. "I know what you're going to say. But don't worry—I'm fine. I'd love to go down to the beach if that's okay. The water is so calm and beautiful—maybe I can spot a dolphin." She continued down to the boardwalk.

Brad said, "Hi, Roger. It's good to have you all here."

"Good to see you, Brad. By the way, Eileen is joining us for dinner. I hope you don't mind. Crystal invited her before your invitation came. We should have called you—sorry."

"Eileen, my foundation director? Oh, that's fine, I should have thought of it myself."

❧

A couple hours later, after everybody had settled in, the family regrouped for cocktails at the terrace. The sun shined in golden streaks over the blue water and started its slow decent. Brad looked out for Laura, but couldn't find her.

"Martha, have you seen Laura since breakfast?"

"No sir, I haven't. I thought she was taking a nap. But we expect her to join us for dinner, correct? I have already set the table for her, right here next to Eileen."

For this festive afternoon, Martha had changed into a traditional servant's uniform, a black robe with a white apron. She artfully arranged glasses, ice and napkins to give the cocktail bar the final touch.

"Most definitely, she is expected!" He wondered if he should go up to her room and ask her to join them for drinks. He had invited her, hadn't he? He thought he had. But it never crossed his mind that she would hesitate to join the private family gathering.

"Martha, may I ask a favor? I know you are busy, but could you go up and ask her if she is all right? And please let her know that you have a seat prepared for her at our dinner table. I would like her to join us tonight."

"Mr. Coleman, I'll do that right away. That poor woman. I hate the idea of her being alone in her room." And she glanced upwards to Laura's balcony. "Don't you worry. I'll take care of it."

Martha asked Jacqueline, who was also dressed in black and white, to start serving the cocktail punch and the gourmet appetizers. Everybody looked so eager to try the delicious-looking hors d'oeuvres and mesquite-grilled starters.

And so the party began as Martha climbed up the wide marble staircase to check on Laura. She found her fully dressed with perfectly styled hair and makeup in front of her laptop. Laura was looking at candlestick charts. She looked so calm, peaceful and fully engaged in the moment.

"Laura—Mrs. Winchester, the party has just started, and Mr. Coleman asked me to check if you are ready to join them."

Laura looked up, surprised to see Martha.

"Oh, Martha, of course. Is it that late already? I thought I would get dressed early because . . . you know, all these dresses are new. We just bought them yesterday, and I'm not used to them. The style—well, you know, it's quite a bit different from what I was wearing a week ago . . ."

Laura laughed, squinting her eyes in a smile. Humor helped her to cope with moments like today. Thanksgiving dinner parties always brought back treasured memories of her life that was now gone.

"Anyway, isn't it gorgeous?" Laura stood up and turned around in her formal dinner attire. The dress was made of luscious, rich fabric in a soft rose tone matching her hair, in an elegant up-do with youthful thick, eye-grazing bangs.

"Oh, Mrs. Winchester. That is quite a dress." She touched it carefully. It was a beauty. A luxurious, light cream silk organza dress featuring ribbon and rose embroidery. Perfect for a stunning party, but perhaps a little too much for the small crowd downstairs. But this was so Laura Winchester.

Martha was taken back to the times when the Winchesters

threw their big end-of-the-season party, right before they left for Montana. Each time, she needed about a week to get the house back in order. But it was a good time, a very good time. Laura was always the driver.

She and her husband, James, loved to bring back the Roaring Twenties. And so she did today, with her stunning dress and the long white dinner gloves she was slipping into right now.

"Martha, I don't want to keep you any longer, I'll be downstairs in five minutes. What was Brad's sister's name, Chantal?"

"No, it's Crystal, her husband Roger, and their daughter Ivy. Ah, and there is Eileen Walsh. She works for Mr. Coleman."

"Thanks, Martha! You're the best."

Laura wasn't afraid to meet Brad's family. No, she was looking forward to meeting them. Brad was the problem—she didn't want to take time with his family away from him, didn't want to be in the center of attention tonight.

Over the last couple of days, she'd come to like him and had gotten used to being so well cared for, to draw so much attention. He'd fulfilled her every wish—new clothes, a laptop, and a generously funded brokerage account. But more important, he'd spend every free minute with her and didn't seem a bit tired of it, even after her endless bitching and moaning about her situation.

And then there were those long walks on the beach, mostly during the afternoon into the early wintery sunsets. She loved those. But it wasn't true care—she was sure of that. It was more out of respect of her dependency. And it couldn't last, she knew that too.

However, she wasn't sure about her own feelings. Her own need for security, companionship and love. Anyway, there was nothing she could do about it right now. Time would tell how deep his feelings for her truly were.

With a sigh, Laura saved her work and closed the laptop. She swirled around to straighten her dress, double-checked her makeup and hair and left the room to head downstairs. She walked slowly, step by step with her long dress trailing down the staircase. Out the window she saw a pink Cadillac parked in the driveway.

Wasn't that the car of the blonde who had left her in the rain last Sunday night? She heard voices. Brad and a woman were entering Brad's office.

This must be Eileen, his foundation director. That was probably her car . . . Laura stopped abruptly as she overheard Eileen screaming her name. Brad closed the door, but now Laura was more than curious. What had Eileen to say about her? She moved closer to the office and tried—totally gracefully of course—to catch a word or two.

"No, Brad, I won't understand. What is she doing here? You don't owe her anything. Why don't you give her some money and let her go. If it's the foundation's money, I don't mind. But I do mind that she's living here—with you—under the same roof."

"Eileen, please, I just want to help. She needs a little time to adjust—"

"Adjust! Adjust to what? To your lifestyle? I mean, it isn't hers anymore, is it? She doesn't have a dime. She doesn't belong here anymore."

"That's enough."

"Brad, let me finish," she snapped, "just yesterday, at our monthly book club, Lady Cunningham expressed her deepest concern about this situation. And she was mortally embarrassed to have run into you and this homeless person in a highly questionable moment of intimacy at the beach."

"We just saw a green flash at sunset. You know how special that is. And so I hugged her and threw her around in the sand. It was like playing with a child, nothing more."

"Okay, then let her go. Promise me! Otherwise, I can't join you at dinner tonight. I thought we would tell your family about us and would set the date for the wedding."

Laura suddenly had to hold onto the banister—she was shaking. Eileen and Brad were getting married and Lady Cunningham had referred to her as a homeless person and was concerned about her living here in this community.

But the worst part was that she totally misjudged Brad. She thought she saw something flashing in his eyes when he looked at her, something deeper than just wanting to help her.

"You must be Laura, Laura Winchester?" A young woman, tidy, blonde and lovely, with a soft voice said, "I'm Ivy Brooks."

Laura sized up the elven princess in a light yellow tulle dress who was standing at the bottom of the staircase, reaching out to her.

"Ivy?" Still shaken by the conversation she overheard, Laura slowly continued her descend.

"Yes, I'm Laura, it's nice to meet you. Your gown—it's the most beautiful thing I've ever seen!" Laura took her tiny hand.

What a lovely, graceful girl, she thought—and a dainty eater too, judging by how bony her hand felt.

"I was looking for Brad. Dinner's ready. And my dad is hungry. He probably smelled the turkey roasting in the oven for too long. Anyway, would you like to join me?"

With no chance to offer an excuse, Ivy led Laura into the dining room where voices saluted and Crystal waved her over.

∾

A few minutes later, Laura was sitting next to Brad and Eileen at a festively decorated Thanksgiving dinner table with Christmas garlands, flickering candles and the soft sounds of holiday carols on the stereo mixed in with the everlasting song of the ocean.

With warm words of welcome and a broad smile, Brad introduced her formally to his family and to Eileen.

Laura didn't notice any change in his attitude toward her, and obviously, there was not much intimacy between him and Eileen either—they looked and acted like business associates.

Brad had introduced Laura as an old friend of the family, not mentioning anything about what had happened to her. However, of course, her reappearance had made headlines, on paper, TV and the internet, and she could feel the eyes on her.

Never mind, she told herself, she would concentrate on formal conversation with Crystal and Roger, who were seated across the table from her.

The first course was a delicious-smelling New England-style clam chowder with Maine surfer clams in tender diced potatoes with a delicate blend of onions, herbs and spices.

"Laura, you look gorgeous in this dress—where did you get it?" Crystal asked while Jacqueline offered a basket filled with freshly baked dinner rolls served with the first course.

"Oh, it's from Missy Dress on Third Street, downtown Naples." Laura looked over the bread basket and decided on a whole grain roll. "Thank you, Jacqueline, this looks delicious."

"Missy Dress, hmm, I don't know if I've ever been there. Naples has such a great selection of fine stores. Isn't it very unusual for such a relatively small city to have Tiffany, Gucci and Louis Vuitton next to each other?"

"I've never really thought of it that way. But you have a point. Our Waterside Shops, The Village, Third and Fifth Street offer the most luxurious brand stores in the country within a convenient distance. No need to fly out to Miami or New York for shopping."

Laura placed the roll on her side plate and reached out to take a rose-shaped pat of butter and a little salt.

"Crystal, if you like, we could call the store tomorrow and have some dresses delivered to the house for you to have a look at them."

"What a wonderful idea—you think they would do it on Black Friday?"

"Oh yes!" Laura buttered her roll. "Missy Dress is not a store that is very much effected by the spending spree."

"I thought we'd all take the boat out tomorrow." Brad interrupted. He had been eating silently for a while. He was delighted to have Laura next to him, but felt a little uneasy about how his sister might take the situation.

Was it to intimate to invite Laura and have her seated next to him? And Eileen? She smiled whenever Roger asked her a question, but he could feel she was seething with anger and disapproval.

He was certainly not going to announce any fantasy engagement plans of hers, since that's what it was. She had feelings for him, and they'd been out on the boat a couple of times, but he never felt close enough to ask her to take Regine's place. Wouldn't think of it, especially after that scene in his office.

"The weather is supposed to be perfect, a calm sea with a light landward breeze. We'll start early to watch the dolphins. Roger, if you like, we can take the fishing gear, catch a grouper and have lunch on a secluded beach." Brad looked over to encourage Roger and Crystal.

Crystal poised a spoonful of clam chowder. "Hmm, delicious. I mustn't forget to ask Martha about this recipe."

"Hey, sounds good to me—let's spend a day fishing in the sun!" Roger enjoyed the idea. He felt tired from the drive down to Naples.

They lived in St. Petersburg, where he and Crystal had built a real estate office over the last fifteen years. Hard work with long hours and many ups and downs through the years had left marks on his face.

He was looking forward to spending a couple of days in the world of the super rich without a worry. A couple of years ago, he had been thrilled with Ivy's success in golf. His girl had really taken off, and he started coaching her—together, they traveled to all tournaments around the globe. It was perfect, and she was so happy.

But the attack earlier this year made him realize how fragile happiness was. In a split second, a beautiful world turned sour. To see Jason die and her suffer without being able to help. For the first time in his life, he started questioning, what's the purpose, why did it have to happen? His little girl had worked so hard, and she was still so young.

"I'm not going. I'll take a walk on the beach," Ivy said quietly. "I can't stand hurting those beautiful creatures."

And with these words, Martha rolled in the serving cart loaded with the golden brown roasted turkey.

"Martha, how wonderful it all looks," Crystal applauded to save the moment. She knew that these family gatherings were very special. However, only too often they were interrupted by sparks of regret and sorrow. She looked over to her husband, then to Ivy. She knew that, despite the sorrow, after a few years had passed, these memories would stand out as very special treasured events.

And so the family dinner continued, with Martha busily carving the bird while Jacqueline prepared the plates with all the delicious side dishes. There was stuffing, gravy, mashed and roasted potatoes, tender asparagus, French green beans, Brussels sprouts, cranberry sauce and much more.

When everything was served and the glasses refilled, Brad looked around the table and caught Laura's eyes. She smiled, a little starchy, he thought, but she was probably missing her own family. With sparks of unexpected love, he smiled back at her. She would get through it, he would take care of that, and then he would make this her new home, her new family.

"To us," he said, raising his glass, and the family feasted on a very special meal.

SEVEN

What a special place this is, Laura thought, lying in her bed—restless again, turning from side to side to find comfort and sleep.

She couldn't. Too much was buzzing around her head. Memories. Good and bad, joyful and remorseful. Images from the past. Her childhood with Mom and Dad at the ranch, despite the tough times. Thanksgiving dinners with James and his family, where she was welcomed with infinite prosperity and abundance.

Only too clearly, she remembered her first visit to Holly Grain. A late summer barbecue. As she drove through the gate, a whole new world opened up to her. Lavish crop fields and rich pastures with cattle and horses as far as the eye could see. Lush fruit trees surrounded the banks of a lake fed by a river winding through rolling hills.

Every detail was put in place with perfection. The farmhouse with barns and staples was surrounded by flourishing flower and vegetable gardens. And the barbecue—a live band was playing popular country music, and it seemed like hundreds of people were having a great time watching the rodeo. This was where she first met James.

James, where are you? Her thoughts spun around, and tears seeped into her eyes. These old memories gave her comfort tonight.

The farm was always magnificently decorated in festive colors, with freshly planted flowerpots and patriotic garlands lining the long driveway to the house. The main house opened itself through an iron-cast mahogany door, giving sight to old antiques, original artwork, and modern sculptures.

The mansion was detailed with rich fabrics—leather, silk and linen-trimmed walls and checker-board marble floors. Every room breathed luxury—the world of old money.

She kept thinking.

What had she felt when she first encountered the world of the wealthy?

That deep-seated wealth, showing off in their surroundings, behaviors and activities created a sound feeling of belonging.

What impressed her most in the beginning were the different dress codes. There was a morning dress code, a formal dress code, semi-formal, informal and active attire. Being well dressed was part of the occasion—be it Sunday church, the Country Fair, the Cattle Barron's Gala or the yearly barbecue.

Not so for James—he was much more grounded, happy in a shirt and jeans. And he was so fit, trim and tanned from his hard work as a farmer and so sensitive and humbled as a market trader.

Laura rolled around and adjusted her pillows. She belonged here, too—at least she had. Now, everything was lost. She didn't belong here anymore.

The only thing left was her ability to trade. At least, she hoped so. The stock market—was it still the same? She had taken a quick look this morning, the market was ranging sideways, but otherwise, it printed a very familiar picture.

But how could she be sure that she would be successful again? And there it was—her first doubt. About her existence, her right to belong, her future success. Her confidence had taken a deep dive.

And probably more so since she would be taking Brad's money. She would depend on him. She had never traded other people's money. Would she have the same aggressiveness to put on large positions? And if so—did she have the guts to let her winners run to earn real money?

With a deep sigh, Laura turned again. Her thoughts wandered to her mother. Then to Curley, to James and back to her mother. They had told Laura that her mother was dead. She hadn't had a chance to say good-bye.

Did her mother know how much she loved her? When was the last time she told her? What did she write in that last email as she sent the picture of the sunset from the beach?

Enough! Laura pushed back the heavy duvet and got up. She opened the French terrace doors and walked out into the night. She took a deep breath of the fresh sea breeze and tried to enjoy the wonderful scenery. She looked up to the moon and the stars, infinite space. Curley, James, where are you? How small it feels when you lose everything.

"Okay, stop right here and focus on what you have!" she disciplined herself out loud.

For her own sanity, she needed to get away from

everything—at least for a couple of days. To run. To cry. To clear her mind. To let it all out. She needed to find herself—her true self—without being pressured to explain. She wasn't a victim. No, she was a victor!

Laura felt relieved after this outburst. She decided to sneak down to the kitchen and get a glass of hot milk. It had always helped her to find sleep. But suddenly, she had another rush of feeling that she did not belong.

She didn't want to sneak into somebody's kitchen. She wanted to go rightfully down to her own kitchen, make a lot of noise, turn on the TV, and feel alive.

However, for now, this was the only way. With this in mind, she put on her silk morning robe and tip-toed down to the kitchen.

❧

With a glass of warm milk in her hands, she felt much better. She traipsed toward the fireplace in the living room, and as she put her glass down in front of the crackling fire, she heard soft sobbing coming from one of the oversized armchairs.

Looking around, Laura didn't see her at first. But then she noticed Ivy curled up in the chair under a fringed Western-style blanket.

Her face looked tired and sad. She had been crying, Laura could tell from the tears dried on her cheeks. She wasn't sure if she should silently retreat or take a more straightforward approach. She decided to go for the latter.

"Ivy, are you okay?" Laura kneed down to her. "Can I get you something?" As awaken from a trance, Ivy looked up with blurry eyes.

"No, I'm fine. Thank you, Laura. I thought you might have been my mother, and I don't want her to see me like this."

"But Ivy, you're not fine, I can see that. Come over to the fireplace, I'll get you a cup of hot milk and we'll talk."

"Thanks, but I don't wanna talk. There's nothing to talk about."

"Oh, yes there is. There is always something to talk about, especially when young and beautiful teenage girls curl up under a blanket and cry."

Now Ivy had to smile, a soft tender smile. It gave Laura a deeper impression of how pretty Ivy was, with her ivory, soft face and her rainbow-colored eyes. Strong healthy eyes that could measure the distance from tee to flag on a golf course with supernatural precision.

"It hurts inside, still after all those months, but I don't know why I keep crying. I'm okay now. I just can't stop it." Ivy sobbed into a tissue she held crumpled in her hand.

"I know exactly what you mean." Laura took her hand, squeezing it. Wasn't she in the same sort of distress just minutes earlier?

"You know my story, don't you?" Ivy looked up straight into Laura's eyes. Searching, scanning for help, understanding, perhaps love.

"Sort of . . . but not really, I think." Laura wasn't sure, but she knew whatever Ivy was searching for, it could only be found within herself. Ivy grabbed another tissue from a box she must have had hidden under the blanket and sobbed deeply again.

"See, this is one more reason to join me for a cup of milk or hot chocolate and I'll tell you my story first and then, if you want, you tell me yours—deal?"

"I'm not good at keeping my word these days, but I'll try."

"Okay, milk or hot chocolate? I'm going back to the kitchen anyway to heat up my milk."

Laura reached out to hold Ivy's hand. The tiny hand with long fingers was ice cold and bony, no muscle strength. Where was the athlete? The high performer? The number one golfer? Ivy was probably anorexic or something like it, Laura thought—didn't anybody else notice?

"I'll take hot chocolate, no sugar and very hot, please, if you insist." Ivy got up, stretched and looked out into the dark night.

"Will do." Laura went back to the kitchen. A few minutes later she came back with a silver tray loaded with milk, hot chocolate and a plate with freshly baked holiday cookies she found on the kitchen counter.

She and Ivy settled in front of the fireplace on blankets and cushions. Laura loaded more wood onto the fire. Then she took a cookie and a sip of milk and told Ivy what had happened to her. Soon, the sobbing stopped and Ivy listened, entranced, to what Laura had to say.

When Laura came to the end, Ivy couldn't hold it any longer. Questions came bursting out of her. She wanted to know all the details, her feelings, her thoughts and how she's dealing with it now.

"You've lost it all? Do you get your name back? I mean, can they revoke the death declaration?" Ivy had totally forgotten her own misery.

"Yes, I'm waiting for my ID cards. With a little luck, I should get my new passport tomorrow morning." Laura paused.

She was exhausted from reliving those events again. But she'd shared all of it with a newfound lightness and sense of possibility. Ivy was a good listener, and Laura knew that she had found in her a believing soul mate.

"Your passport? Why? Are you planning to go away? Do you need money? I can lend you some." Ivy burst into tears again.

"I've been thinking of going away for a couple of weeks. I too need to clear my mind. Find out how my future life should look. I'm not sure yet what I'm going to do."

Laura reached out for another cookie. "Okay, now tell me about you. I've heard you're real talented when it comes to golf, this is quite a gift. Tell me what set you off balance. Why is it that you're so sad? You know bottling up negative emotions can be very harmful."

Ivy still hadn't said a word about herself, hadn't touched her hot chocolate, but she listened.

Laura continued. "They told me so on Monday, when I refused to see a psychiatrist. They called it perpetual emotional suppression, and it can lead to potentially serious mental and physical health problems. Here, try a cookie, they're quite good."

Ivy picked one up, crumbled it with her fingers, irritated, and tasted a small piece—it felt like a lump in her throat. She coughed and took a tiny sip of hot chocolate to clear her throat.

Laura tried to get her to unfreeze, to relax and to open up. "What would you do tomorrow, if nothing had happened? If nothing had changed?" She sensed an inner connection with her and truly wanted to help. She thought it might help her, too.

"Tomorrow, what would I do?" Ivy looked at her, thinking.

"Tomorrow, I would fly down to Rio."

"Rio! Brazil. That sounds great!" Laura said cheerfully.

"Yes, in fact, if everything was normal, I probably would be down there to play the season's last tournament." Ivy's face gloomed for a short moment, and more tears filled her eyes.

"So, now I'm really curious. Why not go there? What is holding you back?" Laura leaned back against the sofa and encouraged Ivy to continue.

Ivy crumbled with the cookie and glanced back at Laura. What was holding her back? Huh. Why can't she just break through that invisible wall around her, that terror barrier, which only kept her in distress?

"Do you really want to know?" Ivy took another sip of her hot chocolate. "My story, I mean?"

"Yes, I'd like to." Laura's curiosity rose.

"Mmm, this is good." And with another mouthful of the sweet hot drink, she leaned back against the wall next to the fireplace, stretched her long legs and brought the tragic events back to life.

"I can tell you my story, but I'm not sure what's still holding me back."

"Okay, go ahead. The story first."

"At the end of January in the West Indies, we were playing the final round. It was the season's opening tournament. Great location and a wonderful course. It was so unbelievably peaceful. The smell of passion fruit and hibiscus—the air was so crisp. I clearly remember that day."

Ivy stopped. Her eyes filled with tears, and she pulled a couple of fresh Kleenex.

"With the morning dew, the grass was a little slow, but I like it that way. I can play with a little more strength without the danger that the ball keeps rolling on for too long. Early on, I was leading the field."

She sniffed and took another cookie, dipping it in her hot chocolate. The hot beverage and the cookies were doing her good.

"It all started at hole thirteen, where they had a special price for a hole-in-one. A brand new red Porsche Cabriolet, it's called the GT3. And I wanted to win it—for Jason, my fiancé. I had a very good start in the season, I felt confident about my game and my swing was better than ever before. On New Year's Eve, Jason and I had decided to get married this year. I was so happy. We flew out to the tournament earlier to take a couple of days off. Swimming in the ocean, hanging out at the beaches, relaxing, enjoying each other. And to get me a super good start to the season. Every day, I played the course in the early morning hours and then spent the rest of the day together with Jason. It was all so perfect. It all seemed so normal, so easy."

She cleared her throat. "Laura, I want those normal days back. The hole-in-one was the beginning of the end."

"What happened?"

"All right then. As we got to the tee, there was a crowd, people, TV reporters, and there was the Porsche. They'd set up a public bleacher right behind it. Anyhow, it seemed there was less security than on the other tees. I didn't notice it back then as much as I do now—anyway. A par-3 with 226 yards of distance, I knew I could do it. I mean the hole-in-one. I was so focused—truly in the zone—you know what I mean?"

"Oh yes, I do know." Laura nodded while she warmed her hands on her milk mug—trading was all about being in the zone.

"Anyhow, I just hit it. Hit the ball straight down to the green. About two feet off the hole. The ball rolled, bounced off the flagstick and landed in the hole."

"Wow!"

"Yes, it was all over. I was thrilled. Not only had I won the Porsche, but this was an eagle, two strokes under par. And gave me two additional points on my score card—I was already leading by five. In this moment, I thought I had it all. My golf I loved so much, and Jason. My life was bliss. It was so natural for me to play, to practice for hours without ever getting tired, never getting enough. Always the first up in the morning and the last to walk back from the course in the dark. Especially during the time at the academy."

"The academy? Is that where you were trained?"

"Yes, up in Orlando." Ivy stretched again, needing to move. "We just called it the academy. Most pros have gone through it. Some managed to stay longer than others. It is a real boot camp. Hard—very intense. No excuses. I lived on campus since my tenth birthday. Practiced in the morning before sunrise, went to school, came back, practiced until sundown, homework, sleep and all over again."

Ivy glanced over her tights. Her legs were so thin. Would they still support her in a five- to six-hour game? She needed to get back in shape, put on some real muscle soon. But what for?

"That must have been tough on you."

Ivy looked up. Laura had just stopped her from being miserable again. "You'd make a good coach."

"Well . . ." Laura smiled.

Ivy paused, took a sip of hot chocolate and grabbed a

gingerbread cookie. She looked so happy, captured in those memories. Laura wasn't going to interrupt again, although she was truly interested to learn more about Ivy.

"Okay, where was I? Oh, yes. I had just hit this hole-in-one and was comfortably leading the game. Jason was with me then, and he was overwhelmed with joy."

Ivy put her mug down, moved closer to the fire and added another log.

"You know, I haven't told anybody what I'm going to tell you now. I don't know you—well, I mean, not for very long—but still, I feel I can tell you everything. It's just that it stuck inside me for such a long time. Ten months now. Anyway . . ."

Ivy circled around with her words, but Laura was patient, knowing that this wasn't only about telling her the story. No, it was also a very important step toward recovery.

Facing the truth, recalling the details, bringing back the feelings could end the suffering. The first step on the road to reconciliation. The road Laura hadn't even found yet.

Ivy took a breath and continued. "Jason and I were high school sweethearts at the academy. However, he quit pro golf and wanted to become a sports doctor. He'd just finished medical school and was about to start clinical residency this summer. Anyhow, we were thrilled after my hole-in-one shot. I walked towards the green to pick up my ball. At some point, the way was blocked by the Porsche, so we all had to walk around it. Some volunteers were trying to hold back the crowd. They were all excited, cheering me on, asking for autographs. Then, all of a sudden, I felt a sharp pain in the back and I crouched down. I remember a beautiful yellow hibiscus bloom in front of me and thought, that can't be it. And then, everything went black."

"Do you know what happened?"

"Only later. I can show it to you, it's all on YouTube. They had it live on TV, millions watched it. The next thing I remember is people screaming, two paramedics around me, holding my head and my legs. And there was Jason, lying on the ground. He didn't move. His eyes were focused on mine . . . I didn't know what it meant. I had no idea."

"Although, I saw the blood—no, I smelled it even before I saw it. There was blood everywhere and high-pitched screaming. I wanted to move towards Jason, to touch him. I tried to say something, but I couldn't speak. One of the paramedics did a pupillary light reflex. They held me down so I could not move. But I had to. I needed to check on Jason. He wasn't moving. He was just looking at me. I'll never forget his beautiful brown eyes, so open, alert and full of love."

"I bent over to him, kissed him. He whispered something I couldn't understand, and then he said, 'Good-bye, I love you!' Later, I woke up in a hospital bed. First, I thought, we all are going to be all right, and it was only hours later. But then the doctors told me that they couldn't save Jason. He had lost too much blood."

"The knife hit my left shoulder blade. The wound was severe but not life threatening. Later I learned from the police that Jason must have thrown himself over me, to protect me, as the attacker stabbed a second time. He thrust the knife straight through his rib cage, directly in his heart."

Ivy put her face in her hands. "Oh Laura, it was so horrible."

Laura didn't know what to say. What a tragedy. She took Ivy's cold and shivering hands, trying to give her comfort. But the best she could do was encourage Ivy to finish her story. To let it all out.

Ivy wiped her tears.

"A couple of days later, I was transferred on my own request to a clinic in the States. It took me six months to heal and recover. The doctors there were very supportive and understanding. The whole staff was great. Over the summer, my mom and dad rented a house, and we spent a couple of months together. A true family vacation. I loved it. Hiking, and dad went fishing a lot—then he grilled the catch of the day. They did a great job keeping everything away from me."

"So who did it? Did they catch the attacker?"

"Oh yes, they arrested him on the spot. Apparently a psycho, a madman, and a crazy fan of Julie Ferguson."

"Julie Ferguson?" Laura was curious.

"Yes, Julie is also a pro golfer. Actually, she was the number one, before I took over, and I believe she is back on the top now. This weekend at the season's ending gala in Rio de Janeiro, she will be the star and receive the big check. Oh well . . ."

"I see."

"Anyway. I recovered fully—at least physically. And I was in a good enough mood to decide to get back to the game again, it was the only thing I was ever interested in doing. I was ready to get a coach and start practicing again. I thought I was going to be okay and could make it to the Olympic team and play in Rio next year. That was my goal."

"But golf isn't part of the Olympic program, isn't it?"

"No, it's back on, for the first time after a century. Golf was last played at the 1904 Olympic Games in St. Louis, Missouri. Back then, the U.S. and Canada were the only competing nations. But this time, there will be at least thirty countries in the golf competition." For the first time, Laura could see a real sparkle in Ivy's vivid eyes.

She continued. "Going for the gold medal. That was my dream."

"And? I think it's a great idea—why not go for it?"

"Hmm . . . yes." Ivy took another sip of her chocolate. "I found this coach who trained track & field Olympic athletes in Aspen, Colorado. He said he would take me on his team for the rest of the summer, and so, I went through a ten-week drill and practice program with the Olympic team."

Ivy got up and walked over to open the french doors to the terrace. She took a deep breath before she added more wood to stir the fire. She seated herself against the stone wall and continued.

"Training was so intensive. No time to brood and agonize. Up before sunrise and back at camp after sunset, and it was exactly what I needed. I needed to work every bone, every muscle in my body, feel it all come to life again. It reminded me of my earlier days at the academy. My mood was lifted, and I slept better. After those ten weeks, I was in great shape."

"So?" Laura looked up. It sounded good to her, the right thing to do.

"To make a long story short," Ivy walked up and down now, "about two weeks ago, on my way back from Aspen, I broke down again."

"What happened?"

"I was sitting at the airport in Denver waiting for my

connection. I felt great and full of energy, and then they broadcasted the news about the trial on CNN. They'd let him go. The madman had been set free—after all he had done to us. He killed Jason, destroyed my life, but they let him go free."

"But wasn't it attempted murder—at least in your case? He was trying to kill you, wasn't he?" Laura was upset. This didn't sound right.

"We certainly thought so. But apparently not the judge, and not the jury."

"Now what?" Laura was touched as Ivy mentioned the trial and the verdict. Injustice being served. Obviously. Can it be undone? Was injustice being served in her own case also? Perhaps. She knew all too well how this felt.

Instead of being embraced by the world, you are regarded as the one who caused the trouble. And it will never be the same. All is lost, broken, and shattered. Only this feeling of betrayal and anger remains and occupies your mind. But who is responsible? Will they be held accountable?

Suddenly Ivy jumped up.

"Take a good look at me," she said, "I lost weight during this intensive training, which was good. I built muscle. But since that time, I haven't been eating well, and I still keep going with the hard training. It keeps me occupied and my mind off brooding. But I'm losing too much weight. Somehow I can't stop it. And by now I don't care anymore. It doesn't matter, nothing does anymore."

Her hands covered her face while she slipped back down the stone wall. She sobbed like a baby.

"And Rio, the Olympics?"

"Nope."

"Ivy?"

"I wanted to go, but something deep inside me has a stronger hold on me. Can't put it in better words. And they won't let me play anyway. I dropped too much behind. I—"

"Ivy," Laura got up, she was excited and thrilled. "Sorry to interrupt! I just got an idea. I'll go—I'll fly down to Rio and investigate on your behalf!"

"What?"

"Yes, I like the idea more and more. I can go as soon as I have a passport. Most likely by tomorrow."

"And then?"

"You said the season's last tournament is currently being played and the race will end in Rio with a red carpet gala on Sunday night, right?"

"Yes . . ."

"See, you know my story, don't you?"

"Yes, but— "

"I was hurt, I lost it all and I have no place to go. And," Laura looked around, "I don't belong here, Eileen is right."

"Eileen? What's she got to do with all this?"

"Never mind, but I don't want to be in anyone's way or dependent on anyone. Listen, I lost it all, and so did you. Why can't I help you to find answers, since there is absolutely nothing I can do here for myself? I just can't stand this any longer. The press, old neighbors and friends. Their sneering looks. I do not belong in this class anymore. I'm poor, homeless. See my engagement ring? That's all I have left."

"Laura, come off it!"

"Oh no, I don't mean to be bitter. I'm not. I will survive, whatever it takes, and I will build my life back with my wealth. That's for sure. I'll work harder than I ever did. But before I even begin with a fresh start, I need to overcome my past."

"I see."

"Please, let me go to Rio for you!" Laura entreated urgently.

"But I hate to lose you, it's good to talk to you. Why don't you stay over the weekend? I think Uncle Brad really likes you, I see it in his attitude. He'll support you. He'll give you money. He is well connected."

Ivy was puzzled. Of course, she had listened to Laura's story, but she was so deeply involved in her own dilemma that she didn't realize how dramatic the circumstances were for Laura right now.

"Ivy!" Laura took Ivy's hands and urged her again. "I need to get away for a couple of days, maybe a week or two, to clear my own mind. Rio would be perfect. And honestly, I think you're right about the injustice. Perhaps there is a hidden truth behind the crazy fan—who knows? Did anybody investigate it thoroughly?"

"The police, the prosecution, I think."

"You were in Colorado in rehab while the attacker was brought to trail, right? And all this time, you thought the authorities would bring this to a fair end. So far they haven't. Now it is your turn."

"What do you mean?" Ivy didn't get it.

"You're in charge of your life, your career and your happiness. It's your responsibility, and I'm going to help you."

Laura was thrilled to bits. She walked around, collecting wet tissues and empty mugs and closed the french doors. This was what she needed. She could feel it, sense it, and it charged her with tremendous energy.

"Let's go get some sleep. We need to start fresh in the morning."

"Start? With what?"

"Solving a murder mystery."

"Are you serious? I mean, you think there was a reason for all of this?"

"Perhaps, perhaps not—but I've got a hunch, you know. Big boning knifes are not lying around openly on golf courses, do they?"

"No."

"All right then. Let's see what I can find out in Rio." Laura was more than determined and finished cleaning up after their ladies' night.

"I'll come with you!" Ivy was electrified by Laura's energy—it was like a spell over her. "Yes—the two of us should go to Rio! All major players will be there, all coaches, managers and officials. Big money—big time! It's the best place to start. I know most of them and can give you insights."

Ivy hurried and followed Laura, who had already shut down the lights and was on her way to the stairway.

"Hey wait, I'm coming with you!" Ivy shouted again.

"I can hear you. And I like it—with you, I don't have to pawn my engagement ring for airfare and hotel," Laura joked and waved her stunning 12-karat diamond ring at Ivy.

EIGHT

M a'am, would you like another glass of champagne? We'll be landing in Rio de Janeiro soon, and this is our last service round."

The steward's soft voice woke Laura, and the hum of the aircraft flying smoothly at 30,000 feet above sea level brought her back to the present.

"I'd rather have a coffee and some juice, please. And could I have a glass of water, sparkling, with some lemon, too?"

"Sure. Anything else?"

"No, thank you."

The steward handed her the drinks, and Laura placed them on her small table. She looked over to find Ivy still stretched out behind her curtain, sleeping. Although these first-class sleeping seats were very comfortable, Laura struggled to sleep much on their eight-hour flight from Miami to Rio.

She was too excited. Everything had turned out so well. She'd received her passport and preliminary papers quickly, they'd caught this night flight to Rio, and they should be well on schedule to watch the final round before joining the gala at the

Grand Palace Hotel.

Brad hadn't been thrilled about this whole idea, but Crystal was. She immediately noticed the difference in Ivy and her newfound thrill and excitement to take her destiny back in her own hands, and so she approved.

Now, Laura leaned back, gazing down at the Brazilian coastline and enjoying her hot coffee. She felt like a warrior, with Ivy as her companion—two warriors against the rest of the world. Yeah, we'll bring justice where justice belongs. She toasted to the approaching skyline of Rio.

This is the last day I'll play the role of a gunman, he thought, smiling. After all, that was what they called him since the end of his short childhood.

He started out young to become a professional. This was his true calling, and he would finish this job as he had finished so many before. Men, women, and children, clean, with no traces left behind, according to the demands of his masters.

However, this job was different, and he hadn't liked it from the beginning, but the contract conditions were too good to pass up.

Still, he had to kill in public and let himself get arrested for it. This would put a lot on him, but it was part of the deal. He'd taken the blame as a madman, not knowing what he was doing.

"Haha, not knowing what I was doing," he said to himself. "Like that would ever happen." It was all part of the plan to act that way—even the judge probably knew . . . although he couldn't be sure of that. Still, he'd sweated heavily as they made him stand up for the pronouncement of judgment. But his lawyers were the best that money could buy, and they had gained him acquittal from all charges.

It's all part of the deal, he repeated to himself, and the handsome compensation included a new identity and enough money to ensure a comfortable living until the Lord would call his name.

With his face obscured by a baseball cap and dark sunglasses, he sat quietly amid the crowd at the 18th hole reserved seating and watched the first group of players come into sight.

Tonight, as soon as Julie Ferguson took the Vare Trophy in her hands and was honored as the LPGA Rolex Player of the Year, he would be awarded too, richly, with a final check and a new passport. And then he would celebrate dearly his early retirement.

Now, all he had to do was sit there and wait for the hours to pass.

"Hurry, hurry," Ivy called over from her suite while quickly unpacking her luggage. "It's getting late, and we want to see the final groups arriving."

"All right, I'm all set." Laura appeared in the comfortable salon of her oversized penthouse suite at the Grand Palace Hotel. They had booked adjoining suites with a connection door so they could leave the passage open for a more home-like feel.

"Okay, let's see. Where are my black sunglasses? And I need my cap. I don't want to be hassled by paparazzi, and I surely don't want to be recognized by my old peers."

"Soon to be your new peers. Remember, I'll need you back on the tour next year. I need somebody to cheer me up. To be my hero!"

Laura spun around, enjoying her new role, enjoying her youth and determined to make a difference in Ivy's life.

"Sunglasses and hats will be our warrior outfit for this afternoon. Glamour and glitter will do it tonight at the gala. I like it."

"Laura, I still don't get why all this is necessary. First you want to mingle with the crowd instead of taking our seats for the finals in the VIP lounge, and then we attend the gala tonight in full glamor as if nothing has happened. As if everything was normal. What's the point?"

"Are you afraid of the crowd, being around other people?"

"No, not anymore. I had therapy for that, and I've worked through it."

"Okay then, let's go, and don't worry. I have a plan. Trust me! Just take your iPhone and be prepared to shoot a lot of pictures. Let's go now, I'll explain later."

"All right then."

They left to join the walking spectators for the final round of the LPGA tour.

It was a beautiful afternoon in late November, and the sun towered brightly over the *Marvelous City*. A pleasant breeze rolled in from the ocean, and the air was filled with scents of rose and gardenia. Just perfect.

The atmosphere was electrified by the excitement of the crowd as the last two groups approached the final holes. TV sports channels from all over the world joined sponsors and golf fans to cheer for their favorite players.

Ivy was thrilled. Although this was the first time after the incident for her to return to a major golf event, she was immediately thrown back into the game.

The fascination of performing under pressure, in all weather, with spectators constantly shouting and TV crews filming, was intense, and she needed to calm her mind, block it all out and strike the ball to perfection. Straight forward into the hole. The hole. The only focal point in her mind she would allow herself to be concerned with.

They'd asked her why she didn't see the attacker coming. She remembered how she'd stumbled in court to answer this question. But now she knew. She was so preoccupied with teeing off that nothing else mattered. The rest of the world was left outside. She was completely calm. And she felt the hole-in-one before her club even hit the ball.

To be the best, to perform at your best, you have to control your mind and your body to work in perfect harmony.

"Are you okay?" Gently, Laura touched her shoulder as if she wanted to awaken her from a sleepwalk.

They were standing at the tee markers of hole 17, waiting for the final flight to arrive.

"Yes. Yes, I'm fine. I was just daydreaming. Oh Laura, it's so good to be back. Back at the links. See the beauty of this golf course?"

"Yes, is this a links course?"

"Yes, indeed it is. A coastal course designed between dunes, with deep bunkers, few water hazards and few or no trees like the historical St. Andrews Links."

"I see." Laura took a couple of pictures of the course.

She did play golf during the winter season in Naples as a social event, and she was quite good at it, but it never made it to the top of her list. She was always preoccupied with trading and horses.

Finally, the players arrived, with Julie Ferguson leading the way. Apparently, she had just shot a birdie and was now leading the field. The crowd applauded. She was closely followed by her caddie and the other players of her flight.

It was quite a sight, her long blonde hair pulled back to a French braid, her stylish golf gear from head to toe—and she had the body to show it off, toned and in top shape, the natural way.

"Laura, look, isn't she great? Can you feel the arousal of the players? The smell. The sounds. I just love it. And I've missed it so much. I'm not sure if I can ever go back to playing at my best, but I'll try. Yes, I will. I can't wait to start practicing again." Behind her black sunglasses tears of joy were forming.

"Ivy, you're so sweet!" Laura hugged her like a little sister, and as Ivy looked up with a big wide smile and honest, pure, open eyes, she felt on top of the world.

"Thank you so much for bringing me back. It was the right thing to do." Ivy was holding Laura's hand. "You know, I just can't believe what happened. Look at me—my arms, hands and fingers are so tiny, so weak. How could I have let that happen? I need my strength back, have to build up muscles. And energy." Tears were running down her cheeks.

"We'll do it. We'll get you back to the tour. Soon. I have a plan." More like a vision, an intuition, Laura thought as she squeezed her hand in encouragement and pulled a Kleenex out of her bag.

"But first things first," Laura insisted. "Let's walk with the final group to the end. And watch Julie closely. I noticed something a little earlier, and I want you to take videos of each of her shots. Focus on her body. And after the stroke, focus on her face. Get it zoomed in as much as you can."

"No problem. But why? We can watch this all later online or on the TV replays."

"No, we can't. Not the way I want it. Only Julie. Her swings, strokes, her face. Focus on her."

"What did you notice?"

"Hmm, I'm not quite sure yet, to be honest. That's why I want you to have those videos so I can study them later. Oh, get ready, there she is, ready to tee off. And take the practice strokes too."

"Okay, on your command." Ivy got her iPhone out of her pocket and started to position herself to have an unobstructed view of Julie, who selected her driver for the first shot.

And Julie was at her best. She played the par-3 hole with one stroke onto the green and with the confidence to play her third birdie in this final round.

Nobody would take glory and triumph away from her this year. Nobody. She played -1 and was cheered by an increasing group of fans who followed her to the final hole.

Later, as Julie was holding her trophy up in the air to share her joy, Ivy had to close her eyes. Although she admired and loved Julie and wished her nothing but the best, at this moment, her hands formed to a fist while she remembered only too vividly how she felt a year ago, right here at the finals.

How did they put it? "The race ends here—the winner takes it all." Yes, she desperately wanted to come back, to show the world what was still in her, and how she would win future races and Olympic gold.

Golf was her passion, her true love, and the only love left in her life, now that Jason was gone.

❧

As expected, the gala was in full swing as Julie and Marilyn arrived in the foyer. Reporters immediately flocked around them, followed by the media glare, and they started questioning everything they had missed asking at the press conference just two hours earlier.

But the big news they expected wasn't out, yet. Was it true that Julie Ferguson and her long-time fiancé were planning to get married during the winter break?

For weeks the subject was viral in the tabloids, and everybody was waiting for the official announcement.

"Smile, my dear. Just smile." Marilyn walked one step behind Julie, who still wasn't used to all this glamour. Julie scanned the foyer for Dustin Cooper, her husband *in spe*. They were going to announce the wedding date tonight, and this lightened her mood.

"Do you see Dustin?"

Julie looked around. She couldn't possible face the reporters without him by her side.

"Smile, my darling, just smile. A happy confident face for the bold headlines tomorrow. Dustin may be already at the table. We'll find him, or he will find us. Let's try to get to the crowd. Keep smiling, and don't comment on anything they ask. Wait for your time at the podium, where all can hear what you've got to say. Huh, they will love it. You and Dustin, I'm so happy for you, darling!"

"All right." Julie smiled like a clown at the circus. "You're right, it's show time—I just wish you could stay a couple of days longer and enjoy Rio with Dustin and me."

"Darling, I've got to go back. Tons of work is waiting, and besides, I've a wedding to plan. My flight leaves early in the morning."

"Yes, it's only three weeks, I can't believe it. The pressure of the tour is fading, and all it leaves is pure joy—I did it! Wow!"

"Yes, you sure did, my darling."

"Thank you, Marilyn, without you, I wouldn't be holding the check in my hands tonight."

"And you won't, unless we move quickly to the ballroom and the podium."

"Why don't you take the lead, and I'll follow you." So Marilyn edged her way through the excited crowd toward their table.

Julie continued to look for Dustin, and with some caution, she tried to see if her father was somewhere in the audience. Whoever sent her the note must have seen him here. Or could he be so impertinent to write the note himself?

All those years, he was her big hero, her mental coach, her trainer. She'd lost her mom to cancer when she was only seven, but her dad was always there for her. He was the only person who devoted total commitment and confidence in her talent.

However, since she started earning good money, he'd changed. He'd signed too many sponsor contracts without consulting with her. He was accused of verbally abusing officials, manipulating his daughter's schedule to preserve her ranking and performing illegal coaching during the game. Most notably, he got into a fistfight with an American millionaire at an international tournament.

All that could be explained away with overprotection and love for his daughter—at least that's what he'd told her. But then, last year, their relationship turned sour when she was questioned about a criminal tax scheme she had no idea about.

Her father was accused of mismanaging the millions his daughter had won, and at one point he was said to be carrying around her winnings in paper bags.

Later that year, he was convicted of failing to pay two million dollars in taxes on her earnings and attempting to evade another five million through a tangled scheme of mock companies and tax havens. He was sentenced to pay a heavy fine, served six months in prison and is out now on probation—or so she heard.

Luckily, she was completely exonerated by the court. Nevertheless, the tax issue had alienated father and daughter, and it was a low point in Julie's career and her personal life. She'd lost on the tour, and she'd lost her father.

Where would she stand today if Marilyn hadn't stepped in at the right time, earlier this year?

Julie hurried through the crowd to catch up with Marilyn, who already arrived at their sponsored table.

"Hello, hello, see who finally made it. Congratulations again!" Harry Butcher, her main sponsor, kissed her cheeks and gave her a hug.

"Julie, my superhero! Let me take a look at you! Wow, your dress, your hair—you look like a Hollywood star tonight! Now that's what I call a red carpet beauty. Here, take this seat, we'll leave this one for Dustin." He swirled her around and appointed the seat next to him.

"And Marilyn, why don't you sit right there, next to my wife. Donna, I'd like to introduce you to the golfer of the year and her coach." Harry directed a waiter to open the magnum bottle of Dom Pérignon, which was sitting close to him in an ice cooler.

Marilyn took her seat. "Harry, good to see you. Mrs. Butcher, Donna, so what do you say? Julie amazed us all today, didn't she? My little darling gave a wonderful performance to the end of the race."

Julie was still glancing over the festively decorated ballroom, looking for Dustin. Music filled the air, and waiters were busy serving delicious finger foods and cocktails to the continuously arriving guests.

Finally, she spotted him—yes. He was sitting at a table in the back row. He had his back to her, but she was dead certain it was him. But wait. Who was sitting next to him? Wasn't that her dad? Hmm . . . she tried to get a better look, but still, she couldn't be sure.

The ballroom was packed with people, and the lights were already dimmed. The award ceremony was about to begin.

"Julie, take your seat. You'll get your chance to stand right up there on the podium, holding the Vare Trophy and your check soon. Now sit down and toast with us."

Harry raised his glass.

"To Julie, my protégé, my favorite golfer and her team. To her very successful year and many more to come!"

Julie sat down and took her champagne glass. "Harry, thank you for your ongoing support. Marilyn, thank you for stepping in with full devotion. I owe my success to all of you!" And she toasted to the table round.

Dustin hurried up. "Wait! Where's my glass? Sorry I'm late, princess—some reporter kept me busy. Are you ready for the show?" Dustin hugged her and whispered, "I've missed you. You look terrific tonight." His lips softly touched hers.

Julie felt warm and cozy, her nervousness drifted away. Dustin's upfront, candid manner gave her comfort and strength. He was always so content, and his pleasing words were sometimes too flattering.

But she liked it—it certainly helped with the press and the sponsors, and she knew there was a much deeper, meaningful side too.

"Just be yourself, and all will fall into place. You'll see. I love you!"

He kissed her again, this time on her forehead.

As a former professional golfer, he still kept his body in perfect shape and with his soft brown hair, his tanned smooth face and his dark eyes, he was irresistible. Nobody could be angry at him for long.

"I love you, too."

She took his hand and held it tightly. She wanted to ask him if he had seen her father, but something held her back.

Maybe later, she thought. The pure idea of her father watching her tonight made her feel unsettled and more nervous than she already was. But she had to pull herself together and to concentrate on her display on stage.

The show had just begun, and thunderous applause spread through the crowd for the LPGA commissioner, who had appeared in the spotlight to open the Rolex award ceremony.

❧

Ivy and Laura were seated at Ivy's sponsor table. Laura noticed how the sports manager was checking out his former number one star—he wasn't all pleased with her overall physical condition.

Oh well, Laura thought, weak muscles and sore tendons were certainly trainable, but a damaged mind was not so easy to repair. Somehow, that was her job, she concluded, and so far she'd enjoyed it. Rio was just the start.

If she could bring clarity to the real motifs and shed light on the people behind the attack, it would help Ivy to get back into the game, and it would be for her own good.

Maybe, just maybe, she would then find new meaning for her own life.

❧

"Julie, my darling, it's time. Are you ready?" Marilyn turned over to her, double-checked her makeup and corrected her hair. All looked perfect. But her eyes had a slight shadow of sadness.

"I'm nervous as can be. My heart is pounding."

Her name was called.

Dustin squeezed her hand encouragingly and gave her a quick peck on her cheek as he pulled her chair back while she got up. Flash bulbs started their dance, and Julie showed her biggest smile.

All of a sudden, a shooting pain fired through her lower back. For a slight moment, she faded. She couldn't breathe and wanted to sit down, but she couldn't move.

"Darling, keep breathing—in and out. Yes, that's fine—in and out."

And so she tried. Her eyes were open, and she was facing the flashes from the photographers. Is pain visible? That was the only thought she had. She kept breathing—in and out . . .

"Yes, that's good." Dustin balanced her, but everything seemed so distant—so far away.

"Concentrate on my eyes, Julie, look at me." He held her tight. "It's just the nerves, isn't it? Keep breathing."

"I can't move. I just can't. The pain—"

"Dustin, why don't you escort her to the podium? Start with your wedding date announcement and then kiss her officially and let her accept the trophy and the check."

Harry Butcher was taking the lead now. Beads of sweat appeared on his forehead. Harry wasn't amused, and he was close to losing his temper. He had come this close to a massive celebration, and now this. His superstar wasn't fit for the media.

He needed to work on this immediately. There was too much at stake. Julie's schedule of public sponsorship appearances was bursting at the seams, and he needed her to perform well—super well and fit.

She had to live up to the expectations of a superstar, a hero for the teens and an idol for the chaps and bobbysoxers of this world.

Was that so complicated?

Under cheering applause from a very appreciative audience, Julie managed to get up to the podium, where Dustin took the lead and announced their wedding date—Sunday before Christmas. This was a crowd-pleaser and set the whole room on fire.

The whole room?

Not quite. One person in the back did not respond favorably. He'd hoped for a different partner for his daughter—not Dustin. He knew too much and would always be a threat to him. But why was she hesitating to get to the podium alone?

What was wrong there? Julie's father saw the pain in her eyes. How he wished to be up there with her at this moment. His little baby. She'd made it all the way through. And if he had smoothed the path a little, so what? Wasn't a father supposed to do all he could to make his offspring bloom?

A couple of tables to the left, Ivy didn't feel so thrilled either, but she applauded anyway as Julie stepped up the red carpet stairs onto the podium. She knew that feeling—the slow pace to the top and then the sudden spotlight.

Oh boy, how she'd hated it last year and wished to be at a thousand different places while she stood up there. And now, she was hiding in the dark, unnoticed, a loser, a total failure.

She fought hard to keep the tears back, but the moment when Dustin released the date of their wedding, she couldn't hold on any longer and they flooded her eyes.

"What's wrong, Ivy? Honey, what's the matter?" Laura didn't understand.

"Oh, it's just that date. Jason and I were planning to get married that day too." Ivy looked pale and fragile again.

"Laura, I miss him so much. Why did he have to die so young? And how can I go on, knowing that he gave his life for me?"

"Listen, Ivy, not now. Pull yourself together. We're here on a mission, and this includes getting justice for his death. To learn why he had to die. Why somebody tried to kill you. Now I need you to be strong—can you do that? The press has certainly gotten wind that you're here, and we don't want to make headlines—not yet. Let's stick to our plan and keep a low profile. At least for tonight. Okay?"

"Yeah, okay." Still sniffing, she took her glass and toasted toward Julie. "To her success and to us for a successful outcome of our project, whatever that means."

"That's better! And to your successful comeback next year."

"Hmm, we'll see."

"Sure!" And Laura raised her glass, "Cheers!"

Julie received her trophy and the check. She waited for the applause to die down. With tears of joy, she looked forward to the speech she'd prepared during the previous days.

But the crowd kept cheering her, rising to their feet. What a moment, she thought. Forgotten was all the pain, the note about her father. This is it! Was it worth the effort? Yes! And yes, she needed that encouragement tonight to keep on going despite her back pain and the enduring training and practice sessions.

She would continue, definitely. The room was filled with hundreds of supportive fans, peers and potential sponsors who would support her.

Suddenly, her eyes spotted a familiar face in the rear, dimmed at the dark end of the ballroom. There was no mistaking it—her father was standing there, applauding and toasting to her when their eyes met.

So he was actually here tonight, attending the show, celebrating what was once his.

But why hadn't he contacted her and congratulated her directly for her success? Granted, she wasn't so thrilled to talk to him since his conviction. But time goes by, justice was spoken and if he walks free and has good intentions, she'd forgiven him, wouldn't she?

She never forgot that it was he who encouraged her to swing the club, again and again and again. It was he who had planted that seed in her. To do something special, to be excellent, to become number one in the world.

But wait, she thought, who was that guy standing to his left? She saw his face only briefly before the man turned and walked swiftly towards the rear exit. This face—she'd seen it before. She was not sure when and where, but it made her flesh crawl.

But now the crowd was awaiting her oration.

He was very upset. This hadn't turned out as planned—he carefully checked if he was alone in the marble men's room. Then he splashed cold water on his face. Looking into the mirror, he could still hear the crowd cheering.

This was all his doing, wasn't it? Julie climbed the top, and her success made her sponsor, boyfriend, manager and father rich men.

But what about him? Instead of receiving his final payment, he had been accused of not having performed up to the expectations—of not doing his job right. Nonsense. He had delivered.

He injured her enough that she couldn't continue golfing this season, perhaps to give it up forever. That's all. The killing of her boyfriend wasn't even part of the original package. He did that as a freebee.

And now they were going nuts, telling him he should have killed her. But that was never the plan. The goal was the right shoulder blade—from the back. He was supposed to use a boning knife instead of a gun, his normal joystick.

He wanted to kill and to do it his way. That's what he was good at—killing people without a trace. Smooth and quick—no big bang. But this time, they ordered a public job, a scandal was needed.

And this was what he delivered. Final payment was due tonight, right after Julie received her honors and awards. Instead, they had kicked him out.

Why was Dustin so upset that Ivy Brooks was here tonight? She is not coming back to the tour, she will not qualify for the Olympic Games, and the way she looked tonight, she probably will never again be able to hold a golf club longer than a minute.

But they would not get away with it.

Not this time. He was too exposed to the media. His face had been all over the world. There was no way that he could continue to earn a living in his old profession.

They had an obligation to take care of him, good care, and he would make them pay.

Harry Butcher was disappointed with Julie's performance on stage, and it showed all over his face. Marilyn noticed it, and so did Dustin and the others at their table.

The band started playing and invited the first eager dancers to the floor, while most guests remained to enjoy their desserts. Julie returned to the table, proudly holding her trophy in one hand and the check in the other. She was still shaking and tried to relax after that disaster on the podium.

She had hoped that her nervousness and pain attack weren't too visible down here in the audience, but that hope faded the minute she saw their faces.

Those looks spoke for themselves. She just wasn't born to speak in public, and tonight, she was closer to screaming in pain than interacting with the audience.

Sure, they had expected a hero, a glamorous celebrity. The perfect role model for all the products she signed sponsor contracts with—golf gear, shampoos, makeup and watches. Most of them were pushed by Dustin, her father and most recently by Harry.

Clearly, they needed somebody who would connect with the audience through strong charisma and appeal, someone who would shine and make others want to be like her.

Maybe this needed to end anyway. The back pain had become excruciating—she wasn't even sure if she could swing a club with speed and power again as she finally sat down in her chair.

That wasn't her only concern.

She would deal with her pain when she got home. Maybe back

surgery could fix it during the winter break.

No, she was more concerned about her father's doings. Why was he in Rio? And who was the man he was talking to?

She didn't like it at all.

NINE

The crowd screamed louder and louder, and the applause was deafening. Thoroughbreds could be seen in every direction.

Laura stood in the Winner's Circle and embraced *Pieces of Eight*, her own champion, who was draped in a blanket full of red roses.

The run for the roses.

Yes, she had done it. Her filly won the Kentucky Derby! James and her mother applauded excitedly. Suddenly, a deep ominous rumble distracted her from the sweet, soft smell of the roses.

Thunder.

Heavy drops of rain began to fall down on the pretty silks and glamorous setting. People tried to cover themselves with the derby's brochure, and umbrellas were opened in panic.

A sharp bolt fired through the sky. Expressions of surprise turned to terror as *Pieces of Eight* suddenly whinnied sharply and started kicking out before collapsing and burying her under a thousand pounds of dead horse flesh.

"*¡Buenos días!* Room service. May I come in?" A voice jolted her awake.

Where am I? she thought. She was covered in cold sweat from a restless dream that had ended in pure horror.

Where is *Pieces of Eight*?

Where is James?

Slowly she regained full consciousness. She wasn't in a hospital bed and was nowhere near Louisville or the Kentucky Derby. She remembered—Rio de Janeiro—did they have horse races in Brazil?

"*¿Cómo está usted?* How are you this morning? It is a wonderful day. Where would you like the tray, ma'am?"

The service attendant presented a silver tray loaded with fresh juice, coffee, steamed milk, croissants, jam and butter. Strange enough, there was also a single red rose in a small crystal vase . . . and a greeting card.

"Thank you!" Laura hoisted herself up in her king-sized bed and leaned comfortably against five silk-covered goose-down pillows. This must be part of the private butler service Ivy mentioned yesterday as they checked in.

"Why don't you put it right here on the coffee table?"

"Anything else you would like?"

"No, thank you, it looks delicious. What a lovely courtesy." Laura signed the check and added a nice tip.

"*¡Muito obrigado!*"

"You're very welcome."

What better way to wake up from a nightmare than this nice surprise? she thought. The terrifying events of her dream faded slowly away.

This girl was trying everything in her power to make Laura's life as comfortable as it could be. Actually, in this case, Laura was trying to do the same for her. Yet what did she have to offer? Definitely no money—all she had were nightmares, visions and headaches.

At least she would be there for Ivy, give her support and understanding and listen with an open mind. This was new for her—her new world—and she'd come to like it more and more.

Perhaps this was a second chance, not only to live the good life but also to do something more meaningful. Not that her life with James was not fulfilled, but she was always referred to as Mrs. James Winchester. Was that really all she was?

Now she could help somebody else, help Ivy to get back on the grounds.

By the way, where was Ivy?

Laura looked at the neat breakfast tray and reached for the greeting card.

Laura, I'm already up, couldn't sleep. Look out from your balcony to the golf course. The pink polo is me. Yeah, I'm on a full round this morning! I needed to know how it feels, after all this time. See you later. Enjoy your breakfast! Ivy

So she's playing again, what a brave girl, Laura thought and recalled how hard it was for Ivy to attend the red carpet gala last night.

With a cup of hot coffee in her hand, Laura opened the french doors and stepped out on the balcony into the fresh early-morning glow. If Ivy was busy playing golf, she had some time to do more research on their case, and she needed to speak to Julie before she left town.

Way back in the distance, she saw a tiny pink dot in the first golden rays of the morning sun.

Laura waved but wasn't sure if it was Ivy or if she could even see her.

But yes—Ivy waved back, and that brought tears to Laura's eyes, joyful, meaningful tears. Yes, a new life had come into existence, and who knows what it might have in store for her. Her eyes followed the lovely golfer for a while as the phone rang.

"Hello?"

"Laura, is this you? It's Brad."

"Yes, hello."

"How are you?"

"Oh, we're okay, everything is going well here. How is everything at home?" She felt an intense stab in her stomach. Unusual for her. She wasn't that attached to him, was she?

"Well, everything is fine here. Ah, by the way, your accounts are now open and fully funded."

"Wow, thank you!" Laura laughed. She was surprised by her feelings for him—were they really that strong? Was it because he was out of reach? A loaded trading account was so out of her focus right now.

"It's really the least I could do . . ." Did she hear insecurity in his voice?

"Brad, thank you—this means a lot. I'm excited to get started."

"All right then. How's everything going?"

"We're having a good time down here. Ivy is hitting the links this morning. Would you like her to call you back later?"

"No, it's okay. I just wanted to know if everything is all right. Wait—Ivy's back on the golf course? Now, that is good news! Laura . . ."

"Yes?"

"You need anything, you let me know, will you? I mean anything."

"Oh, sure. Don't worry. I'll be fine!"

A few minutes later she hung up, but her thoughts stayed on Brad for a while. Did she miss him? Maybe—this fluttering inside her stomach made her feel like a teenager again.

Why not? There was nobody to judge her, and if he wasn't free, that left her with an unrequited teenage crush. That wouldn't be the worst thing, right? Laura picked up a golden brown croissant, topped her coffee cup and whistled on her way to the bathroom.

She sounds so happy, Brad thought as he walked over to the bay window overlooking the gulf coast with its calm turquoise waters. He watched a sea gull feeding on fish, and the deep lines on his forehead began to relax. Still, he felt an urge to light a cigar and pair it with two fingers of old Scotch.

His desk was loaded with the morning papers, reminding him why he had called to check on Laura. The press had picked up her story. Somehow it must have leaked, as it always does.

Breaking news it was, and breaking news sells. He scratched his temple. Headlines were teeming with terms like "sensation," "miracle," and similar phrases. Most articles included a color photograph, a snapshot from ten years ago of Laura dressed in a laced pale suit with a straw hat.

The picture was taken at a charity auction, probably at the Winter Wine Festival the year she disappeared. It was the same picture they used ten years ago in the search for her.

It was good she had left the country. He would have a hard time shielding her from all the reporters and paparazzi who were surrounding his house at this very moment. Intrusive and bothersome. The sharks were circling at the front gate, at the beach boardwalk, to broadcast the miracle exclusively.

Well, he would make sure that it stays at circling and proceeds no further.

Brad was concerned that the attention would make Laura a target for kidnapping—hadn't it been foul play when she disappeared?

But who was behind it, and why? A ransom was never demanded, and with this thought, he picked up a letter from his desk and read it once more. It was delivered express and strictly confidential this morning, which made him more uncomfortable than all of the paparazzi combined.

He knew the old-fashioned handwriting only too well, although he hadn't heard from this friend in years.

The letter came from James, asking about Laura.

❧

The receptionist had told Laura that Julie Ferguson could be found in the spa area, since she was booked for a ten o'clock massage, but only after Laura had lured the information out of her with some compliments about her wonderful service.

Huh, not my regular style, she thought. She felt like a private investigator sniffing around, but it was for the best intentions of all involved.

So she put on her bathrobe, left a note for Ivy and went down to the underground waterworld and spa lounge. She pondered whether she should go for the medical facial or the ionic foot detox as she opened the milky glass doors leading into a temple of pure relaxation.

The sounds of soothing background music, a running waterfall, the sight of colorful tropical plants and the scent of aromatic flowers mingled together and enlivened her senses. A servant, dressed all in white, offered Laura green tea and tropical fruits on a bamboo tray while she awaited her first treatment.

The air was filled with eucalyptus and mint flavors, and she enjoyed the relaxing ambiance. To her left were treatment rooms with people coming and going. They were dressed in spa robes, and most had their faces covered with thick green, brown or red mud.

She had no clue how to find Julie.

But then, she had a stroke of luck. Julie Ferguson entered the spa area, dressed in jogging gear, her hair pulled back in a tight ponytail, and her face looked tense and sweaty as she quickly entered treatment room number two.

Apparently she'd come alone, and this was a great advantage, since Laura wanted to start off with some small talk before entering into a more serious discussion. Equipped with two cups of green tea, she went after Julie.

"Good morning, are you the ten o'clock full body massage?" Laura set the tone straight as she entered the treatment room.

"Yes, that's me," Julie called from the steam shower. "I'll be with you in a minute. I just finished my morning workout and need to freshen up."

"Take your time. This is your time to relax." Laura smiled when she heard herself talk like a seasoned pro. She lit a scented candle and dimmed the overhead light.

"Here I am." Wrapped in a towel, Julie took the cup and sipped her tea. Slowly, she sat down on the massage table, holding her back in pain.

"What's wrong with your back?" Laura was honestly concerned.

"Oh, I don't know. Nothing serious though—too much stress, I think. That's why I need a massage. I can't stand still, and I can't lie down. It hurts all the time."

"All right, try to lie flat with your face down on the table. the massage therapist will be here shortly." Laura tilted her head downwards to face Julie and took the seat next to her. Knowing that Julie couldn't escape, she started asking questions.

At first Julie seemed wary of Laura, but then she recognized her as the companion Ivy brought to the gala last night. Somehow she liked her, for a reason she couldn't quite place. She closed her eyes, relaxed and opened up about her youth, her golf affection, and endless practice sessions. It felt good to talk to somebody.

Suddenly, she stopped. "Who are you?" she asked. "You can't just come in here and ask me all these questions. This is so wrong."

"I'm just a friend of Ivy's, and I want to help her. She needs to understand and wants to know why this has happened to her." Laura felt uncomfortable because she knew only too well how unfair it was to intrude into somebody's privacy. However, she was on a mission.

"Nobody knows, nobody will ever know why that madman was so affected by me and tried to hurt her so much. Let the past go." Julie shook her head.

"That's exactly why I want to help. To let the past go. To find peace. Ivy needs to know to get on with her life." Laura looked at the clock hanging on the wall. She only had about five more minutes until the therapist was coming in, and she was not sure how she should continue.

She did not want Julie to become upset. On the other hand, this was important and could be the only chance she got to ask Julie about the event.

"Julie, I know it wasn't fair to drop in and question you like this. I'm sorry."

"Don't worry. It's okay. You know, I'm just not feeling well this morning, and I'm really looking forward to the massage." She lay flat on the table and tried to relax.

"I have an idea! Why don't you join us, Ivy and me, for lunch today? They have a pool-side Tiki bar where they serve salads and sandwiches. Should we say around noon?"

"Okay, let's do that."

"Okay, sounds like a plan." Laura said, stood up and walked to the door.

"All right, see you later."

Julie closed her eyes and smiled. Maybe it would be good to talk with Ivy to make peace with the past. It was true that she had felt very uncomfortable with Ivy's presence last night.

As Laura exited the room, she almost ran into the massage

therapist, who seemed to be in hurry. He was a strong man with an artificial smile on his face.

At this moment, Laura had a strong vision. She could see the same guy, not dressed in white but in black. He held something in his hand—was it a gun? She couldn't tell. Strange. She hadn't had a vision like this in a while. But here it was. But this time it felt different. There was something strange about it—a feeling of fear. No, not just fear—real danger.

❧

There she was! A beautiful young lady lying on a massage table, waiting for her therapy. She had no idea what kind of therapy he was going to give her.

He had planned it all out, and it was the right thing to do—that he knew. A therapy she and her father would never forget.

"Good morning, ma'am."

"Morning," Julie murmured. She was tired and did not even bother to look up. Very well, he thought, you spoiled brat. We'll see what a morning this will be for you.

He pulled on his gloves, took a cloth and reached for the bottle of chloroform on the bench behind him he had placed there earlier.

"All right, what will we be doing this morning? Yes, I see, a full body massage, right?" He spoke as naturally as he could with his slight accent.

"Yes, and please start gently, my back hurts so much, and I need to . . . hey, what are you —"

He quickly pressed the chloroform-soaked cloth onto Julie's

face.

She saw the world around her fade, confused about what was happening. The last thing she recognized were his dark eyes. She had seen them before . . .

She blacked out.

Carefully, he cleaned the doorknobs and everything either one of them might have touched. He didn't want to leave any traces behind.

His plan did not include carrying her unconscious out of the hotel—he knew that wasn't possible, with the celebrity she was.

No, he would give an example how a true professional worked. After he had cleaned everything, he dressed her in a bathrobe, then tightened her hands with a hose clamp in front of her.

From the back of the room he pulled out a wheelchair which he'd placed there ahead of time, opened it up, and maneuvered her into it.

After a thorough cleaning of the table, he pulled a straight razor shaving set out of his back pocket. He opened it on the bench and prepared everything to work on her scalp. Oh yes, he would take his time, and he would make nice, clean cuts. A contemptuous smile crept onto his face.

With long, straight moves, he shaved off Julie's hair, lock by lock, and placed it carefully in a box. He needed that later. He then cleaned everything very carefully and covered Julie's head with a white towel.

A look at the clock told him that he had about twenty-five minutes left before the next person would enter this room.

Now, he had to prepare her face to make her unrecognizable.

He walked to the sink to mix a heavy green mud mask, which

he then painted over her face. That's good, he thought, I've never used that technique before, but it works great! As soon as the mud is dry she can't move her face, can't speak and nobody would notice anything. To be sure this was the case, he put cotton balls into her mouth so that she couldn't make any noise, even if she wanted to.

"All right, young lady, we're almost done."

A last look around the room ensured him that everything was as neat and clean as it had been before. He was very satisfied with his work.

"I must admit, the green mud looks very nice on you. It gives your face such a smoothing touch."

He stored all utensils in the wheelchair, took out a blonde wig and put it on his head, applied a mustache and covered his eyes with stylish sunglasses. After the final check in the mirror, he was satisfied with his cover.

"Okay, young lady, we're ready to rock'n roll."

He opened the door and wheeled Julie out of the room. He tried to look casual as he pushed her through the hallway towards the elevator.

Kids were playing in the pool, and people were relaxing in the open spa area. Nobody took notice of the good-looking blonde man who was wheeling his client to her next appointment.

Ha, ha, this was clever, he thought, as he pressed the elevator button to the underground level.

TEN

Hibiscus blossoms filled the air with their sweet scent, and a light breeze from the Atlantic ocean made this last day of November perfect for outdoor activities.

The poolside cafe and Copacabana Tiki bar were bustling during the lunch hour—people came and went, some in bathing suits, others dressed for tennis.

Laura watched the area, sipping a cold mango iced tea as she waited for Ivy and Julie.

"Hi Laura! What a beautiful day it is." Ivy took a seat across in an oversized rattan wicker chair and snapped her finger to get the attention of the waitress. "I'm exhausted and hungry."

"Yes, you've had quite a morning. And thank you for the breakfast surprise. I saw your note and saw you on the green!"

"It was good for me to go back to the links," Ivy said. "I didn't sleep very well last night—too many memories were buzzing around in my head." She arranged the silver around her plate.

"I was up early, and when I saw the golf course from my window, I felt his sudden urge to go down and play."

She took a long gulp of ice water. "As strange as it is, I haven't had this energy in a long time. It was as if a higher power was driving me, showing me the way. What could I do?"

She put her glass down.

"Sure enough, I called the pro shop for a tee-time and a set of clubs. First time I rented clubs—can you believe that?"

Ivy laughed. She played with the napkin as the waitress arrived and ordered an iced tea as well.

"So how was it?" Laura asked, interested.

"Oh well, in the beginning, you know . . . but I got into the flow, and it was pretty nice. It felt like playing golf for the very first time." Ivy stopped fidgeting and looked straight into Laura's eyes. "Laura, this is what I need to do, my purpose."

"Ladies, are you ready to order, or do you need a couple more minutes?"

The waitress set down Ivy's iced tea.

"We're waiting for one more person, but I think I'm ready to order," Laura said. "What about you?"

Ivy focused on the menu. "Hmm, I'm having a Caesar salad with chicken."

"Sounds good to me too." Laura handed the menu cards to the waitress and took a look at her watch. Julie should be here any minute.

"Maybe we should have waited to order until Julie joins us," Laura said.

"How was your talk with her this morning?" Ivy asked.

"It went okay. I think she's looking forward to coming today." Laura checked her watch again and became concerned. Ever since her vision on the way out of the massage room, she'd had this strange sensation. She wasn't sure if it was the person with the piercing dark eyes or the general situation that made her so uncomfortable, but this tingling sensation wouldn't let up.

Relax, she told herself and took another sip of her iced tea. Give it a couple more minutes and Julie will be here.

Ten minutes later, the waitress returned, holding a tray loaded with their Caesar salads. "I'll be right back with your refills. You guys need anything else, just let me know, okay?" She rushed back into the kitchen.

Laura's brow furrowed.

"Ivy, why don't you go ahead and start eating. I'll peek inside and see if I can find her. Perhaps she left a message for us at reception." Laura got up from her seat and hurried into the lobby before Ivy could even reply. But she was very hungry and the salad looked delicious, so she was happy to dive in.

She didn't notice how much time had gone by before Laura returned from the lobby, running.

"Ivy—she's missing! I just spoke to Dustin Cooper, they haven't seen her for several hours."

"Maybe she's out spending her prize money." Ivy knew what Julie liked to do the day after her big win. She took another bite of her salad.

In the underground parking lot of the Grand Palace Hotel sat a white van with a colorful label that read *Catering Express*. Inside, Julie was fettered to her wheelchair, still unconscious. The man in the driver's seat closed a brown manila envelope, addressed in bold capital letters to the hotel management.

The content of the envelope was simple: it included a photo of a ransom note and a picture of Julie before he'd shaved her head, taken using a disposable camera.

This was clever, he reasoned, since there was no trace of fingerprints or identification. He played with the idea of including a strand of her hair but decided otherwise. It was too early.

Five million U.S. dollars' worth of rough diamonds, rare white, and one million U.S. dollars transferred to his Swiss bank account. This was the amount that was rightfully his and would give him the advantage he needed to fulfill his dream.

The hacienda up in the hills he was about to buy last week was the perfect location for his retirement. But then everything changed when he didn't receive his payment.

It wasn't fair, and he didn't like to be fooled. He had to make sure that, from now on, they played by his rules. He put on his sunglasses, and with a disdainful grin, he started the engine.

Slowly, he drove out of the parking garage. He didn't want to draw any attention to himself. On the street, he made a right turn and circled back to the hotel's reception line. He stopped in front of the bellboy's desk and rolled down the right-hand window.

"Hey, you there."

"Yes, sir, what can I do for you?" A young lad, dressed in a proper dark navy uniform, answered.

"Here, pass this envelope on to hotel management. They're waiting for it. I'm in a hurry." He avoided looking up and spoke slowly, knowing that his accent was not easy to understand for the untrained ear.

"Sure, no problem. Is there anything else I can do for you, sir?"

"No, thanks." He rolled up the window and drove away at a controlled pace. Before he turned onto the ramp to the highway, he heard some shuddering in the back of the van.

Must be the breaks, he concluded—it was simply too early for the girl to be waking up. The dosage he'd given her should last at least one full hour. And by then, she would be safely tucked away in his hiding place.

Julie struggled to open her eyes. She felt sick. Everything hurt, especially her arms and wrists. They were tightly bound to the wheelchair, and she couldn't move an inch.

Her head felt strange. She was used to a facial masque, no big deal, but her face felt like a brick wall, and there was something else not right, she wasn't sure what.

She was too numb to think clearly. Her back hurt again, and darkness closed in around her.

She dreamed she was in her hotel room taking a hot bath. She was tossing back a handful of those painkillers Harry gave her occasionally and drinking a gallon of water.

She woke up with an abrupt shake. Dizzy, she tried to concentrate. Where was she?

What Julie could not see was that he had gone around the car and removed the magnetic signs and the fake license plates. After that, he got back in and made the short drive to a rented wooden shack, deep in the forest.

Finally the car stopped. All she could hear was an owl hooting in the distance. The silence made her anxious. Then the sliding door of the van opened.

"Well, young lady! I hope you had a good drive." The sound of his voice made her shiver. She tried to speak, but she couldn't.

Her mouth was full of cotton balls.

He looked around. The forest appeared very dark. Only a few sunbeams found their way through the dense foliage. The old hunter's cabin was small but got the job done.

"Let's go. We have to talk." He pulled her out of the van and wheeled her inside the cabin.

It was furnished with an oversized iron cast stove embedded in a small kitchen, a fireplace surrounded by a stone wall, and logs neatly stacked in front of it.

He parked her across a coffee table, away from the windows. Then he cleaned her face with a wet towel and removed the cotton balls.

"Please, I need water, I'm very thirsty."

Julie was not yet able to speak clearly. Her wrists were bleeding, and she had a pounding headache. Her scalp was burning, and her head felt cold. What had that bastard done to her?

"Okay, lady, I'll get you some water. And you keep your mouth shut or else!"

With strong steps, he walked into the kitchen, which was hidden from her view. There was no way she could see what he added to her water.

He brought the glass to her mouth for her to drink.

"Thank you, but can't you free my hands? They're hurting so much. I'm not feeling well, I'm so tired." Her words came out slowly, and she felt dizzy again.

"Sorry lady, can't do that."

"Please, just my hands," Julie tried once more. She felt heavy and drowsy. Her back was in agonizing pain.

He walked back into the kitchen, waiting for her to fall back to sleep. His plan was to keep her sedated as much as possible to avoid any trouble.

"Hello . . . are you still there?" Julie called with the little energy she had left. "Please let me call my father . . . He'll give you money . . . He'll give you anything you want. He is in Rio, in the Grand Palace, I—"

"Your father is who brought you here. And I will call him when the time is right."

❧

"He wants what? That's ridiculous!" Harry Butcher shook his head and looked up from the photographed ransom note.

"Five million dollars' worth of raw diamonds, and one million dollars transferred to a Swiss bank account. Can you believe it?"

Henrik Ferguson paced back and forth in Julie's hotel suite. He felt like a caged tiger, not knowing what to do first, not knowing where to turn.

"He must have lost his mind. First he shows up last night, asking for more money, and now this!"

Henrik looked over to Inspector Corelli who was standing at the window.

"He's going nuts—kidnapping my little girl!"

Exhausted, he lowered himself into a leather armchair next to the coffee table.

"We don't know yet if it's really him, do we?" Harry pointed out. "It would be too dangerous for him to do such a thing. He is still on probation, remember?"

"Gunman on probation," Henrik countered, "that doesn't mean anything to him. He is a professional killer. And he was very upset last night."

In disbelief, Harry looked out of the window, where the late afternoon sun bathed Rio's surrounding mountains.

"How perfect the world would be if only Julie were here, alive and well. I wanted to make peace with her, I wanted to make up for everything. I can't believe what's happening right now." He buried his face in his hands. "It's him. I know it."

"I would agree with Mr. Butcher. We cannot be certain that it is the same man who lead the attack against Ivy Brooks and killed Jason Briggs earlier this year."

Inspector Corelli, a well-dressed, dark-haired athletic man in his early fifties spoke up from the back of the room, where he stood silently and observed the scene.

He was called in by hotel management when they found the ransom note, and he sensed that he was not welcomed here.

Leandro Corelli had been too long with the Rio Police Department not to know that, in most kidnapping cases, the families wanted to pull it off on their own—a fatal mistake.

Suddenly, the door opened, and Ivy and Laura burst in.

Ivy was furious. She looked around the room and approached Julie's father directly.

"Are you behind all this? Tell me, are you behind all this? I saw you last night on the same table with him, the madman. Tell me the truth, Henrik, right now."

"Well, why don't we sit down and go through what happened this morning, step by step." The Inspector started by introducing himself to Ivy and Laura.

"Oh, I'm glad you're here. I'm glad they called you. You'll take care of it, right? And my friend Laura and I will help you as much as we can."

"Sorry to interrupt," Harry Butcher stepped in, "but these two ladies here have nothing to do with our situation, and I won't discuss anything with them in the room."

With a deep red face, Harry pointed toward Ivy and Laura. His heart was pounding fast, and he could feel his blood pressure rising to dangerous levels. Normally, he knew how to control his temper, but as Ivy walked into the room, he couldn't hold it.

He took a deep breath and clenched his fingers. After all, Ivy was the point of origin of this bloody mess. If she hadn't outplayed Julie, this whole thing wouldn't have happened.

There was too much work, money and effort involved to push Julie Ferguson to the top. Now she was a superstar, and he'd recognized her talent early on.

However, without his management skills, providing the right resources at the right time and calling for sponsorship when needed, Julie would never have reached the top. That was clear.

Then, finally, as the money poured in, Ivy Brooks appeared out of nowhere and won over the tournaments and the hearts of the people. She attracted the most desired sponsors—intolerable.

He knew that Henrik felt the same.

He glanced around the room. Nobody was moving, so he approached Ivy, took her by the shoulder harshly and tried to escort her out of the room.

"Hey, don't touch me! Do not ever touch me again." Ivy whirled around. "Please, Inspector, I think Laura and I have something to contribute to this matter. Laura, why don't you tell

Inspector Corelli what Julie told you just this morning?"

Ivy took a seat on the leather couch.

Now all eyes were on Laura, who didn't know what to say.

"Ladies and gentlemen, please, let's all have a seat, and then we will go through the events of this morning."

Inspector Corelli's hands pointed down for everybody to sit. He took his seat at the head of the table.

"Mrs. Winchester, when did you see Julie Ferguson, and why don't you tell us what you discussed?"

～

There was a knock on the door. He put down his newspaper—old fashioned, he knew, but he liked to spend an hour each morning studying the headlines.

What he didn't like was the continuous newsfeed on his smartphone.

"Good morning, sir! Here comes your coffee, hot and fresh, and some messages." A young lady dressed in fashionable business clothing, smart and eager, placed a transparent tray in front of him.

"Do you need anything else at this moment?" she asked in her lovely Swiss accent.

"Thank you, Vanessa. In fact, yes, I need a secured phone connection in about five minutes, could you arrange that?"

He took a sip of his coffee, strong and hot with lots of crema on top of it, and turned back to his smartphone.

Julie Ferguson kidnapped in Rio! The events down there were getting out of control. Couldn't they do anything right?

Something needed to be done—and quickly, before his private investors got wind of it. They sure didn't like local authorities sniffing around more than they already did.

"Ah, Vanessa!"

"Yes, sir."

"Could you please check if the private jet is ready for a flight to Rio de Janeiro tonight, just in case?"

"No problem, I'll get your phone line first, and then I'll check with the airport."

Although he didn't like it, he might have to intervene personally—he had no choice.

As soon as the green line on his phone began flashing, he picked up the receiver and dialed an unlisted number he'd wished he had forgotten by now.

≈

Sitting at the kitchen table, he disconnected his anonymous IP address, which he used with a prepaid air card. He was satisfied—one million U.S. dollars had been deposited in his Swiss bank account.

"So, this is working fine, just fine," he murmured to himself and stood up to walk over to the counter. Julie was still asleep, and her chin rested on her shoulder. That poor girl, if her father wasn't such an idiot and had paid him what was promised, she wouldn't need to suffer like this.

The least I can do, he thought as he opened the refrigerator, is prepare her a decent breakfast. He retrieved bread, butter, ham and eggs and arranged them neatly on the counter. He reached for his skillet, placed it on the stove, put on medium heat and spooned in a pat of butter.

In a separate bowl, he cracked the eggs, added the salt and pepper and ham, stirred it and poured the mix into the skillet. He put the bread in the toaster and started a pot of fresh coffee. Breakfast was right on its way—I would have made a good chef, he thought.

The delicious smell of hot coffee and sizzling eggs awoke Julie. She rolled her head, tried to focus her eyes. Everything hurt. Every muscle, every bone.

She tried to move her arms and legs, but they were tied very tightly to the wheelchair. She felt terrible. Never in her life had she felt so badly, and while she still tried to find out what hurt most—the headache or the back pain—she noticed him standing in front of the stove.

"Hey, you. I need to go to the bathroom, please. I have to go."

"Ah, good morning, young lady. Hope you had a good sleep. I'm sorry you had to stay in the wheelchair, but you, you know . . . look, I made breakfast—hungry?"

With the skillet in his hand, he scanned over her body. She looked pale, frightened and so skinny.

"My hands, I can't feel them. Please, let me loose, I need to go to the bathroom." Unreal, she thought, what was all this about?

"Just a second. Breakfast is ready in a minute." He set the skillet back onto the stove, walked over to her and rolled the wheelchair in front of the bathroom door. With a small side cutter, he opened the plastic hose clamps around her wrists and ankles.

Immediately, Julie tried to get up from the chair, however, she couldn't move. He kept his hands on her knees and spoke in a frightening voice.

"Young lady, listen very carefully. I'm on a mission here, and I'm a professional. If you think you can run away, you're wrong. Have you ever asked yourself why I don't cover my face?"

Julie was terrified—she had seen enough crime movies to understand what that meant.

"Now, you're free to go to the bathroom. You'll find everything you need to freshen yourself up."

"You must be crazy. You'll be a dead man yourself if you kill me."

"We'll see about that."

"I think I know now who you are—you are the maniac who attacked Ivy and killed her boyfriend, aren't you? Did they let you out of jail for good behavior or did you break out?"

"Neither. I never was in jail. Thanks to your father, I had the right lawyers."

"What are you talking about?"

"Do you really think I sent you those fancy love letters? Did you never question why a crazy fan would know all the places you stay during the tour?

Anyway, we'll talk about that later. Now get into the bathroom before I change my mind."

That was her stalker. What a nightmare. And what was he saying about her father? She knew her father. He would never do anything to hurt her or anybody else, would he?

With great difficulty, she got out of the wheelchair and hobbled to the bathroom.

Only a few seconds later, he heard a horrified scream through the bathroom door, and he smiled, knowing he had done his job right.

ELEVEN

I think it's him." Laura concentrated on her putt, focused her eyes on the ball, and gently moved the putter. "Who?" Ivy followed Laura's ball, which was slowly rolling towards the hole. It circled around the rim but did not drop in—still a pretty good shot.

They enjoyed a round of golf in perfect weather conditions, with a bright sunny sky and a nice refreshing breeze from the ocean.

"The criminal who kidnapped Julie. I think it's the same guy who attacked you earlier this year."

"You're sure?"

"Yes, I watched all available videos from the attack. It was on television."

"Of course." Ivy looked dazed. She had a strong feeling that it was he who she saw in the ballroom the other night.

"As I told the police, I saw a man entering Julie's massage room right as I left. I thought it was her massage therapist. What I didn't tell them was that I'd had this vision that something was wrong. I couldn't make much out of it at that time. But now I understand—I've seen that guy before, that's what it is."

Laura picked up her ball from the hole and put the flag back in.

"Pretty darn good, eh—what you think of that?" Laura rolled her ball in her hand as they walked back to their cart.

Ivy wrote down their scores.

"It can't be him."

"Why not?"

"He was lucky to be sentenced with a two-year probation only. Why should he risk his probation by kidnapping Julie? To me that makes no sense. Not to mention the fact that I was his target and not Julie."

Laura thought about it.

"You know what, maybe it makes sense. See, he was crazy about Julie, and now, she's number one, right? It's sick, but wouldn't it make sense that he would kidnap her to have her for himself?" Laura took a couple of notes in her small notebook.

"So, where are we now?"

"Hole 16, it's a par-5, 475 yards."

As the cart stopped, Laura jumped out and put on her glove.

"Let me try to make birdie here."

"Hmm, a birdie! Let me see if I can top that."

Ivy took the *Big Bertha* driver out of her bag and walked up to the tee.

Puzzled, Laura looked at her. She couldn't believe how lightly Ivy had taken their conversation. It was amazing how much she'd changed over the last two days.

Not quite a week ago, she was a skinny and very frightened person, and now, after two days of playing golf in the sun, her face was tanned, and she had the appetite of a lumberjack.

With determination and self-assurance, Ivy checked the flag position and measured the distance with her GPS watch, then she teed up her ball and took position.

She made a concentrated practice swing.

Seconds later, she literally exploded into her drive—her stance, alignment and body rotation worked in perfect harmony and her swing looked world class. The ball shot high up in the air, dropped on the green and rolled to within 10 feet of the pin.

"Wow, what a shot!" Laura was flabbergasted and, with a little heads down, she walked up to her tee position, which had a shorter distance to the hole—the women's amateur tee.

She gave her best and was satisfied that she had hit the ball straight, and with a landing of about 180 yards into the middle of the fairway, the shot wasn't that bad at all.

"Nice shot," Ivy affirmed.

They got into the golf cart and drove to Laura's ball position, where she stepped out to make her next shot while Ivy waited patiently in the cart.

Later, they reached the putting green, and Ivy picked up her ball from the hole after she had managed an eagle on this par-5 hole.

"Maybe it is him. But then, if he really was so confused and mentally disturbed as everyone believed, how could he plan a kidnapping like this? How could he have planned to attack me in the first place? You know, over the course of two trials, he was deemed to be so deranged as to be incapable of reason and no longer a threat to anyone. Huh, can you believe that?"

Ivy cleaned her putter with a towel and continued.

"The way he did it. The way he must have planned it. I can still see the hatred in his face when I turned around. And he served not a single day in jail. Since he was free, I was afraid to go out in public. I saw him everywhere, watching me, stalking me. So I retreated into my own world, which became more and more dominated by darkness and self-pity."

Now she looked Laura straight in the eyes.

"Not anymore, not a minute longer. I'm still afraid of him, but I will not allow him to take control over my life for a second time." She took a deep breath. "Did you see that, I mean, the eagle?"

Laura walked over to Ivy, and without any word, she embraced her and kissed her on the forehead.

"Yes, pro, I saw that—it was magic! Don't you ever think about giving up on golf again, promise?" She pulled out a Kleenex. "Now, let me finish my hole—gracefully."

Laura walked to her ball, which was waiting about two feet from the hole, and with her fifth and sixth shot, she finished with a bogey.

Half an hour later, they were on their way back to the pro shop.

"Ivy, I can't stop thinking about it. Wouldn't it be possible that he had somebody helping him, planning it for him?"

Ivy pushed the breaker so hard that the golf cart stopped, and the clubs rattled in their backs.

"What do you mean? Are you saying that there is somebody behind all this, like a conspiracy? How sick is that?"

"I don't know. Not yet, but we'll find out." In her notebook, Laura put down some of her thoughts and said,

"Let's forget about it for now. What would you say if we indulged in a special treatment? Soothe our tight joints and muscles? Let's go to the spa and see what they can do for us. I've studied the brochure, and I'm more than ready for a relaxing deep muscle massage, a hot stone treatment and an algae facial followed by a steam bath before we order a fully loaded salad and some fancy tropical drinks. Sound good?"

"Sure does! Let's do that." Ivy returned the clubs and the cart to the pro shop, took her scorecard and followed Laura to the spa.

❧

The girl isn't well, he thought, looking over at Julie while he prepared his backpack for tonight. She hadn't eaten or drunk anything since she had been with him. He'd sedated her most of the time—that was the plan, and he always stuck to his plan.

The last time she was awake, in the early morning hours after a restless night of pain, she begged him to let her go or call for medical assistance. She said her back was killing her, and the pain was too much. But he couldn't let her go, and he couldn't call for help.

Not today. A few more hours, and everything will be fine. He handed her another bottle of water, spiked with even more tranquilizers than before, and she was so thirsty that she didn't notice them.

However, the sweat on her face and her cold body seemed serious.

It didn't matter. The ransom was to be collected tonight. In only a couple of hours, he would be on his way to his final destination. They'd never find him, he was damn sure about that. He would leave her where she was and give them a couple of clues for how to find her. That should give them just enough time to get her help.

But now, he had to concentrate on preparing everything for tonight. First things first, he thought, as he picked up the phone. A final surprise for sweet Ivy . . .

❧

Meanwhile, at the Grand Palace Hotel, Harry Butcher was out of control. He paced ceaselessly in his suite.

"What the heck is going on? It can't be that hard to get raw diamonds."

Red-faced and swinging both arms, he finally maneuvered himself into an oversized armchair.

"What a freaking nightmare!" He looked at Inspector Corelli and over to Henrik Ferguson. Henrik's face was ivory pale as he put down the receiver.

"He said he wants the diamonds by four o'clock. He said he'll give us the details later."

"What a load of—"

"Harry, please! I don't have a good feeling, something must have gone wrong. I don't know what, but he sounded very weird on the phone." He looked over to Harry. "My God, he wouldn't dare to kill her, would he?" He started crying.

"Gentlemen, the diamonds are not the problem. We got the diamonds. However, we want to mark them with a laser before the transfer, and this is technically difficult in such a short time," Leandro Corelli explained in his calm and solid voice.

"I must say, in all my years with the police department, this is the very first case where someone asked for rough diamonds in this quality," Leandro Corelli sighed and took a sip of his coffee. "We're obviously dealing with a highly professional subject—why should he make an unintelligent move? Like killing Julie before he has received the diamonds."

"I sure hope that he knows that rule," Harry Butcher interrupted sharply.

"Of course, we can never be sure about that. But tonight, at the transfer, we'll have everything covered and—"

"Just make sure the diamonds are ready then," Henrik cut him short. Just the thought of Julie being dead—killed by the man he had hired himself—made him lose his mind. All his fault. And they have no idea whom they're dealing with. Maybe it was time to tell the truth.

As if reading his mind, Harry gave him a sharp look, got up and walked over to him.

"Henrik, can I have a word?"

"Of course, go ahead."

"In private." He walked out of the room.

"Harry?" But Harry was already down the hallway, in front of his room. He opened the door.

"Get in there. No more word in public about this. Or to the police." He banged the door behind them and put on the *do not disturb* light. Then he walked straight to the mini bar, filled a glass with ice and selected a mini Jack Daniels from the fridge.

"Do you want anything?"

"If you got another, I'll take it. Otherwise, Jim Beam will do."

"Here you go." And Harry handed him his drink.

"Now, please sit down, and listen, Henrik, do listen carefully."

"Okay." Henrik sat with the whiskey in both hands, which

were shaking and causing the ice cubes to clack.

"Relax—relax! Henrik, you and I, we go back a long way, right? Sunday night, at the red carpet event, you didn't treat him well enough, so it seems. Now we know—a little too late." He took his drink in one go.

"He must have been dissatisfied with what we offered. Didn't you notice? Henrik, tell me, what happened?"

Harry, the cool and smooth businessman, flopped exhausted onto his bed and stretched out. He should have done it himself. No need to have such an enemy out there. Too much is at stake here, he thought, closing his eyes.

"Yes, yes, you're right. I know, now I know. He left angry, but how should I've known that he was that angry? I mean, he was asking for the full amount plus bonus, but, of course, I would have given him more."

Harry sat up.

"Okay, let's not talk about the past. Focus on the here and now. First, we need to give him what he wants. That clear?"

"Course it is!"

"Secondly, we don't want Inspector Corelli getting him behind bars. Can you imagine if he talks? He knows way too much. We don't want to have anything to do with it, with him. There is no connection between Gunman and us, that clear?"

"Clear! What we gotta do?"

"We do what we gotta do. Let me fix another drink. Then, we'll go back and you make a point, clear and sharp, that you're very concerned about Julie and you do not want anything delaying or compromising the ransom delivery tonight. Is that clear?"

Harry walked over to the mini bar and pulled out two more

whiskeys.

"Sounds like a plan!" Henrik cheered up to Harry. He had gained his confidence back and was enjoying his drink.

"Think about it, in one or two days, Julie will be back, and Gunman will be gone, hopefully satisfied this time. And we're where we want to be—at the top in ladies professional golf! Nine months before the summer Olympics. Ad agencies and sponsors will kiss our feet. Open the money bin and let the gold nuggets run."

"Harry, you're right—our dream is coming true! You had it all laid out, from the first minute you saw my Julie on the course. You were the first who truly recognized her talent. And I want to thank you for that!"

"Ms. Brooks, Ms. Ivy Brooks?" Laura looked up. After two hours of deluxe spa treatments, Laura rested comfortably, relaxed on a sunbed. She wore a silky pink dress over her bathing suit, which seemed perfectly suited for that summer day at the poolside cafe. She had a cappuccino with whipped cream topping in front of her and waved to the waiter who obviously was looking for Ivy.

"Here, what is it?"

"Ms. Ivy Brooks?"

"No, I'm Laura Winchester, a good friend of Ms. Brooks. Ms. Brooks will be joining me here any minute."

"Oh, then I guess it's okay if I give you the greeting card." And he handed Laura an oversized white envelope, *Ms. Ivy*

Brooks—personally was written on it in bold black letters.

"Thank you, I'll give it to her as soon as she arrives. And by the way, could you bring us a large bottle of mineral water and two glasses, please, ah, with lemon wedges."

"Would Pellegrino be okay?"

"That would be fine, thank you." The waiter was about to leave, as Ivy arrived, still wearing her white spa robe. "Hey, not so fast. I have a Caipirinha, not too much alcohol, though. *Muito obrigado!*"

She took the seat next to Laura, "Huh, I'm overheated, I think. Too long in the sauna. But it felt so good." She settled back and stretched out, her hair was wet, and beads of sweat pearled on her forehead.

"Laura, I'm sorry about what happened to Julie. I just wish she could be with us right now. It's so horrible what this man is capable of doing. But soon, it will be all right, am I right?"

"I hope so, Ivy, I sure hope so." Laura took her hand and squeezed it.

"Going to Rio was the best thing that could have happened to me. I already feel much stronger, and can feel my muscles fortifying. So, what should we do this afternoon?"

"Oh, I almost forgot, Ivy, here, this is for you." Surprised, Ivy took the envelope and examined it.

"From whom?"

"I don't know, the waiter just brought it."

"All right then, let's see . . ." Ivy opened it and found a clown card. She quickly read it.

"Oh my God, it's from him!" She threw it at the table as if it were poisoned. "From the kidnapper. It's him, the madman. He wants me to deliver the ransom, tonight. He wants me to be in the *Restaurante da Dourada* down at the beach. At seven-thirty. I can't believe this. Why me?"

Her newfound confidence seemed gone, and her face was as pale as the robe she wore. Her eyes scanned the pool lounge.

"He might be right here, watching us." She wandered around the lounge again. "Laura, what shall I do? I feel sick."

"Listen, try to stay as calm as you can. You may be right, he could be here right now, watching us. Let's display strength, and let me see if I can find the waiter who brought the card." Laura looked around and waved him.

"What can I do for you, ma'am?"

"The envelope you gave me, the one for Ivy Brooks?"

"Yes, ma'am."

"Who gave it to you? Do you remember what he looked like? Or where he is?"

"Oh, I'm sorry, ma'am. It was given to me at the reception desk for delivery at the poolside cafe. That's all I know. You may want to ask there."

Laura knew they needed to inform the police as soon as possible. "All right then, please bring us the check, we are in a hurry, as we need to get back to our rooms." The waiter left and she turned to Ivy.

"I'll go!" She murmured with a low voice. "Don't worry, I'll go."

"I come with you. I'm not hungry anymore."

"No, you don't understand. I mean I'll go instead of you tonight, handing over the diamonds."

"Laura, you can't do that."

"Oh, yes I can. I have to do that. As a matter of fact, it was my idea to go to Rio, and now you're in this mess again. No way will I let you put yourself in danger. I gave Brad my promise to take good care of you, and that's what I'll do." She sighed and smiled. "See, it's a brilliant idea, it will weaken his position, and I'm sure he won't hurt me. I'm not his focal point"

"How can you be sure?" Ivy didn't know what to think or say. Deep inside she felt relief, but could she really let Laura do this for her, or for Julie?

"As soon as he has the ransom, the diamonds, his only focus will be on getting out of here. Why should he kill me? That would be stupid." She finished her coffee. "And apart from that, you know what I think? I don't buy the claim that he is a madman. I do believe that there is more to the story than we know."

"Like what?" Ivy looked stunned, and slowly, color came back into her face.

"Ivy, let's not waste valuable time here," Laura urged as she signed the check and passed it on to the waiter.

"Let's go up into our rooms, change and call the Inspector. And we need to prepare for tonight. I'll explain later. It's a puzzle, and I'm still missing some important pieces. And tonight, I have the chance to find them."

❧

A couple hours later, Laura was sitting outside at the *Restaurante da Dourada*. The building used to be an old fisherman's cottage, and it was charming with a great view of the beach and the ocean.

The dress she had chosen for tonight was a classic golf outfit, a simple pink polo shirt, white pants and a light down jacket with a lot of zipper pockets. It served several purposes. First of all to cover the microphone and speakers the police wired her with, and secondly it came equipped with a smartphone and a microchip that signaled her precise location at all times.

In addition, this golf dress made her look like Ivy. They did a great job, she thought, makeup and hairstyle did wonders, and with the sunglasses, her cover was perfect.

According to his instructions, she carried a black backpack loaded with the diamonds. She had it placed on the chair next to her, casually, not to draw too much attention to it.

The atmosphere in the restaurant was awesome, the place was packed with chattering, laughing people who were enjoying the marvelous sunset on the beach. A small two-man band played classic pop songs of the eighties in the background.

Only a few minutes ago, Laura was almost the only person sitting at the table, but now, the crowd flocked in, searching for table and chairs, shouting out for waiters, ordering drinks and food. She knew that the crowd included not only hungry tourists but also some local police officers.

Inspector Corelli had prepared well for tonight. Members of a special task force were placed strategically around the perimeter and inside the restaurant.

The instructions the kidnapper had given had been very specific. At eight o'clock, she should order a drink, a Batida de Coco, from Ronaldo, who was obviously a waiter here. It was seven-thirty now, this gave her time to adjust and to wait. She was nervous.

"One, two, three, sound check please!" From the tiny wireless speaker attached in her hair behind her ear and hidden by a cap, she could clearly and distinctly hear the Inspector's voice.

"Yes, I can hear you." Laura whispered without any body movement, just as she had been trained earlier this afternoon in the conference room at the Grand Palace Hotel.

"Please remember to speak as relaxed as you can and slow. Do you remember the code words?"

"Yes, I do."

"Okay, do you want to repeat them right now?"

"No, I remember them. I'm nervous, and I would like to concentrate on the surroundings here."

"You look very stiff. Relax and smile. Concentrate on the music and get your order in, it's almost eight. Good luck and over."

"Yes, I will. Thank you." She waved Ronaldo over and ordered her drink.

The staff was very friendly, and the food looked delicious. At the neighboring table, Falafel appetizers, small pizzas and lots of skewer seafood dishes were served. Portions were very large, and it smelled really good.

Laura was getting hungry. She hadn't eaten anything since breakfast, and now she wished she had heeded Inspector Corelli's recommendation to take a couple of power bars with her.

The place was getting packed. Some people were dancing between the tables as the band started to play Felicita.

She hummed along with the melody, "Felicita e un bicchiere di vino con un panino," happiness is a glass of wine with a slice of bread, "Senti nell'aria c'e gia," you feel it in the air—or something like that. Her Italian was far from perfect.

This song reminded her so much of a romantic dinner with James about two years ago in Venice, Italy. They'd just completed a two-week trip through Europe and decided to extend a few more days at the *Danieli* in Venice. It was their song.

She had tears in her eyes as she saw the waiter approaching with her cocktail.

Next to the drink was placed a note: "Don't talk to the police. Go to the ladies' room immediately. Alone. Don't forget the diamonds."

La felicita e una mano sul cuore piena d'amore!

The music continued as Laura stood up to leave the terrace. She couldn't risk Julie's life, so she followed his orders.

"Laura, you're okay? Where are you going? Give us the word and we'll move in." Inspector Corelli was concerned, but he didn't want to escalate the operation.

"I'm okay, really. I can handle it. Don't worry."

Laura disappeared from view.

"Where are you going?" This time, Corelli got no answer, only background noise. He had to make a decision—quickly.

"He'll take her and the diamonds." Corelli was tempted to give the command to close in. However, something inside him told him that this would be the wrong move. And another voice inside him told him that he cared about Laura.

A little too much.

TWELVE

Rio at night had a life on its own. As darkness closed in over the ocean, the colorful, vibrant city seemed to be just awakening from its daydream.

Festive, costumed Samba dancers were singing on the street. Elegantly dressed couples were rushing to their dinner destinations, and some of the younger folks just enjoyed themselves on the sidewalks or in one of the many open-air bars along Ocean Drive.

Joy and happiness are so close, Laura thought as she watched the scene rolling by like a movie. Not so for her, she was inside the madman's van, speeding fast through the night.

"Who are you? I can see that you're not Ivy Brooks. What's your business here?" His strong, dark voice with its Eastern European accent made him sound like a comedian, but Laura could see that this couldn't be further from the truth.

"I'm Laura Winchester, a friend of Ivy's. Where're we going?"

He'd waited for her in the bathroom and forced her into his car with a gun, but not before he removed her surveillance gear, including speaker and microphone. She also carried an RFID tag affixed by the police for geolocalization—downright ridiculous, he thought. After all, he was a professional.

"Laura Winchester! I think that rings a bell."

"So what's the point in taking me, you've got the diamonds. The police are following you, and I'm just slowing you down. Why take the risk?"

Her mind was working like a machine. She tried to be as reasonable as possible and give her voice some extra strength. Her hands were cuffed behind her back, and she knew the car was locked.

"Of course, we have to deal with law enforcement, but see, that's where you enter the picture—individual protection, you know."

"Again, there is no value for you in keeping me. Besides, nobody will care about me here in Rio or elsewhere. Nobody will pay ransom money for me."

And this is the truth, she thought, staring out of the window through the darkness into an emptiness she'd never felt before.

"Why not? You look decently rich."

"Yes, that may be so, but I'm not rich." Laura paused. She wasn't sure if it was a good idea to fill him in on her personal situation. However, she couldn't find any reason for him to take her in custody, no point there.

"Laura Winchester—aren't you that missing lady who reemerged out of the blue after ten years?"

"Hmm, yes, I'm a lone ranger, back from the dead and nobody cares."

"Listen, as soon as we arrive at our destination, I'll call the cops and leave them a clue for where to find Julie. They paid for her, and I stick to my word, like every honest businessman does."

They drove silently through a deserted area with only a few lights to the right and left. Just a few minutes ago, they were in the middle of the city with its glittering nightlife, and now, it seemed they were entering the rain forest.

After another turn, they reached a rusty iron gate that blocked the road. He got out and opened it. Laura could read *Tijuca Forest* on one of the signs.

"Is Julie here, in this forest? Did you hide her here?"

"No. But this is where you will go. And now shut up, I'm getting tired, and you're talking way too much."

He continued the drive on a wet overgrown dirt road, leading even deeper into the jungle. A while later, the van came to a stop in front of a small building.

Another car, a black SUV, was parked outside. There were no lights and no signs of any people. Far in the distance, the illuminated statue of Christ the Redeemer was shining down on them. She hoped that was a good sign.

Laura tried to concentrate, and listened to determine if the police were on their tail. However, when the engine stopped, the only thing she could hear were the sounds of the nocturnal activity in the jungle around her.

"Wait a minute—you're saying that the police lost him?"

"Yeah, they only found some equipment, microphone and wire, and they have no clue where he could be hiding."

"That's absurd! Now, he's got everything. Julie, the money and the diamonds, and you sent him this other lady, the one who made headlines all over the world. Do you have any idea what that means?"

He didn't bother to listen to the hectic babbling voice on the other side of the line. He'd heard enough, and he needed to focus on his next steps. Maybe it was time to cut his losses. He could stay here in Switzerland and make a decent living. But no way, there was too much at stake, and he would never give up, would he?

He got up and poured himself two fingers of Irish whiskey. It was of utmost importance that his role in this mess would never be uncovered.

"Hello, are you still there?!" Harry Butcher's keyed up voice was screaming on the other end.

"Harry, I'm here. So, what about Gunman? Does he know about the organization, the lobbying, or my name?"

"I don't know, I don't think so."

"Harry, this was all your idea. You brought the man in, and he was supposed to hurt Ivy to give Julie a chance to get back on top. And what did he do? He messed up and killed her boyfriend instead. It cost us quite a lot to keep him out of jail. And now he's kidnapped Julie. Our two best shots are out. Harry, the Games are next year—I need gold for the U.S.!"

"Yes, sir, I know."

"Harry, do me the favor and bring this to an end. A clean cut, or heads will roll. I must say I'm very concerned."

"I'll do my best. But I'm on the line here, too."

"Do whatever you have to do to get this mess cleaned up. And leave my name out of it. Remember, you cannot afford another mistake."

Frowning, he put the receiver down. He knew they'd reached a crossroads. He poured himself another whiskey and rolled the glass in his manicured fingers, watching the ice cubes mingle with his drink. A clear, focused mind was what he needed.

A few minutes later, he picked up the receiver again. He checked to see if his private jet was ready, and then he made a second call.

❧

"Uncle Brad, you're here! I'm so happy to see you." Ivy stormed after him in the hallway.

"Hey! Look at you, young lady. You're looking so good. It seems the climate down here is just right for you," Brad said cheerfully. He was always amused when she called him "uncle." It made him feel his age a little.

"Oh, Brad, I'm so glad you're here. I wanted to call you, but I didn't know what to say, how to explain."

"Explain what? I just tried to call Laura this morning but couldn't reach her, so I decided to take a couple of days off and join you at this wonderful place. Maybe we can learn more about this beautiful country together."

Brad was overwhelmed to see Ivy so splendidly recovered. But the truth was that he'd missed Laura very much, and he felt so lonely in Naples, so he had taken the next flight out on a private charter.

"Ivy, give me a couple of minutes to unpack, and then we'll heading downtown, where I made reservations for the three of us at *L'Atelier du Temps*, a French Restaurant. I hope you like traditional French Cuisine—I know Laura does. I was told they do have a great selection of vegetarian meals. And a fine wine list!"

He handed the luggage boy a handsome tip and closed the door.

"The three of us! Haven't you heard? Oh Brad, you don't know, do you?"

"No, what is it?"

"Laura! She's missing!"

"What? That can't be! What happened?" With his face frozen and pale as snow, Brad had to sit down. He was in shock. Anxiety was building up inside him and tightened his throat. He knew it, he knew something was wrong, he felt it all along.

"You must have heard about Julie's kidnapping, right?"

"Yes, I . . ." He couldn't speak, he couldn't think.

"Well, it's a long story, but since the kidnapper asked for the ransom, he wanted me to deliver it. But I was frightened, and I didn't want to go. So it was Laura's idea to go on my behalf."

"What? Are you all nuts? Didn't you just survive this horrible attack? I am happy to see you fully recovered. And now Laura is in the hands of this killer!"

He mastered his anger. He breathed out, loud and slow. Ivy sat next to him and took his hand.

"Laura felt so guilty about bringing me down here. She was afraid you might abandon her. And I know she likes you, even after she learned that you and Eileen . . . oh, Uncle Brad, please don't throw her out. I really do like her, and she has nobody besides us." She squeezed his hand firmly before she let go.

"Me and Eileen? Where did that come from? There is no me

and Eileen, never has been, never will be," he said dryly. Ivy's heart made a big leap.

"So you won't let her go—you like her, even just a little bit?"

Now he was smiling. He had no intentions of ever letting her go again. Not in this life. But then, his eyes narrowed in concern.

"Tell me what happened, step by step."

After relating the story, Ivy stopped and shook her head. "I just got the information from the police. They have lost contact with her. They stopped the search and will resume at dawn. He took her and the diamonds and disappeared."

"And when was this?" Brad checked his watch. It was 9:00 p.m. There must be something they could do tonight.

An owl was calling in the distance as Laura slowly recovered consciousness. A sharp pain throbbed in her head, and the wet and stinky mud reminded her of how he'd hit her and threw her out of the car. It was totally dark, but she was not alone, that she could hear.

There was a deep thunder rumbling, slow and far away, and she was shivering as she got up. The last thunderstorm dated back only ten days and had changed her life dramatically.

Count the good things, she told herself. She was alive, and relatively intact—she had some bruises and dirty abrasions, but at least she was untied.

But where should she go? There was no trail, no road. He must have dragged her through the undergrowth and left her in the middle of nowhere. In the distance, the tropical thunderstorm was building up.

Not again, she pleaded.

❧

Not too far away, in a wooden cabin, Julie woke up, soaked in sweat. She'd had a horrible nightmare, but it was the pain in her back that had made her wake up.

Vividly, she recalled only the last scene: her father covered in blood, holding both of his hands over her head, blood dropping from the knife he'd held down toward her face, as he moved to kill her.

How horrible, she thought. How could she dream something like this? As far as she could remember, her father had always been her best friend, her coach and her trainer. He was the one who spent every minute of his free time to teach her how to swing a golf club.

She didn't know exactly when he started teaching her. The first time she remembered was on her fifth birthday, because it was the last birthday her mom was there. She was hitting golf balls in the backyard and she wouldn't stop, even as guests arrived and everybody was sitting down at the table.

Yes, she'd never forget how her mom picked her up and carried her over to the table so she could blow out her birthday cake candles. She had the golf club in her right hand and the golf ball in her left as she blew out the candles with all her strength, and she accidentally hit her grandmother with the club.

Oh, she has not forgotten Grandma's face and her black eye, even weeks later. Of course, that story was told over and over again on every birthday—always a sure bet for some laughter and fun.

But it truly was her father's drive that made her what she was today, more so after her mom's death. Shortly after her fifth birthday, her mother developed a very sincere blood anemia and died.

Ivy blocked out that time of her life, probably because of the pain she felt, hearing their constant fighting. She couldn't recall what had started first, mother's sickness or their fighting, but it was never again as it had been before.

Then it was just her father and Ivy. He pushed her when she was tired, he encouraged her when she was down and he celebrated her when she was at the top.

She believed nothing of what that criminal had told her. How could her father be involved in something so horrible, and why?

Julie looked up, surprised to find herself alone. Apparently, her kidnapper had taken all of his belongings with him. He even had cleaned out the kitchen. Slowly, she tumbled up and moved to the bathroom. Water, she desperately needed water and painkillers.

The cold water felt good on her face. She drank from her hands, and for the first time in two days, she felt somewhat relieved.

As she looked up into the mirror, she still couldn't believe what she saw. Only two days ago, she was so wonderfully styled for the red carpet gala, and now she was gaunt, pale and BALD!

It's only hair, and it'll grow back, she told herself as she searched for pain relievers in the bathroom cabinet, but there weren't any.

The pain was killing her. She felt dizzy again, and she needed medical help, soon.

Only then did she notice something was wrong with her right foot. She couldn't walk freely. What was this? And to her horror, she saw that she was on a sturdy tie-out cable with just enough room to go to the bathroom.

He'd leashed her like a dog.

✒

Meanwhile, Laura was getting more and more worried about the approaching thunderstorm. Lightning became much more vivid, and the thunder had escalated into deafening crashes right over her head.

The air was packed with humidity, thick and warm, which made it hard for her to breathe. The pressure was on. It was only a matter of minutes until the sky would open up and release the moisture it had collected during the hot summer day.

Otherwise, it was pitch dark. However, the jungle nightlife was very active, and that made her very uneasy.

✒

Brad walked over to the window and let some fresh air in. The air was sticky in the conference room.

He needed a clear mind, he needed to think.

"Inspector, there must be a plan B. You can't just sit around the phone and wait until he calls. Why would he? I don't think that we will ever hear from him again."

He took a deep breath of hot, humid air. "He's kidnapped Julie, and now, he has the ransom money, the diamonds and Laura. What does he need us for? Maybe he'll dump them somewhere on the road as soon as he has made enough distance."

Now he turned and faced the room where Inspector Corelli, Henrik Ferguson, Harry Butcher, Dustin and Ivy sat around the oversized coffee table.

It was still early, but everybody looked tired after a restless night with no news of the whereabouts of the two hostages. The police had searched all night with track hounds after he'd put some pressure on, but unsuccessfully.

"Sure, he'll dump them. It will be too much of a hassle for him to keep them with him. Too dangerous. From what I've heard so far, he is a professional, so he'll know that the manhunt will never stop until Laura and Julie have been found. So I believe he's going to release them sooner or later. Also, I don't see the need for him to kill them."

"He better not!" Ferguson said furiously. He wanted to continue, but Harry kicked him hard under the table.

"Mr. Coleman, I'm Harry Butcher, Julie Ferguson's manager. I don't think we've met. I must say that I'm impressed about how you see the situation, and I couldn't agree more. There's no need for him to kill. The question here is what can we do to find them ASAP?" And with this, he looked around the table and fixed his eyes on the inspector.

"I have my men out there, searching, and we'll do what we can to find them quickly."

"I need you to find my daughter. The last time I spoke to her, she wasn't well. This season was very hard, and she needs to rest.

Please let us know how we can help."

"Mr. Ferguson, please stay calm, and don't interfere with our investigation. We'll do what we can." Inspector Corelli was well aware of the fact that, at this point, the trail was already cold.

Angry but controlled, Brad stepped in. "Sorry, Inspector, but this isn't good enough. And whether you like it or not, we have to do more to find them, to find Laura."

Loudly, he closed the window and turned to Ivy, who was close to tears. "Let's get out of here. I can't breathe anymore. I need fresh air, and from the look on your face, I would say you do too." He took her by her shoulders, and they left the room.

Outside in the hallway, he stopped and turned to her. "Ivy, what is going on?" He still had her hands on her shoulders, and he looked her straight in the eyes. "These people have something to hide. Some of them clearly have a hidden agenda. They aren't telling the truth. So what is it? Do you know?" He let her go.

"No, but you sound like Laura. Brad, please, I'm so concerned about Laura, and Julie, of course. I don't know what to do."

"Why don't you start by telling me all you know. What did you and Laura do? Whom did she talk to? Please remember, it might be important."

A cleaning crew appeared at the end of the hallway, opening two guestrooms, and they started vacuuming.

"Brad, do you remember Thanksgiving after dinner? I couldn't sleep, and I was sitting in the study, crying. And then Laura walked in."

"So?"

"We started to talk, and she told me what had happened to her, and then I told her my story. It was good for me, a huge burden taken off my shoulders." Ivy searched her pockets for a tissue, because she felt tears coming up, and she felt terrible about bringing Laura into all this mess.

Brad gave her one of his ivory silk tissues with his initials engraved, and as Ivy saw this, she had to laugh.

"You still have those? I remember them when I was very little. When you gave me those with your initials on them, I thought you were a very important person. And I guess you were."

Now Brad was smiling. Having no children of his own, he always considered her his little girl.

"That's why you came up with the idea to fly down to Rio, I see," he said, shaking his head. "What was the purpose behind it?" He was curious now, since he hadn't really given it a thought last week. He was under the impression that they needed a break and chose to fly down to South America, not much more.

"After I had told her my story, she wasn't quite convinced that this was all there was to it. Too her, it sounded too easy. The attack, the smooth police investigation, and only after a few days in court, he was out of prison."

"Actually, it had been Laura's idea to fly down to Rio, to attend the gala and to investigate these events further. She had already started to dig deeper into the happenings of the events prior to the attack. Honestly, I don't know what she found out. I was thrilled with golf again, and I spent most of my time on Monday on the links. You know that golf is a discipline at the Olympic Summer Games, next year, here in Rio? I was imagining playing here and started dreaming about how it would be to win a medal."

She sniveled into the tissue and continued. "Well, come to think of it, Laura was always working on her laptop, and I thought she was setting up her trading account. But when I spoke to her, she always talked about the case, and as the kidnapper handed us the note that he wanted me to deliver the ransom, she jumped on it immediately."

Ivy was worried. Now that she remembered how Laura reacted, she must have come up with something.

Why hadn't she talked to her about it?

Brad furrowed his brow. "What were you thinking? That was stupid. Did she have any solid evidence, any proof?"

"She found out that he had $20,000 in twenty-dollar bills in a plastic bag as they arrested him. I don't know more, but she thought the kidnapper was the same man who attacked me. This was her last lead."

Ivy was feeling sick—she shouldn't have agreed to let Laura go. He wanted her, Ivy, and he must have been furious when he found out about the replacement.

They'd tricked him, and maybe that drove him over the edge.

However, she couldn't let Brad know about her fears. He cared too much about Laura, she knew that. She'd never seen him before talking about another person for more than thirty seconds unless he was seriously concerned.

"You see, she's got a theory that there must be a conspiracy behind all this."

"A conspiracy?"

"Maybe I can help with this," Dustin cut in, "but not here. Can we go somewhere where we can talk more privately?"

"Dustin?" Ivy looked sharply at him.

"Yes, let's go into Laura's suite," Brad took up, "we can talk there, and I want to check Laura's laptop, her emails and her latest files. Maybe we can find more clues."

Brad lead the way to the elevator. He only hoped that all this was pure imagination and fantasy, because otherwise, much more trouble could be on its way.

THIRTEEN

Greeted by a gust of humid hot air, he left the airport and got into the first taxi available. He hated to arrive midday in a hectic city after spending more than thirteen hours on a transatlantic flight.

But what annoyed him most was the fact that he had to play an active role in this unfortunate scam, and to his unpleasant surprise, the man selected for this delicate job had made a mess with an uncertain outcome.

This, he could not tolerate.

He checked his Rolex. Within the next two hours he should have completed his job down here. And if everything went according to plan, by tonight, there would be no trace of his involvement whatsoever.

Smiling dryly, he put on his black sunglasses and the brand-new tan Fedora he had acquired at the airport shop to make him look like a local business man. However, he couldn't resist selecting the stylish model with the pale blue band.

In the backseat of the taxi, he stretched his tired legs and enjoyed the scenic ride along the Atlantic coastline toward his destination.

❧

Lunch time. It got busy at the snack bar at the Port de Azuçá, approximately sixty miles south of Rio, where many large cargo vessels fetched heavy loads of iron ore bound for western European ports. Port de Azuçá was one of the largest ports in Brazil, and it was the perfect place for money laundering.

And Manuel Gustavo Rodrigues knew the trade.

Due to his scarred face, he was called Cicatriz Cara, or short *Cica*. He had gone underground, as he was the most wanted person in Brazil. For two years, he was now working as a hired hand loading maritime freight. Hard work. He didn't mind.

Nobody questioned his dark glasses, the mustache and the cap he always wore. Nobody questioned the gloves he used to hide some very distinguishing tattoos, which could easily reveal his identity.

The clock behind the counter turned to one as he finished his espresso. Soon, he would receive his payment. The job was easy—three million U.S. dollars black money had to be placed in exchange for a bag of rough diamonds—$100,000 in cash for him.

Little did they know, however, that he planned to cut a little extra from both sides. Call it arbitrage. Call it commission.

What was strange was the request for hidden passage on a certain freighter to São Paulo. But he had been in the business long enough to know when not to ask questions.

He ordered another double espresso. With all that money he

was making, he could splurge.

❧

"Curley, Curley Marie, stop licking my face. I'm waking up, it's okay. Hey! Stop licking my face." She saw her Golden Retriever jumping through a watering fountain in the sun onto a trail and disappearing. A trail? And the sound of water, no, it was rain, lashing rain.

"Ouch!" Laura tried to turn her head to see where Curley was going, but there was a sharp pain on the left side of her head. She carefully touched it with her hands and felt a clot of blood. Cold and dry.

She looked around, searching for her dog. Was it true? Was it Curley Marie licking her face, or was it just another dream? Her head was hurting badly and she was disoriented, couldn't see clearly.

Lying on the rain-drenched, wet ground, Laura shivered with cold. But where was that sound of streaming water coming from? It was still dark, but it wasn't raining anymore.

Some images flashed through her mind. Last night, she had been at a restaurant, and then he had taken her in his car, they drove through the dark forest to a cabin, and from there on, it was a total blank.

No, wait, she recalled the thunderstorm approaching and the need to hide. She couldn't walk, but she had crawled into a hiding space. It was too dark to see where she was going.

Her eyes slowly adjusted to the darkness, but where was she? Then she realized where she was—she was lying on bare stones in a cave behind a steep waterfall. That was the sound of gushing water.

Water drops were splashing down on her head. So that's what the licking really was, she concluded. She must have sought shelter in that cave as the thunder came closer. And that's why she was so cold and wet.

Suddenly, it hit her—déjà vu. A horrible feeling knotted in her stomach. What date and year is it? Am I back? What is happening to me?

Blood shot through her brain. Her head was spinning, and she faded back into a heavy dream. This time, she was in her childhood. She saw her parents and the ranch. There were many horses there, but only one stood out—*Pieces of Eight*. Alive.

James smiled at her with his loving brown eyes, smiling and squeezing her hands. They were sitting together, holding hands, on top of the Corcovado mountain, looking down at Rio and the beaches, and of course, there was Christ the Redeemer.

Again, Curley Marie jumped through the water, and the last thing Laura remembered was a luminous light and the sharp, cracking sound of thunder.

She slept for hours, and as she finally awoke, she could see the sun glaring through the waterfall. Were those people's voices?

Her dream. It had felt so real. Was it a dream, or was it another vision? James and Curley showing her the way out? She would rather not deal with these mind games right now.

However, she'd done too much research on time shifts and paranormal sciences lately to ignore it completely. Why was James with Christ the Redeemer? They'd been in Rio before, yes, but only a couple of days on their honeymoon, a cruise from Miami to

Buenos Aires.

Closing her eyes, she listened carefully. In the distance, behind the waterfall, she could hear children laughing. And there was something else. She could hear a hissing sound. A train? Was there a train station close by?

She and James had gone by train, a red cog train, up to the top of the Corcovado Mountain. Yes, that was right. It was a very busy tourist attraction. She remembered it clearly because, at first, they didn't want to go. The train looked overloaded, bursting on its capacity, but then they decided to take the chance and got on.

If only I could find the train station or get closer to it so people can see me, she thought.

She checked her body and found no major damage besides the blood on her head and some bad scratches and road burn on her hands, arms and legs. She was sore, but she could move. She got up slowly.

She had no idea how she had found that cave, but it seemed that the only way out lead through that waterfall and a crystal blue lagoon that the waterfall obviously fed into. Here goes, Laura thought, and started—with some hesitation—her approach through the water, not knowing what to expect on the other side.

The water in the lagoon was crystal clear and cold. She cleaned her face and her hands, but even though she was thirsty, she avoided swallowing the water.

Then she approached the waterfall, which roared with the powerfully pouring down of tons of fresh spring water into the basin. Its whooshes and splashes became scarier as she got closer to it, and yet it seemed very relaxing.

Like in a trance, the image of Curley Marie jumping through

the water fountain into the sun came back into her mind, and so, with full trust and all confidence, she took a deep breath, closed her eyes and dived underwater through the fall.

Bright sunlight welcomed her as she surfaced on the other side. The small lagoon had become a lake, and she swam to the closest bank. It was rocky and glittery as she crawled out of the water, happy to be alive and on safe ground. She felt the warm, humid air and gazed at the colorful wildflowers, small scrubs and ancient washed-out rock formations that surrounded her.

However, it took only a few seconds for her to discover that help was not as close as she had expected.

Laura was sitting on an overhanging rock, and it was the only dry spot in the lake, which continued into another waterfall deep down into the forest.

Far away, she could spot the red cog train climbing up a mountain crest, loaded with tourists going up to the Corcovado mountain. That had been the source of the echoing sound of children's laughter.

With both arms she waved toward the train and called for help as loudly as she could, but the train continued its slow ascent. It was just too far away. She repeated her appeals twenty minutes later as the next train rolled by.

Nobody noticed her. Totally exhausted, she leaned back and tried to get more comfortable and safer on the small overhang. This isn't working, she thought, looking around for an alternative. Rocks and water. No way out, it seemed.

However, even though her location was scary, it wasn't life threatening, and she could rest on that rock relatively comfortably. How long, she had no idea, but so far, it looked stable enough to hold her.

The sun was slowly rising, and Laura realized how rapidly the heat was drying her out. Soon, she would need water. She decided to give it a try and drink the water from the lake. It was risky, but what other choice did she have?

＊

"I saw you play the other day," Dustin said with a genuine smile to Ivy as they walked into Laura's suite. "And it looked real good. In fact, *you* looked real good."

"Thank you! I feel great, and I want to come back to the game as soon as possible." Ivy smiled at him. She never thought much of Dustin since he seemed to be a shadow of Julie's. However, as she had watched him closer over the last couple of days, she even found him attractive. This was a first since Jason's death.

"So what are your plans?" He held the door open for her.

"My plans? I'm not so sure right now. I would love to play at the Olympics next year." She turned her head and her eyes twinkled. "Do you think I'd have a chance?"

"Sure you do. I think that is a wonderful idea," Brad stepped in, touched her slightly on her shoulders and shoved her into the room. "But right now," he continued, "let's think how we can get Julie and Laura safely back. That should be our first priority." He closed the door and took the lead.

"First, let's go quickly through all the details and facts. Dustin, you mentioned that you knew something about a conspiracy? What information do you have?"

"I'm not sure if it means anything, but a couple of days ago, I overheard a conversation between Harry Butcher, Julie's manager, and her father."

Dustin sat down in the armchair by the window, while Ivy got busy starting up Laura's laptop.

"What conversation? What did you hear?" Impatiently, Brad walked over to the minibar and took out a mineral water.

He was nervous. He glanced back at his watch and looked out of the window into the hot summer day—close to a hundred degrees, one of the hottest days this year. No clouds, only bright sunshine.

He knew they had to find them soon. If the kidnapper dropped them without proper shelter and supplies, especially water, they might not survive that heat.

"I overheard them talking about the incident earlier this year, and it seemed to me that they have some kind of business relationship with the killer, who supposedly is also our kidnapper."

Dustin felt uncomfortable. He was very sure about what he had overheard at the time, but now, a couple of days later, it was much harder to tell what was true.

"What do you mean? What kind of relationship?" Ivy looked up from the laptop screen. She was frightened, and she wished she had known more about Laura's ideas about all this.

"I couldn't hear clearly what was said. However, to me, it sounded like both of them were very familiar with the events, the attack and the kidnapping—both of them. Somehow, it was clear that they were not surprised by what was happening. And they talked a lot about money. Black money."

"When was this? Did you hear any names?" Brad probed for

more information.

"It was the day Julie went missing. I was in a hurry and searched all possible places in this hotel—couldn't find her. So I was running up to see her father and stopped right in front of his room as I overheard them screaming at each other. I didn't think much of it at that time, but now I'm sure they're hiding something. And I'm concerned about Julie, she is—"

"Dustin, you can't possibly think that her own father is involved in Julie's kidnapping?" Ivy interrupted him. She was pale, jittery, in shock. She couldn't think clearly. The attack, Jason's death and now Julie and Laura's kidnapping—was all of this part of a scam?

"Brad, I can't believe that. It's so out of my thinking. But I know that Laura did some research, and the data must be here on her laptop. It all sounded too smooth for her. Too easy. And I've gotta admit, I was so caught up with practicing on the golf course again that I didn't pay much attention to what she was up to. Only that she suspected a network of foul players deep in some organization, and she needed to find out more."

"If I would have known, I would never have let you go. Not with Laura nor alone," Brad responded angry. He couldn't believe what he was just hearing.

Looking over to Dustin and back to Ivy, he shook his head. He had just recently faced a few power strokes backlashing at him as he started to become more active in politics. As soon as money and power were at stake, it wasn't going to be a fairytale any longer.

"Okay, okay, I know how you feel, but this is not the right time to be angry with me or Laura. We have to find her. And I think we may get some of the answers here on her laptop. Do you have any idea what her password could be?"

"Try *Pieces of Eight!*" Brad shouted almost unconsciously. He was beside himself—Laura, he had to find Laura. He promised to himself that he would protect her, didn't he?

"*Pieces of Eight*, yes! That's it. It's working! Now I can scan for the last files Laura was using." Ivy clapped her hands as she opened Laura's document folder.

Brad tried to regain his composure and walked over to look over Ivy's shoulder while she scanned through Laura's files. There were a couple of folders dedicated to Laura's trading business, marked *Broker Accounts* and *Scanners*. Then she found two recent files, one was called *PSI* and the other one *IB*, like Ivy Brooks. She double clicked on *IB*.

"Here we go! Let's see what Laura was researching and what she found interesting enough to save." With hope, Ivy looked up to meet Brad's eyes, which had followed her movements step by step.

"Look at these, they are all video clips, mostly from YouTube. Let's watch a couple of those."

She opened the first videos. Dustin walked over too, and now all eyes were fixed on the screen, waiting for the video to load. After the first scenes, they were discouraged, as the pictures showed Ivy playing golf. A couple of shots from the tee and more short game swings close by and at the green.

"Why did she save those?" Dustin asked, surprised. "These videos are probably a couple of years old, and I can't see anything of significance here."

"Me neither." Brad lost a little hope that those computer files would give them more important information. He walked back to the window.

"Hey, look at this one! This is almost the same time frame as the other one, and as I remember, it is from the same tournament—yes it is. I'm sure of it. But here is Julie who is taking shots from the tee and the short game analysis."

She turned around to face Dustin and Brad with open eyes and waited for a comment.

"Why did Laura compare my game to Julie's? Isn't that strange?"

"It really is . . . look," Dustin continued, "here you prepare for your tee off, here you walk, concentrate, and set the ball on the tee. And now the same sequence with Julie."

He took the mouse and double-clicked more videos and all showed the same pattern—tournament after tournament—first Ivy and then Julie, at the same tee, and at the same green. However, neither Ivy nor Dustin could see anything special, just ladies professional golf.

By now, Brad recognized what Laura had pointed out, and he immediately reached his conclusion. He looked at Ivy, and then to Dustin, not sure if this was the right moment for his discovery to be announced.

And, of course, he couldn't be one hundred percent sure. But from what he'd seen in those videos, such a high degree of conformity in stance and body language at something so complex as golf deemed statistically impossible to be considered a random effect.

But that couldn't be true, could it? He needed to talk to Crystal before he let anybody in on this hunch.

He was mesmerized. Only Laura with her excellent pattern-recognition skills as a day trader could have recognized it. What conclusions had she drawn about all this? What would have been her next move?

᠀

Deep in the rainforest, colorful birds were singing in the lush green trees, and sunbeams danced on leafs that were wet from a tropical afternoon shower. The warm air floated in and took the mist off the crowns, and soon the jungle came to life.

Inside the cabin it was dense, only a few streaks of sunlight broke through the wooden slat covering the windows.

Julie had slept with restless anxiety and awoke to find herself fatigued and confused. Only slowly did she remember where she was and what had happened. And she remembered that she had tried unsuccessfully to escape from this cabin.

There was no way out. He must have nailed wooden slats all over the exits and windows. While trying to escape, she'd tangled herself up badly enough on the tie-out leash that she no longer could reach the food and water he'd left for her.

Under normal circumstances, it would have been only a matter of time until she would be found.

Unfortunately, time was running out for her.

She realized now that her back pain was much more serious than she'd imagined. She'd had seizures and shortness of breath. Her legs, ankles and feet were heavily swollen. She was no medical expert, and most of her experience was based on sports medicine, but she was almost certain that she had some severe kidney failure.

After another very painful seizure, she crawled back into her bed, covered herself with all of the blankets she could find. Despite the very hot and sticky air inside the cabin, she shivered badly. She was feeling cold, heavy and very thirsty. Finally, Julie succumbed to her drowsiness and lost consciousness.

All was nice and comfortable, and she felt pleasantly light, even weightless, as if floating in warm waters. The sun was shining bright with clear skies, and there was her mother, laughing and waving, calling her to come.

She looked so young and beautiful. Julie tried to reach for her hand, but somehow she couldn't grab it, couldn't hold onto it.

Julie was hovering. Everything was so light and sunny, and she waved back to her mom.

But something deep inside her told her it was wrong, told her to look down and to go back down. As she turned her head away from her mom in the clear sunny sky, she saw herself lying down in the cabin—a horrible sight.

Only a couple of days ago, a beloved superstar, a celebrity, with beautiful hair and a successful golfing career, now was a gaunt, pale girl with a shaved head lying in a dark cabin in the middle of a jungle, shivering to death.

Julie, go down! Go back into your body! Stand up and fight! Where were those words coming from? She didn't know, and she didn't want to go back. It felt so good being close to her mom. There was no pain—only love, peace and joy. It all was so clear, she could see, hear, feel and smell everything.

Is this how it felt—to have died? It was a wonderful feeling, and she didn't want to give it up. She didn't want to go back into this horrible body.

You have to go back, Julie! It's not your time yet. You have a great future ahead of you, and you will do very well. Julie, go back, go back into your body. Go back into the world, back to your father. He deserves a second chance. Give it to him if he asks for it, will you do that? Will you be my little girl?

Julie, I love you so much, and I'm here waiting for you. But it's not yet your time. I'll be here when it is. Now gather all of your strength and go back.

"Mother, is that you? I want to be with you, I want to stay."

Julie, go back! I love you, and I'll be there for you, always.

And with this, Julie began to feel heavier and colder. Something forceful was pulling her down, she tried to fight it, but all was in vain—it wasn't yet her time.

After endless hours of waving her jacket in twenty-minute intervals to the cog train riders, who obviously were preoccupied with watching the beautiful scenery, Laura finally gave up as yet another red train disappeared behind the trees.

She needed a break and had to rethink her plan. Maybe this wasn't a good idea after all. The midday sun beat down on her head. She was overheated, sunburned and completely frustrated. Help seemed so close but yet she was just too far away for anybody to notice her on top of this overhang.

Would she survive another night out here? Just the thought of spending another night in this jungle and going through another thunderstorm made her whole body shiver.

"There must be a way down to the valley—think, Laura, think!" she called out loud and reconsidered her options as she saw the next cog train steaming into view.

"Help! Please help! Up here, I'm up here!" Hectic and abrupt she got up and waved with both arms for help.

Again, nobody noticed her. How surreal this is, she thought. She could hear them talking and laughing while the train crossed the mountain crest and disappeared into the forest. And she was totally off the map.

Finally, she stopped waving and let herself bounce back onto the rock. This was definitely not working. She had to find another solution. Devastated, she closed her eyes and covered them with her hands to block out the world around her. The darkness felt good, smoothing.

Will she be able to find her family—or what's left of it? Will she be ever reunited with James and Curley? That wasn't likely. Oh, how disappointed she had felt as she saw the picture of James in front of the courthouse after he had gone through with it. With having her be declared dead. Why did he have to do it? Would she have done the same? Wouldn't she have kept waiting and waiting for him to come home?

Maybe he'd married that brunette and they've got children. The ones she couldn't give him. And Curley? What about her? Ten years is a long time for a Golden Retriever. Is she still around, and would she recognize her mama again?

It didn't make any sense. She, Laura, was the problem. Why shouldn't she die right here? Wouldn't that be the best solution for all of them? She had been dead over the last years and the world didn't care, so what's the big deal now?

"Laura, stop it! Just stop this bullshit!"

Wow, this is a first, she thought.

"You have to think out of the box. Think! There must be another solution. There always is. Be strong—you can do it!" Suddenly it hit her. Another vision appeared.

It was summer, and the sun was baking down. She was hiking in the mountains. Her path ran along a steep cliff, and she didn't dare to even look down. She passed a rugged ravine with a small lake and was walking on a beautiful trail up to a scenic point where she had a quick lunch, before she finally set out for the descent to the valley.

But of course! That would work, she thought, as she looked at the rocks and stones around the lake to her right-hand side. She'd been so focused on the way down, she never thought about going up.

It probably wasn't going to be easy, but the way up didn't seem too steep, and if she hiked up carefully, she may find a trail which she could follow until she found other hikers.

Back to civilization.

With new hope, she hiked up the hill for a while. Actually, it wasn't too difficult. She reached a ragged and unkempt trailhead and began her slow ascent. She made good progress, but further up, the incline became steeper, and she was about to give up as she saw a sign pointing to the top.

Then Laura could see the pinnacle, with a stone cap where heavy chains remained anchored along carved stone steps. But to her deepest disappointment, there were no other people, and no train station.

Is that it? she asked herself and sank down to the rocks. The sun beat down even hotter up here. She had no water, and her hands and feet were bleeding. The last incline took all she had left.

And there wasn't a soul in sight.

Laura leaned back against a rock and tried to stay awake. She was so terribly dizzy and tired. Visions raced through her brain, some old, some new.

At least the view was miraculous. It was hard to take it all in, but she could see nearly all of Rio. The Grand Palace Hotel with its golf course in the back and the oversized lagoon pool in its courtyard stood out to her.

What she wouldn't give to be back in her air-conditioned suite, enjoying afternoon tea on the terrace or a lazy swim in the pool. She sighed. And what about Ivy and Julie? Were they all right?

What a wonderful and tranquil place this was. It was not only surrounded by lush green trees and plants and wild life, but it also carried a very special atmosphere. And then, she heard voices. Voices?

This was her last thought.

FOURTEEN

He'd chosen a table in the shade next to the lap pool. He was dressed very casually in white slacks and a navy polo shirt on this hot summer afternoon.

He would have preferred a less public location, but this would do. He nervously checked his watch. His last contact with Manuel Gustavo Rodrigues was last night, shortly after he'd dumped Laura off. They had a quick instant message conversation to finalize the meeting plans for today. After that, he drove nonstop south and checked into a resort-style hotel close to his departure port.

It was all part of his plan. He felt safe here, in the midst of mostly European tourists, too busy spending a few days in the sun to notice him. Flirting with two half-naked French girls, he waived a waiter and ordered a cold draft beer.

He had no idea where Manuel Gustavo got that kind of money. Local mafia? Perhaps. He didn't care. An old friend and trusted source had given him the contact details and assured him of the man's reliability.

As the waiter placed the beer in front of him, he checked the time again. In a couple of hours he would be boarding a cargo vessel and sailing to his retirement estate. Just a quick exchange of funds, and then he was ready to leave. Booze and babes were waiting for him. Today he watched them, tomorrow he would use them.

With a deep, satisfying laugh, he took a first sip of his fresh cold beer and leaned comfortably back in his chair.

❧

The main hotel bar, down in the lobby of the Grand Palace Hotel, had just opened, and some barkeepers were busy getting their stuff ready, making final touches here and there. In only a few hours, this would be the busiest place in the hotel, with people dressed up in dinner gowns, eager to get their drinks.

Glass bowls needed to be filled with mixed nuts. Lemon slices and tropical fruit pieces were cut and neatly stored to chill. Every little detail was arranged in a very personal matter, reflecting the five-star luxury ambiance.

A samba beat played in the background, and lights were dimmed. Henrik Ferguson selected a private corner and ordered a double whiskey.

Silently, he watched the commencing activities of the still empty space. He studied the bar menu—on its backside it explained that the word "samba" was derived from "semba" or "kusamba." It meant something like "to pray" or to appeal for the favor of the gods or ancestors by singing and dancing, as an indispensable part of the religious ceremonies of African slaves who were brought to Brazil by the Portuguese as a work force, first for brazilwood extraction and sugar production and later for gold and diamond mining.

Isn't that kind of strange? he thought. No matter how far humankind has developed in lifestyle and technology—in the end, we are all slaves.

Somewhat depressed, he watched a happy couple walking in, probably coming from a stroll on the beach or from a shopping spree in the most luxurious boutiques in Rio.

Slaves, they were all slaves—of their money or their relationships, their jobs or businesses, and even driven from something born only inside themselves. And as such, they all carried out their traditions and rituals in the guise of parties—hiding, altering their true nature, needs and desire. Modern samba dancing?

Of course, he couldn't possibly draw the conclusion directly, but he felt trapped too. His whole life, he only wanted what was best for his daughter. What had he done?

Julie may have been molested or tortured, perhaps she wasn't even alive anymore—how could he ever have been talked into this horrible scheme? He should have known better. And Harry Butcher, he was a slave too, wasn't he? Greedy and obsessed with money. He'd never be satisfied, no matter how much Julie would have brought in.

"Hello, Henrik, I'm glad we're meeting here. I already called your room. We need to talk."

Without hesitation, Harry sat down. As the waitress approached, he ordered two Irish whiskey on the rocks.

"You look awful. You need to get some sun, some color into your face. Why don't you take a walk on the beach. Believe me, it will do you good."

"Harry, I can't do this anymore. I'm going to talk to the police. Maybe if they know, they will be able to nail him. I need to tell them the whole story—from the beginning."

"That's not an option, and you know it." Harry was getting angry, but he kept a smile on his face while the waitress placed the drinks and a bowl of nuts in front of them.

"First of all, you're still on probation because you dodged those taxes, remember? And secondly, there is too much at stake for all of us. You, the Golf Association and I've invested too much money, resources and time in the development of your child. You know only too well that we left other talents behind to sponsor your girl."

He took his whiskey and leaned back in his leather chair.

"Harry, please, not now!" Henrik sighed. It was all true, but he couldn't handle it right now. If only he could change it, if only he could go back and undo it all, he would do it differently.

"I just want to remind you that, first and foremost, it will be you who's in the spotlight. Your head rolls first, and you go to jail. Not me, not the Association. You're the one who overinsured Julie's arms, legs, accident, dismemberment, and life, remember? You're the one who wrote her the letters which made the world believe that a fanatic, a madman, was after her, which—"

"Please stop!"

"Let me finish, Henrik!" With an underhanded, nasty, slow voice, he slowly continued,

". . . which finally set him free." Sardonically, he sipped on his whiskey.

Harry was well aware that he had his back covered, as he'd

kept verbal and written evidence of all those little nasty details and actions over the past ten years. Their partnership had only one goal—to push Julie up to be the next golf champion, their golden goose, their money-making machine.

"First and foremost, I want to remind you that everything we did was legal and in the best interest of the Association and the public. But then again, it was you . . . or better your bastard, who suddenly and obviously out of the blue showed up and stormed to the top of the player's money list. Just because you couldn't keep your pants on."

"How dare you!" Red-faced and enraged, Henrik flared up, took his glass and was close to throwing his whiskey into Harry's face but instead he downed it all in one go.

"It was your girl who messed it all up. For all of us. I'll never forget when I first saw her as a rookie player. She was a natural, a true talent. Everybody could see that she was going to be a top performer."

"I should never have told you, not that day, not ever. When I saw her at the press conference, I thought I was looking into the eyes of Crystal." Henrik was close to tears.

All his life he had been preparing and planning for his child—boy or girl, it didn't matter—to become a champion. Golf, tennis, swimming or any other sports discipline.

His biggest dream, for his entire life, was to be a world champion, to be at the very top. Nevertheless, early on, he had to realize that he could never reach the top because of his mental weakness. But he knew he had it inside himself, not to be the champion, but to be the perfect coach. The only chance he got was through his child. So he'd put everything he had into Julie, his only child—at least so he thought—until he saw Ivy.

"I was as surprised as everybody else. So what could I do?"

"Anyway, but see, you're not the one who is in any position to go to the police. If somebody would talk to them, it would be me."

"You'd never do that. You are too dead set on the money to risk any of it." Henrik put the glass down, exasperated.

"Come on, Henrik, just let's forget about it."

"Hmm . . . and Julie?"

"Trust me, Julie will be found, she'll be fine. I know it. Gunman wouldn't do anything as stupid as murder."

"You're sure?"

"'Course—the manhunt for murder would never let him live in peace, and that's what he wants most. We made a mistake, should have paid him the full amount."

"Yeah."

"Too late, but he got his final paycheck, with interest, and not too shabby, five million U.S. dollars' worth in raw diamonds. So, since he got what he asked for, why should he endanger it?" Harry gave Henrik an encouraging look.

"Well, you've got a point there, I think."

"Let the past be the past and focus on our future, our bright future."

"But—"

"Nobody needs to know about all this, Henrik. And we continue to focus on our goals for next year. It'll be a big year. Trust me."

Harry tried to make peace. His blood was boiling, but he could not let his feelings overshadow his professionalism. Too much was at stake for him and the Association. He had just gotten off the phone with the president, who again was very concerned about the events taking place in Brazil.

Things had changed—he'd noticed it in the president's voice. It had all started with the kidnapping of his top athlete, which had made headlines all over the world. Sponsors got nervous. It just wasn't good business when the new face of the Rolex campaign and the new Porsche Cabriolet was held captive or could be dead already.

Harry had made a capital mistake by not paying Gunman off. He was too reluctant to give the money away—he realized that by now. And Henrik was a total miscast, not able to deliver the message, he should have sensed the issue and paid off the man.

But Harry had one last ace in his hand, a card he did not play lightly, but maybe it was his last chance to keep his name clean. And with a slight smile, he picked up his smartphone and sent a short text.

Harry looked up to see Dustin cruising through the lobby towards them. "Hey, I've got good news. The police just called, they've found Laura."

"That's great news—how is she?" Harry got up and let his smartphone slide into his back pocket.

"Oh, she is fine. Some hikers found her in the Tijuca rainforest and brought her to the hospital where she got a throughout checkup—she was released a few moments ago. She's with the police right now and will be arriving soon."

"Dustin, did they say anything about Julie? Did they find her too?" Henrik bolted up, nervous. God, they had to find Julie soon. It's been two days and two nights, she needs water and food. What had happened to my little girl?

"No, sir, I'm sorry. I'm very concerned about Julie. I don't know if you noticed, but she hadn't been feeling very well over the last couple of days. This year's season was exhausting, especially last weekend with the final tournament and the red carpet celebration and the gala night on Sunday. She looked so pale and fragile on Monday morning. That's why she decided to spend some time in the spa."

Laura was found. But that didn't matter to Harry. He needed Julie alive and well. Or he had to quickly change hands and take Ivy Brooks under contract. With a little nurturing, she could perform very well next year. Anyway, he had all under control now.

"That's all you can remember, Mrs. Winchester?" Inspector Corelli flipped through his notepad after he had quickly summarized what Laura had told him.

"Yes, Inspector, that is all. I know by now that he must have tranquilized me. I don't think I had any amnesia, and I feel fine now."

Finally, Laura was back in her air-conditioned suite. She was sitting straight up in her bed with huge pillows stuffed behind her back, and she answered the final questions from the Inspector.

She was grateful to him, since he had rescued her from an over-committed, though very supportive hospital staff. When the

Inspector arrived, she almost wished she had not disclosed her identity to the nurses.

American tourists had found her, and of course they knew what had happened. They had already soaked her in and gave her all—if not more than—the attention she wanted. And then the hospital . . .

"Inspector, I'll be staying here in Rio for a while, at least until we know what happened to Julie and hopefully get her back safely as well. So, if anything comes up, I'll sure give you the first call. You'll be the first to know, I promise. I owe you."

"No, you don't," he played it down with a slight smile, already guessing what she meant.

"Don't laugh, I owe you big time. Without your strict interference, I would definitely be today's megastar on Facebook and Twitter."

"All right, then, you got my number, and I think it's now time for your family to see you."

"My family?"

Corelli walked to the door. He looked back once with a twinkle in his eye to that beautiful lady which was out of reach for him. Then he opened the double doors to let Ivy storm in, closely followed by Brad. Ivy couldn't contain herself, and she jumped right onto her bed.

"Laura, I'm so happy that you're back. Are you all right? Did they treat you well in the hospital? Brad insisted on going there right away to get you out, but the police wouldn't let him."

"Oh, Ivy, give me a hug. I missed you so much, and I'm so happy that I've got you and Brad." She looked over to him, and a tingling sensation arose in her stomach. Was it the two dozen red roses in his arms or rather the dearly warm look in his eyes?

That wasn't all—to her great surprise, the hotel attendants entered the room and brought in an overflow of flowers, colorful balloons and a slew of teddy bears—she once told Ivy how much she loved them.

Tears welled up in her eyes as a silver tray was finally rolled in. It was overloaded with tropical fruits, a cake, ice cream and a bottle of champagne.

What a stunner! This was totally unexpected, and now big joyful tears were running down her cheeks. Had her dreams come true? Had Curley Marie brought her back to her family?

It seemed, though, that she had finally found her family. Isn't that all I could ask for? Laura thought, searching for a Kleenex.

"Here." Brad handed her his silk handkerchief engraved with his monogram. He too was more than relieved that she was finally back. The last days had a profound effect on him, and he was now certain of his true feelings for her. He would never let her go again.

From the moment she stood in front of his home in Naples, he had felt something so incredible that completely baffled him. He had heard about that sort of feeling, but never really understood it.

But now he knew. He just knew. And he wanted to tell her, to say out loud how he felt for her, but he couldn't find the words. Nothing seemed right. So he just took her hands and kissed them.

"Brad, thank you. I missed you too," Laura fell into his arms, welcomed and wanted.

Brad gazed at Laura. "Forgive me for what I said back in Naples. To Eileen. I wasn't thinking clearly that day, and she was so—" Softly, Laura put her finger on his lips.

"It doesn't matter, not anymore." She beamed at him, and he bent over, as it seemed to be the right time for their first tender kiss.

"Not so fast!" Ivy squeaked up. "I'll leave you both alone now. You probably have a lot to catch up. But I—hmm, I need to take a piece of that delicious cake with me."

Ivy placed a huge chunk of double chocolate cake on her plate, kissed Laura on her cheek, whispered, "Everything will be all right," in her ear and rushed out of the room.

In the hallway she was almost run over by Dustin. "Hey, careful! Look at this awesome cake I have here. Do you want to try?" She balanced the plate in front of his nose.

"Ivy, I'm sorry. The cake looks great, sure does, but I'm going to pass." He looked real sad.

"Any news on Julie?"

"No. You know, I'm really concerned about her. Does Laura know anything? Is she all right?"

"Dustin, I'm sure the police will find her soon. Based on what we know from Laura, the kidnapper left with the diamonds."

"And Julie?"

"Not sure. Laura recalled that they stopped at a cabin. She doesn't know much detail because he'd tranquilized her. However, she remembers that, after he got out of the cabin, he heaved a big bag into the trunk. And a little later, the car slowed down and he hit her on the head. When she woke up, she realized that he must have dropped her in the woods. And when she heard thunder approaching, she crawled into a cave for shelter. That's her story."

"And nothing on Julie?"

"I assume that the police is looking for that cabin. Hopefully they'll find it soon, with Julie in it."

"You know, Ivy, I'm very sorry about what happened to you and Jason. And I know that Julie was horrified by these events too. She didn't mean to take any advantage of the situation. She's always respected you and admired you for your natural talent to play golf. I even think she was—she is—your biggest fan. I just wanted you to know that."

"Oh, Dustin, that means a lot. Thank you."

"No matter how this ends, I want you to keep her in good memory, and please pray for the best." Dustin took her by her shoulders, hugged her and kissed her cheek before he heavy-heartedly withdrew to his room.

Manuel Gustavo Rodrigues had strict orders, and he intended to follow them. In his way, and according to his standards. He saw himself a loyal and trustworthy businessman, and he would never double cross anybody or risk his reputation and only reported to one master. Today he would do the same.

As he walked through the lobby toward the pool, he caught a glimpse of himself in one of the wall-long mirrors and smiled. He liked what he saw.

Although he couldn't change the scars on his face, the brand-new silk suit, the fancy light-brown English leather loafers and a tan Fedora with a white band made a big difference. He had to have it, because his master had one with a pale blue band today.

These clothes, they made a new man out of him—a true gentleman.

"*Olá amigo, como está*—how are you?"

"Manuel, or should I call you *Cica*? You're late, and I'm not a patient man. Do you have the money?"

Using a red bandana, he dried his sweaty forehead. He had boiled for too long out there. Even in the shade it was close to a hundred degrees, and he was irritated to have been kept waiting.

"I'm doing very well, thank you for asking. You can call me Manuel."

"Do you have the money?"

"Do I have the money? Of course I have it. Do you have the diamonds?"

"All right, I'm sorry, I've been waiting too long in that heat. And I suppose I have to trust you anyway, 'cause my life lies in your hands right now, doesn't it?" Gunman flicked his fingers and pointed down to his beer to order a refill. "What would you like to drink?"

"I'll have a double espresso, *por favor*."

The waitress took their orders, rearranged the umbrella slightly so that her guests were sitting in the shade and left for the hotel bar.

"All right, I have the money and everything else is well prepared. Where are the diamonds?"

"They are right here in this backpack."

"All right, then, let's do the exchange first, and then I tell you what to do." Manuel took a key out of the inside pocket of his silk jacket and placed it on the table in front of Gunman.

"This is the key to a safe deposit box here at the hotel. It's in your name. The name you gave me. It contains the money in a waterproof box, all in twenty-dollar bills, unmarked as per your request. Go now. I'll wait here keep an eye on the diamonds."

"I'll do that." Gunman got up, took the key and walked to the reception desk.

During his absence, Manuel quickly called in to confirm that everything was on track. He had also received the latest information on the departure time of the cargo ship, where he had reserved a special cabin for the man.

A superior balcony stateroom in the rear end of the vessel, where he could hear the calming sound of the sea and enjoy the breeze. Ha, ha. He was sure this gentleman would definitely enjoy his journey—and a little seasickness was included in that fare.

For now, Gunman looked very happy. He returned to the table with dollar signs in his eyes.

"Perfect, everything has worked out well so far." Gunman sat down and took another sip from his beer.

Soon his dream would come true, and he would be sitting in a rocking chair on the veranda of his hacienda. He gazed straight toward the blue waters of the Atlantic Ocean, and it gave him peace of mind that he had resisted the strong urge to kill the two women.

In his earlier days, he would never have left any witnesses alive. No way—that was unprofessional.

It was the right time to stop, to retire. He could feel it in his bones. His heart was getting weaker, too, and he'd become more emotional about the killings. So, in the end, it was the right decision to let go. And with all the money he had earned over the years and with what he was getting now, he could finally enjoy his life.

He had just finished his beer as Manuel touched his shoulder and brought him back to the present.

"Muito bem, very good!" Manuel checked his watch and looked up into the sky, almost another hour until sunset. Perfect cruising conditions, and the timely departure of the cargo vessel to São Paulo was confirmed.

He was eager to get going—to secure the diamonds.

"Time to go. Your ship leaves at eight o'clock. Why don't you go back into your room, pack and rest for a while. The driver will pick you up at seven."

"Good." Gunman stood up, finished his beer and handed him the bag. "And the diamonds, don't you want to check them?"

"Oh, I'm sure they're okay. I'm going to check them later. It will be better for both of us if they're what they're supposed to be—rough diamonds of highest quality." Manuel got up and left fifteen Brazilian reals on the table.

"Be ready in the lobby at 7:00 p.m. A black Range Rover will pick you up. Have a nice trip!"

He picked up the backpack with the diamonds. As his fingers slid over his silk jacket to straighten it, he felt he'd stepped up to the top of the range, to the top of the top.

This was his first deal with that distinguished gentleman whom he'd met today for the first time, but as agreed, it wouldn't be their last arrangement.

FIFTEEN

At 7:00 p.m. sharp, Gunman was ready. He'd checked out and was waiting for the arrival of the black Range Rover. With only a small suitcase containing the waterproof metal box with the money and his open-waters snorkeling gear, he'd decided to travel light.

During the time he spent getting ready, he had gotten rid of his car, cleaned his laptop and smashed it to pieces to eliminate any compromising data. Finally, he thoughtfully cleaned his room in order not to leave any fingerprints or traces of DNA behind.

Now he was ready and eager to start his journey. With this in mind, he stepped quickly outside, just as the black Range Rover rolled into the driveway.

Soon he would be boarding a huge cargo ship to São Paulo, and as Manuel had confirmed, he was booked for an abaft balcony stateroom at the rear end of the ship. That was special—he was well aware of that—but his plan included an early exit, shortly before the ship moored the next morning in the port of São Paulo.

With a nod, he acknowledged the driver, who had opened the passenger door, and he got into the car, his mind focused on his trip. Sitting on a balcony that overlooked a ship's wake was the closest thing to a Zen-like experience—mesmerizing and calming at the same time.

He'd seen that once in a movie. Since then, he had dreamed of that feeling, to be out on the water, feeling the gigantic power of the ship and the ocean droplets softly touching his skin and sipping champagne in the moonlight.

Soon it would be his reality.

They drove silently along the beautiful coastline back to the port. A glance at the driver assured Gunman that he belonged on Manuel's team.

Boy, that man had an eye for picking up the bad guys. Just the looks of the driver could scare people away, and he didn't have even one scar on his face. However, his monstrous stature was one of a eunuch monk with iron-strong muscles. His veined, bald head made him look like a refugee from Frankenstein's lab. His eyes, focused on the traffic, were covered by black sunglasses.

Around the world, Gunman had worked with many different warriors in the underworld. He had tasted bony fists and fire-hot pistols, he'd danced with martial artists from China and Japan and he had wrestled those who had attained the highest mastery of combat skills. Clearly, he knew quite well that this guy was one of a special kind—he was certainly not somebody to be trifled with.

Gunman tried to keep his focus on the outside scenery. A railroad bridge to the port came into view.

No 5-star cargo cruise liner was in sight. What type of ship had Manuel mentioned in their online chats? He couldn't remember. He had been under the impression that it was a nice modern cargo vessel that would provide his final journey.

Okay, a passage on an iron ore freighter, he thought, wasn't quite what he'd dreamed of—forget the Zen-like experience and the champagne—but it was still certainly a safe and clever way to disappear.

Since he didn't know the localities down here, he'd left all the details to Manuel Gustavo Rodrigues.

Therefore, he wasn't surprised as they took a left turn into the woods instead of going straight to the port entrance. Probably, he would be picked up by a jet ski that would bring him to the cargo vessel.

They continued their drive through the woods until they stopped at a small clearing. There was a boardwalk leading to a wooden boat dock, where a small rubber tender boat with an outboard motor was anchored.

Gunman got out of the car and turned to get his travel bag out of the trunk but was surprised to see the eunuch pressing a cold gun into his temple.

"Move! Down to boat." And he pressed the gun a little harder into his head. With no other choice, Gunman stumbled down to the boardwalk.

"I don't understand, *não percebo*. Hey, I'm on your side, I'm one of the bad guys. Please, *por favor*, call Manuel—check back with him, or better yet, let me speak with him."

"Move! Quick, to boat."

"Why? *Porquê*? What's the matter? I'm your *amigo*, your friend."

Gunman started flailing his arms and was trying to play the whole scene down. Something was going terribly wrong.

"No friend, and I speak English, too. Now move, get to boat."

"Do you want money, cash, *grana*?"

"Move! Or I make you never move again." With this, he shot Gunman in his right foot.

Gunman yelped. "Are you nuts?! I'm a friend of Manuel Gustavo Rodrigues, call him—right now!"

In severe pain and unable to use his right foot, he hobbled onto the boat, slipped over something very glittery and fell over onto his back.

"Can you help me, please? *Pode ajudar-me, por favor*? Help me! *Socorro*! Here, you can have it all, it's two million U.S. in cash!" And with his last strength, he threw the bag with the money to his offender's feet.

"Thank you!" With his free hand, the driver unmounted the boat and started the motor, while his other hand held the gun towards the wounded man at the bottom of the boat.

"No! Please!" Helplessly and hopelessly, he tried to stop the severe bleeding on his foot.

"Have a good trip!"

The driver pulled something out of his pocket. It looked like a cigarette lighter, and as the boat was about three feet from the dock, he silently pressed the trigger button.

The glittery thing in the boat was gelignite, blasting gelatin, and it exploded immediately.

"Sir?"

"Yes, what is it?"

"I have a phone call for you. He said it's urgent and he needed to speak to you directly."

"Okay, I'll take it in here."

He sat comfortably in a heavy leather armchair with a forty-year-old single-malt Irish whiskey in front of him and his favorite Financial Times lying next to it. The shades of the small oval windows of this private jet were down. He was on the way back to the States. He leaned over to pick up the phone.

"Hello?"

"This is Manuel from Brazil. The taxi driver—you remember?"

"Yes I do. Did you find it?"

Bravo, Manuel Gustavo Rodrigues, he thought. He was adhering to the rules and to the code they agreed on. He truly liked the man's business attitude.

"I'm sorry, sir, we checked everything—can't find it. Everything is clean and clear. There is nothing left behind. I'm sorry to disturb you, but I thought you should know."

"Yes, thank you, I appreciate it very much."

And he hung up.

Above the clouds, cruising in bright sunshine at about 20,000 feet, the distinguished gentleman with a contented smile sighed with relief. "Finally!"

He stretched his legs and brought his full attention back to his favorite newspaper, in which he had just read the lead article on the recent FIFA scandal.

It was an absolute must for him to clean up his organization, so history wouldn't repeat itself. Especially since he, together with other high-powered golf entities, had successfully lobbied to have golf included as an official sport in next year's Olympic Games in Rio de Janeiro.

Thus another reason he needed a trustworthy business partner like Manuel Gustavo Rodrigues down in Brazil. A man with a professional organization behind him, strong enough to help control medal-hungry functionaries from nations like Russia and China, which were about to invest heavily in the sport and in the country.

People in his position sometimes had no choice. Decisions needed to be made, rigidly and quickly for the good of all parties involved, including, most importantly, the public.

Unfortunately, bribing and money laundering was often part of the deal. The only mistake the FIFA power troop made was that they let themselves get caught.

Uncompromising, he would make sure that this would not happen in his association, especially since murder—too much, regretfully—was part of these dealings.

Clean up, yes, that he would do, and Harry Butcher was next on his list, since he knew way too much. He needed to pull some strings to make sure he would keep his mouth shut.

"Sir! We will be landing in about ten minutes at Palm Beach Airport. Please fasten your seatbelt. Thank you."

Good news, he thought. In about thirty minutes, he would be home, maybe there was time to stop by the country club for a couple of drinks to settle down before heading home to his wife and children. What a trip this had been. As if going to Lausanne for just two days wasn't hard enough, but that step over to Rio was really getting on his nerves.

Laura woke up. It was dark outside, and only a small nightlight gloomed in the corner. She looked around and found Brad sleeping in the loveseat next to her bed. He looked so soft and handsome in his sleep.

Reflectively, she watched him sleep for about a minute or so with a warm affection for him. She really did care for him. She wasn't sure if she was ready to call it love, but she was close to it. She needed to give her new life a good chance before rushing into a new direction.

She saw the balloons and the flowers all over her suite and remembered the wonderful welcome she'd received as she was brought home from the hospital.

Brad turned in his light sleep and recognized that Laura was sitting up in her bed, "Oh, Laura, are you all right? What time is it?" And he checked his watch—it was already past 11:00 p.m.

"Yes, I'm all right, I need to go to the bathroom, but I'll be back soon. Thank you for staying with me tonight. The loveseat looks comfortable, but you could have used the bed."

With a smile, Laura, still a little shaky from the adventures of the past two days, tiptoed to the bathroom. Inside, she turned on the lights and took off her robe.

Carefully and thoughtfully, she examined herself. There were bruises and abrasions everywhere, and some sore wounds were scabbed over, but she couldn't detect anything serious. Nothing that could get any worse by taking a hot shower, she thought, and she stepped into the walk-in marble shower.

As the water started splashing over her head, powerful, hot

and steaming, she enjoyed the wonderful feeling of a total cleanse.

How beautiful her world was right now, right at this precious moment.

She tried all different shower head settings, from massage to raindrop pouring. She even turned on the starlight on the ceiling and the in-room music, humming and dancing along with the song.

She must have shampooed her hair three times and soaped her body at least that many times. She needed that. With every new round of soap and shampoo, she washed away another part of her previous life, freeing herself of those nightmares which wouldn't let her rest long enough to build strength, which haunted her with guilt and regret and made her feel shaky and insecure. She wanted to be ready to continue to exist, to move forward, maybe even into a new love.

First and foremost, she washed away her past with James. That was gone. She scrubbed as hard as she could. Then, the last couple of weeks of her insecurity, and with an extra portion of soap and shampoo, she washed away the trauma of the last couple of days as a hostage and a hobo.

"Laura, is everything okay?"

A familiar voice brought her back. Through the steamed shower door she could see him standing, holding two glasses of champagne and staring at her.

"May I come in? I sure could use a shower myself."

He opened the door and stepped into the steamy, hot shower were he was welcomed by a clean, deliciously smelling, beautiful young lady.

And for the first time they made love—soft and tender. His

hands caressed her entire body as he slowly soaped her—this time it was energizing and empowering.

She felt like a woman again, wanted and needed, needy herself, and then she let herself go. He brought out a side of her which she'd covered up for much too long, she mused, and she let herself fall deeper into the soft rhythmic flow of two bodies meant to melt together.

He took care of her before he came, and then he grabbed her and held her even tighter.

"I love you, Laura, with all my heart. Will you marry me?"

It came over her like a threat, a shock. She knew he meant well and knew she should be delighted, but somehow, it had suddenly splashed away the easiness, the light fullness of that magic moment they'd shared before.

She felt trapped. The shower cabin seemed too small for the two of them. Suddenly, it was too tight for her.

She needed to breathe and wanted to run.

As she scrambled to regain her composure, she reached for the mixer tap and turned on the cold water.

"Ahh!" Brad squeaked and jumped out to get a towel.

"I'm sorry, I just, I don't know. It is all too fast, don't you think?" She'd followed him outside and he laid a warmed bathing robe around her shoulders, and then he saw that her eyes were filled with tears.

"Darling, I am sorry. It wasn't the right moment. I should have known. It was all too much for you. And I was jumping on you like a stallion. I was an idiot."

And he bowed over and kissed her hand and then, with a heartbreaking warm smile, he softly touched her lips.

"I do mean it, though. I am glad I said it. Take all the time you need, don't say anything now. But I do love you." And then he took his bathrobe and went out.

What just happened? she thought. Had he proposed to her? Aren't you the strangest thing, she told herself, not knowing if she meant herself or Brad.

To her surprise, all anger, anxiety and stress gave way to a feeling of peace inside her. She felt loved and that she belonged, which was a wonderful change from the dwindling feeling she had had over the last couple of weeks.

What a shower.

Only once had she dreamed of having sex in the shower. Back then, she was a teenage girl and had just seen it in a movie. By no means did she discuss this with her boyfriend at the time or even with her Catholic parents, and just the thought to suggest it to James made her laugh out loud.

The sound system was still playing at maximum volume, and this was good, because she didn't want Brad to think that she was laughing at him.

She opened one of the luxury body lotions the hotel provided and used it richly on the body. It smelled so good and gave her skin a light, silky tone.

I needed this, she thought, a little luxury indulgence. Tomorrow, she had to go shopping for her cosmetics and beauty supplies. She'd neglected that for too long, and she would take Ivy with her. It would do them good to spend a couple of hours on a shopping spree.

She remembered Brad's question, his proposal. How should she answer him? Did she really love him?

Hmm, she felt a tingling sensation all over her skin. That must be the body lotion, she reasoned. But she couldn't deny that she had strong feelings for him.

Feelings, sure, but love?

She remembered her dreams, as she was lost in the woods, the nightmares but also the dreams of her future, she remembered now the face she'd seen—it was very similar to Brad's.

She put on her bathrobe, tightened the belt around her waist and turned on the blow dryer. In her opinion, there was little more satisfying than styling her hair and witnessing firsthand the transformation back to her beautiful self, or a financial trade working out beautifully, or perhaps even sex at the right moment.

Wow, what a thought. The long shower and the attention from Brad had a very positive effect on her self-esteem.

But what about James? The thought bothered her—wasn't she still married to him, legally? How should she deal with it? He was a real jerk for declaring her dead, in spite of her mother's will requesting trying to find her. He had been grabby, selling off everything they owned together.

Where is he anyway? Why hadn't he contacted her?

He should have seen the headlines in the newspapers too. Was he living somewhere, happily remarried and had totally forgotten about her?

She doubted that. He was a very good and caring man. Still, there were too many unresolved questions.

Her hair was dry and shiny. She brushed over it one final time and used some of the body lotion to bring it a little bit better into shape. She would need to put hair styling products on her shopping list for tomorrow.

Energized, she stepped back into the room, pleased to see that Brad had ordered a light midnight snack from the twenty-four-hour room service. The side table was set up with chef sandwiches, salmon and caviar canapes, cheese, selected fruits and a bottle of champagne in a cooler.

"It's after midnight. Are you hungry or do you want to go back to sleep?" He looked at her with joyful expectancy in his eyes.

"No, I couldn't sleep right now, you know that. And this looks delicious. Why don't we have a good time?" She took the seat he offered her. She felt awkward sitting down with him in her suite at this late hour.

How should she deal with what had happened in the shower? She still wasn't sure about her true feelings for him. And his proposal? Under normal circumstances, men don't commit that fast, do they?

At least, the men she'd known wouldn't have. But then again, Brad had puzzled her before, and the way he looked at her now was so sweet and full of love—that had to mean something.

"Would you care for a glass of champagne?"

"Yes, please, I'd love that."

After filling two chilled glasses with champagne, he handed her one and looked into her eyes. "You know, darling, what happened in the shower was sincere. My love for you—it started way before you stepped out of the police car in front of my house. The first time James introduced you as his wife, I was in love." He took her hands. "There's nothing wrong with you. You just take it as slowly or as quickly as you can. I've waited so long, I can wait longer." He let out a long breath.

"For me, this is real, and I want to marry you as soon as

possible. I love you." He squeezed her hands before he took another sip of his champagne.

"Oh, Brad, I don't know what to say. I'm not sure if I'm ready yet. But I do have feelings for you, and I wish I could say yes right away, but something in me, inside my heart, is holding me back. Give me just a little more time, please. I promise I'll work on it, but right now I feel it's tearing me apart."

Laura took the whole glass of champagne at once. Relieved, she hoped he would understand.

He looked a little disappointed.

She rushed to continue. "I still want you by my side, day and night. I missed you so much when I thought I was going to die, up there in the mountains. You've been the one—not James."

"Laura, I flew down here to ask you to marry me and to give you this." He got up, produced a small red box out of his jacket pocket and put it in front of her. "Open it! This is for you, and I want you to wear it, whether you marry me or not."

She opened the box and a beautiful diamond ring sparkled into her eyes.

"Oh, Brad, I can't!"

"Yes you can, try it on."

It was so beautiful that she had to touch it. She took it out of the box and placed it on her ring finger. It must have been customized for her, as it fit right on. It looked so natural on her finger.

"It's absolutely gorgeous. Okay, I'll wear it, I can't resist. And if I end up not marrying you, I buy it from you." She chuckled. "This ring is mine, I can feel it. Thank you so much for finding something so beautiful for me!" Impulsively, she jumped up and kissed him.

"That is my Laura, the one I love. You're really going to buy it from me, if you don't accept my proposal? Can I get that in writing?"

He was laughing now, and so was she. They laughed off their stress after their first intimate encounter. Laura figured it was probably never easy to become romantic and sexually involved once you're no longer a teenager.

"You know, Brad, I'm glad we had our first time together." Laura smiled and took a canape with caviar. She felt more and more in love with him, and he certainly was worth it to work hard to clear her past and then to be truly free for him.

He was relieved too, more so as he knew that Laura had been a good friend to his late wife Regine.

"Everything is good. Now you should try to get some sleep. You still need to rest, and tomorrow is a new day. They can clean this up in the morning when I pick you up for breakfast."

Still in his bathrobe, he looked over to his clothes—could he manage to escape into his own room without inspiring new headlines about Laura? At this hour, probably. He went to collect his jacket and his slacks.

"Brad, wait!"

"What is it?" He hoped she would ask him to stay.

"I'm still not tired, and I don't have a good feeling about Julie. It's been too long. I know the police are looking for her, searching for the cabin where she may be held hostage. But I doubt they'll find it on their own. I've been dreaming about it, about the cabin where he collected his belongings before he left. I think I may be able to find it if I drive through the forest by myself."

"You can't drive up there, not at this hour. Look, it is pelting rain again. I am kind of tired of this rain, thunder and lightning, we had our share this summer in Naples. I want to go home with you. Leave Julie to the police. They'll find her soon, now that this maniac obviously got all he wanted."

"Still, I can't explain it, but I have this feeling that they don't have much time left to find her."

"Then let's call the police, describe to them where it is."

"That's the point, I can't. This vision I have—it's not real. I mean, yes, it is real for me, but I can't explain it. Somehow, I know that it will show me the way if I drove up there again." She began to feel increasingly troubled and nervous.

"Brad, I need to go, now—I have to hurry!"

Dressed in faded jeans and a T-shirt, she put on her sneakers.

"I need to take the same road at night up into the hills, then my vision will lead me there—to the cabin."

This is implausible, Brad thought, but he was too tired and not in the mood to argue with the woman he loved.

"Okay, okay. Under those circumstances, neither of us will find decent sleep tonight. But I drive, you sit next to me, the same way as it was before. This way, we have the best chance to take the same route and to find the cabin."

"Would you do that? What a wonderful idea. Okay, let's get ready and I'll see you in ten minutes down in the lobby. We can leave a note for the Inspector, just in case."

SIXTEEN

They left the parking garage of the Grand Palace Hotel in Brad's rental car, a black Mercedes sedan. "Tonight, I wished I had four-wheel drive, but this," he said, pointing to the three-pointed Mercedes star in the steering wheel, "is all we've got. So which way to turn, left or right?"

"Let's drive down to the restaurant first. From there I think I can tell you almost every move." She smiled—Brad radiated so much confidence and trust.

What a man, she thought. Never before had she met somebody with such charisma and assurance, and she had met many powerful people.

No wonder he had achieved so much—he always stayed focused and determined and never gave up until things where how he liked them to be.

They quickly found the restaurant—it was completely dark at this time, except for the neon sign. From there, Laura directed Brad on where to go. The rain got heavier as they drove closer to the rainforest. The last right turn brought them onto a small country road she remembered so clearly, and it led the way deep into the forest.

No other car was in sight, and there was no hint of civilization. The tiny winding road had loose shoulders with rainwater canals on both sides.

Brad was right—it isn't so easy to find the same route the kidnapper had taken the other night, she thought as she stared through the foggy windshield into the dark forest. She saw nothing but oversized raindrops. What had made her think that she had a chance to find the godforsaken cabin in this jungle?

But then, suddenly, there it was again—a sensation, a feeling. No, this time it was more. It was a very vivid vision.

In her mind she clearly saw the cabin, with Julie lying on a bed. Something else was there, something that wasn't right, but she couldn't get a clearer image on this yet.

She closed her eyes, trying to concentrate on how to get there. Then, without thinking, she blurted out, "Next one left—it's a gravel road or kind of trail—and be careful, there will be deep water holes in it."

"Laura, are you sure? I can stop here, and we can turn the lights on to check the map."

"No, no. This is the right way. Go on, there's not much time left. Do you see a road on the left side?"

"No, nothing. As far as I can remember from our search yesterday, this is the only road in the whole forest. We did not see any byroads, only trails, but they would be much too narrow and messy to drive with that kind of car."

Brad continued to drive slowly through the woods. The broken road got smaller and steeper—it was already a challenge to keep the Mercedes straight on the narrow pavement.

"Watch for a trailhead sign on the left side."

Laura concentrated again. She had a strong feeling that Julie was desperately trying to communicate with her. But that couldn't be real, could it? How would Julie know that they were looking for her?

"Laura, look, is this what you mean?" He pointed to a small wooden sign leading deeper into the jungle.

He turned the car a little to the left so that the headlights illuminated the sign. And then they saw it—a small trail wound deeper into the dense jungle.

"That's it, Brad—that's what I was looking for! Take it! It will lead us to the cabin."

"Are you sure?"

"Don't waste time!" Laura whirled around, eager to get to Julie. She was absolutely convinced that Julie was in the cabin and that she needed help—badly.

"Hmm, I was going to call Inspector Corelli, but I don't have a signal on the phone. Let me see, I can still send them a text message with our GPS data, so they can follow us once they get the message."

"Brad, we don't need the police, we will just get there, rescue Julie, and bring her back to the hotel. What's the big deal?"

She was getting a little annoyed. Time was of the essence. Julie probably needed water and other help. All she knew was that they had to hurry.

"Laura, we cannot be sure that he is really gone, or perhaps he had come back. Most likely he's armed, and we don't have any weapons. I would rather wait for the police to catch up with us, and then we approach the cabin together."

"Brad—"

"And if this is really the way to the cabin, he may already watching us through webcams or other surveillance equipment."

"But—"

"And then there is this car. I am not sure if that rental can handle this kind of off-road drive. We should turn around, go back to the city and let the police handle it from here."

How could he be so controlled? she thought, a little disappointed. Was he even more similar to James then she had realized? Her vision was so strong. How could she convince him that there was not enough time to go back to the city or to wait for the police?

However, he was right about one thing—they had no weapons, and it was very dangerous to approach the cabin without any.

Concentrate, Laura, concentrate—there must be a way, she told herself and closed her eyes.

"We leave the car here. We go by foot to the cabin. It shouldn't be that long. What do you think?"

"I still think it would be better to go back and have the police handle this. But I realize I cannot stop you anyway, and I will not leave you here alone."

"Right. Now let's go."

"No, I'll go—alone," he insisted. "You wait in the car, close the doors, and if I am not back within twenty minutes, you drive back to the hotel and call the Inspector. Deal?"

"No. I'm going with you." She hopped out of the car into the pouring rain.

"See, I'm already soaked—no point in turning back now. Are

you coming?" She closed the door and started walking down the trail.

"Come on, we'll need to get to Julie. She needs us."

❧

Laura set off at a good pace, and Brad had to hurry to catch up with her. He climbed out of the car and was immediately drenched. He didn't approve of this course of action, but, frowning, he followed her along the dark trail.

They weren't walking for long when a small building came into sight—a wooden cabin behind tangled, mangled shrubs and old, broken trees.

Brad was relieved to see that there was no car parked outside. The cabin windows were dark. They were thoroughly nailed up with wooden boards—not even a dim stream of light was shining through.

"Is this the place where you've been before?" Brad whispered.

"That's it. I remember it, clearly."

"It looks unoccupied and distorted since a while. Are you sure that it is the right location?"

Brad felt awkward and displaced, still not certain if he had done the right thing. What a crazy idea—he hadn't done anything like this since his teenage years, following a girl virtually blindfolded. The outcome was never good—not then, and probably not now.

"Brad, help me! It's locked!" She started pounding against the door. "Julie! Julie? Are you there?"

Silence.

"Julie, please open up. It's Laura and Brad, we're here to help you."

"Laura, wait! We cannot be sure that it is her inside. Actually, we do not even know if she is alone or not."

"Brad, we don't have time. I have this sensation that she's in there and she's not well. Believe me—we have to get the door open, or one of the windows."

Just then, Brad heard a beep coming from his pocket. A new message came through. Immediately he checked his iPhone.

"Good news, Laura." She looked up at him. "They are on their way. They have our exact location through the GPS data system, and they should be here very soon." Encouraged, Laura started pounding against the door again, and this time she heard a faint noise.

"Julie?" Laura hollered. "Julie, are you there? We're here to help."

"Laura, I'm here. I can't get to the door, I'm tied to a leash. Please hurry, I'm not doing very well. I'm running a fever."

"Are you alone, or is he with you?"

"No, no, I'm alone. He left a while ago. Please help me." Her voice sounded eerily weak and far away.

"Julie, hold on—the police will be here any minute, and they have the right tools to open the door. Drink some water if you can and talk to me. Everything is okay now." Laura talked to her in a steady and calm voice. However, inside she could feel how weak Julie really was.

This strange sensation never ceased—it grew stronger from minute to minute, as if she would crawl into Julie's body. It didn't feel good. Laura lost her balance. She reached for the door jamb and had to let herself down onto the wet steps.

"What is it? Laura—what's wrong?" Brad had been looking for another entry into the cabin and rushed to Laura's side.

"Ah, Brad. Talk to Julie, she is fading. Talk to her . . ."

She put up all her energy to even look up. ". . . It's all too much. And coming back to this cabin made me . . ." She tried to smile, though a little unsteady. "I'll be fine . . . I just need some rest." And then she lost consciousness.

In the distance, Brad could hear the sirens of the patrol cars. "Get going, boys!" he hissed, as he knelt down to cover Laura with his jacket. He'd stopped talking with Julie, because as soon as she had heard a male voice speaking, she'd started crying hysterically.

Finally the authorities arrived, and they had an ambulance as well. If he had underestimated Inspector Corelli before, he certainly credited him now.

His men worked as proficiently as a professional U.S. squad unit would have. Quickly they opened the door to the cabin, and a medical crew helped Laura into the ambulance.

A horrible scene awaited them inside the cabin.

That bastard had put a leg iron around Julie's foot and tied her onto a leash. Now, she was tangled in it and couldn't move.

Unconscious, she was lying on the floor, totally dehydrated and overheated. But most shocking was her bald head and her pain-shuttered partly covered with some kind of green paste which made her almost unrecognizable.

"Is she alive?" Inspector Corelli asked the emergency staff.

"Yes, barely. I've got a weak pulse, but her high temperature is life-threatening," the doctor answered as she installed an infusion before they got Julie ready for transport.

❧

From a small balcony, Ivy watched the day come to life. The air was warming quickly. Soon, the heat would simmer again over Rio, brutal but honest.

Inside the hospital room, the air was cold and rotten. But this couldn't diminish the joy on Ivy's face as she watched Laura sleeping.

With some pressure she'd finally convinced Brad to return to the hotel to grab a couple of hours of sleep, but not without promising to keep a close eye on Laura. Oh, how relieved she was that both were alive and well.

Unfortunately, Julie wasn't doing as well. She was barely alive when they brought her in, and still, hours later, she was in a very critical condition in the intensive care unit.

Ivy was convinced that she would make it. Julie was tough and strong. A fighter. She'd known her for a long time, and even though they were competitors on the links, they'd always liked each other very much.

She remembered the very first moment they met. When she first saw Julie, for a quick second Ivy thought she was looking into a mirror—they were so alike in so many things.

Later, she'd admired the grace and style Julie demonstrated. Being only a couple of years older than her, Julie had already found her own way of playing golf, dressing and makeup, dealing with the public or presenting herself to the sponsors.

For a few years they went to the same academy, and Julie was her hero—her role model. They became inseparable friends.

Then, two years ago, all of that changed. Their friendship became rockier, as out of a sudden, Ivy was winning more tournaments, making more points, earning more money and getting more sponsors.

It was nobody's fault, right? That's how things go in life when friends grow up and become competitors. At least that was what she had believed, until the tragic event took place earlier this year.

Not only had she lost Jason, she had also lost Julie as a friend.

From one day to another, Julie seemed to be invisible to Ivy. Not once did she visit her at the hospital, attend Jason's funeral or even reply to any of her messages.

That was hard.

"Ivy, come here."

With a bright smile on her face, Laura held one hand up for Ivy to take it.

"Laura, you are awake! Oh, that's good. That is so good." Ivy came back to the room, sat down on Laura's bed and with both hands she took Laura's and rested her forehead for a few seconds on top of them.

"What happened to you?"

"Oh, I'll be fine, actually, I feel much better already. And you? You look a little bit crunchy, what's the matter?"

"Oh, I was thinking about Julie, you know, and—"

"Hey, hey, don't cry. We found her and she'll be all right. We're all gonna be fine, trust me."

Laura put her left hand out from under the cover, with an IV line in tow. She softly touched Ivy's hair.

"Laura, I just wish we would be."

"Relax. Give us a couple of days, and we'll all be back in Naples, preparing for the holidays."

"You probably haven't heard it yet, but Julie isn't well." Ivy looked straight into Laura's face.

"What? Did he hurt her? What has he done to her?"

"Oh, that. He shaved her head, Brad told me. I haven't seen her. They wouldn't allow anybody in yet."

"He shaved her? You mean her head's completely bald?"

"Yes. Of course, that isn't what's keeping her sick. They're saying that her general condition is very weak, it has something to do with her kidneys, I think. I'm not sure what, exactly. They're doing more tests this morning. Hopefully, we learn more later today."

"Oh my gosh!"

"Laura, they're not sure if she'll make it." Ivy threw herself onto Laura's bed and into Laura's arms. She bawled like a baby.

"You know, we had been friends, I mean, very good friends, like best friends, before all that happened to me. I feel so terrible sorry for her, if only there were something I could do."

"This is indeed very sad to hear. When did you say they will have a clearer picture about what's wrong with her?" With her arms still tightly linked around Ivy's small body, Laura tried to sit up straight in her bed.

She was deeply concerned. She recalled the strong sensation she had that night. If only she had gone faster, or maybe she could have called the police and the ambulance earlier.

Now it was maybe too late.

"We'll have news around noon. Dustin and her father are downstairs in the waiting area. They said they would call us as soon as they know more."

Laura furrowed her brow. "And what about the kidnapper? Any news there? Do the police have any leads—are they on to something?"

"Of course they're doing a broad wanted person search, and they had a report out on two unconfirmed sightings. However, because, technically speaking, nobody was really hurt by him, they don't have the capacity for a massive manhunt. Yes, the diamonds are gone and the money is lost also, but supposedly that is day-to-day business for the police down here," Ivy said.

"So, again, he goes free. A dangerous man roaming free. How do you feel about that?"

"You know, it's funny you ask, because I haven't even thought about that yet. I mean, being with you, and so focused on Brad, you, my family, and going back to golf has occupied my mind so much. I think I'm not afraid any longer. I only hope it stays that way. It feels so good, and I've no desire to go back into depression mode. It's a dark, spiraling tunnel."

Ivy took a deep breath and exhaled with a whoosh.

"And I have made the decision to never enter it again."

Her voice was soft, innocent, but determined. Her eyes and cheeks were still wet from the tears, but she was lightening up now, and she kissed Laura's forehead.

She straightened up and squeezed Laura's hands, carefully, being mindful of the infusion needles. Surprised, Ivy felt something on her hand, and then she saw the gorgeous diamond ring on Laura's hand.

Laura smiled, but didn't say a word. Ivy leaped to her feet. She needed to know everything about it.

"When did this happen? What did he say? Will there be a wedding soon?"

But Laura, silently, just shook her head and put her hand back under the cover. The infusion pump was still running, feeding into her veins.

It wasn't the right moment to talk about engagements or weddings. It was funny, though, she thought that they used the third finger of her left hand for the infusions. The one with the ring. Then it might be true that it was the only one with a vein running directly to the heart.

She'd wondered about it before and wondered again what was in that fusion bag, which by now was almost empty.

"Huh, it's okay," Ivy interrupted her thoughts. "I won't ask anything, at least not right now. Still, I'm really excited, and whatever the rings stands for, it's beautiful!"

Laura pressed her lips together, she didn't want to speak about it. It all seemed so distant now, so unreal.

"Okay, okay, I won't say a word to nobody. Big promise!" Ivy held up her right hand, laughing.

"But did I tell you? I'm going to play in the Olympics next year. I've made up my mind, and nothing is going to stop me. I'm going to win a medal, I want gold. And I want you to be on my side, helping me to get there!"

"Ivy, that's wonderful. What a great idea! Sure. I'll sure help you, and I'll coach you wherever I can."

She took Ivy's pale face into her hands. "Kiddo, we'll bring you back—to golf and to life. Promise!" And with this, Laura pushed the infusion stand and pump a little aside, slipped to the edge of the bed and hopped down.

"What are you thinking you're doing?"

Brad was standing in the door with two dozen red roses while Laura whirled around to find her sneakers.

"We need to check on Julie. It's about time. They should have more test results by now, shouldn't they?" Laura was trying hard to stand up but almost fainted away.

"You rest," Ivy stopped her, "and I'll check on Julie. Uncle Brad, you don't look so fit either, how many hours of sleep did you get?"

"Not more than two or three, I think."

"Oh-oh, I'll see if I can order a decent breakfast for you on my way down."

Ivy gave her uncle a quick kiss, and off she went.

The minute Ivy entered the waiting area, she knew there was something terribly wrong. One look at the doctors' faces made it clear how bad Julie's condition was.

Forgotten was the nasty answer of the nurse who probably didn't mean to be rude. Tired from working overtime, she was simply caught at a bad moment when Ivy asked for a romantic breakfast for two.

Forgotten was the beautiful thought that maybe, just maybe, Laura was about to become her auntie. What a lovely smile they'd shared—they were going to become family.

All this didn't matter anymore.

Never in her life had she seen a stronger, more athletic man than Henrik Ferguson, and now here he was, a picture of misery, sitting down on the small sofa, sobbing in grief. Dustin gazed into space, as if he were on a distant planet.

Immediately, she assumed the worst.

Ivy looked around, not knowing what to do, and then she saw the doctor.

"Hello, please wait!" She ran after him while he opened a milky glass door reading *EMERGENCY UNIT.*

"What happened? Is she dead, I mean did she pass away?" Ivy shook violently—her hands, her feet, she couldn't hold on to them anymore and then it got all black around her.

The next thing she knew, she was looking up from the floor—the doctor she was hurrying after bent over her. Her vision was blurred. She tried to focus on his name tag—*Kirk Matthew Spencer, M.D.*

"What happened? Julie . . . is she dead?"

"Miss, you are at St. Thomas hospital. My name is Dr. Spencer. I was lucky to catch you as you fell." He checked her pulse and her heart rate.

"You are going to be fine, I just want you to relax now. Take a few slow, deep breaths and lie down for another couple of minutes. How are you related to Ms. Ferguson?"

This question made Henrik look up—he wiped his face with a tissue and quickly walked over to Ivy.

"Ivy, what's wrong? What's going on, Doc?"

"Mr. Ferguson, I want you to remain calm. Everything is fine. This lady here came running over to me and then, out of a sudden, she fainted, and I was able to catch her right in time," the doctor said in a fine Oxford English accent.

"This is Ivy Brooks." Henrik Ferguson looked directly into her beautiful, clear eyes. "She is . . . a good friend of Julie's."

Just as he had finished speaking those words, he felt sick. His heart had been torn apart before, because of Julie's condition, which was worse than anybody could have expected. But now, there was more—for the first time in his whole life, he was torn inside out, his whole body felt as if it were burning in hell.

What a terrible mess! He had done things in his life, things he wished he could undo. And most of what people were saying about him was true, at least in part. The tax issues, pushing his daughter over the edge and being a womanizer all his life.

He had to live with those choices. But what was happening here right now was way more sinister. It was evil beyond his standards and something he would never forgive himself.

Would he be able to look into a mirror again without seeing a horrific monster staring back? Silently, shuddering with self-disgust, he walked back to the sofa.

"Mr. Ferguson, she wanted to know about your daughter. What should I tell her?"

"Go, tell her. Tell her everything!" This was not him, couldn't be. All his life, he had imagined how the truth would come out. How he was ever able to talk about it. But he never envisioned it to be that hard, that unfair and despicable.

"Ms. Brooks, why don't you sit up? Take it slow."

"Okay. Huh, this has hit me hard. Okay, tell me, what is wrong with Julie?"

"Ms. Ferguson was brought in early this morning by

ambulance and has been treated for immediate life-threatening symptoms, such as dehydration and severe kidney failure."

"Kidney failure?"

"She became unconscious as she was rushed to the emergency room." He paused. "She still is, but now, we would define her condition as comatose. She is unresponsive. She feels no pain but also does not react to any stimulus in her environment."

"But she's going to wake up, isn't she?" This was like déjà vu. Too clearly she remembered waking up in the hospital, only to learn that Jason was dead. And now, here she was again.

"Ms. Brooks—"

"Please, call me Ivy."

"All right, Ivy. Tests have shown that Ms. Ferguson is suffering an end-stage renal disease or *ESRD*. Her glomerular filtration rate is below 15ml/min. We do have her on hemofiltration, but we need to find a donor quickly. Very quickly!"

He looked at his watch, "Unfortunately, I cannot go into further detail, because I have to return to the ER. Would you please excuse me?"

"But you'll find a donor, right? I mean, she's not just a nobody, she is a U.S. citizen and a world class golf athlete. She needs to fully recover, and she will."

Ivy jumped up, and grasped his white coat to hold him back. He turned and looked her warmly in her eyes, "Ivy, we'll do what we can, I promise. However, we do not have much time left."

"But she is on dialysis, that is working, isn't it?"

"It is for the moment, but her condition is so severe that we have to find a donor as soon as possible." He nervously checked his watch again.

"How much time?"

"Twenty-four hours, at best. Ivy, please excuse me, I got to run—I will talk to you later!" He managed her hand out of his coat and hold it tight. His hands were comfortably warm and soft.

"If you want, you can help. Call your friends and get them tested, and for you, it's the same. You can get tested right here. I will have my assistant take blood from those present."

He straightened his coat and pushed through the milky glass doors into the emergency room.

"That's a great idea, I'll call all the people I know and get myself tested," Ivy said, excited. She looked back to Julie's father and Dustin. "You already got tested, right?"

"They have checked my blood and Henrik's," Dustin confirmed. He looked up at her with red, tear-filled eyes. "We don't match. We'd hoped Henrik as the father could possibly be the donor, but he doesn't match. The best chances for a successful transplant would be to find a donor who's genetically close. But there's no one else."

Henrik Ferguson stood up and took a long look at Ivy. That's not true, he thought.

And then he turned to leave the waiting room. There was one more chance.

SEVENTEEN

He sat in an antique chair next to the escritoire in his hotel room. Good Lord, why wasn't he eligible as a kidney donor for his daughter? That would've been the best way out—for all of them. He stared deep into the glass of whiskey in front of him. It was his second glass, and it wasn't yet noon.

Next to the glass, he had positioned the phone and was waiting for an international call.

During the last twenty years, he had postponed that conversation, had blocked out the whole subject, knowing that the day would unavoidably come. Now it was here, and there was no way to avoid it.

He had let her down twenty years ago. She had told him that she was expecting a baby.

She was in love with him—deeply—that he knew. For him, it was a love affair. Not the first, and not the last.

He was still engrossed in his thoughts as the phone finally rang.

"Hello?"

"Sir, I have your international connection, are you ready to take it?"

"Yes, ma'am, please put it through." A few moments passed.

"Hello—Crystal, are you there?" He cleared his voice and used the short break to slug some more whiskey.

"Henrik, what a surprise! I had no idea that you still existed." Crystal laughed cynically at the other end of the line. This jerk—what in the world did he want from her now?

"Crystal, I know I should have called, I don't know, maybe years ago. I'm truly sorry." Please don't be too hard on me, he thought, sipping from his glass.

"Don't be sorry, Henrik. I've made peace with it a long time ago. And you know, looking back at our time together, you've given me the best gift life ever could've given me. My daughter."

Her friendly openness was only part of the truth. When it came to Henrik Ferguson, she was on alert.

It was true though that the hurt, pain and sorrow were completely gone. And after all, it was also true that he had given her Ivy, and there was no bigger gift in the world then to be blessed with such a marvelous daughter.

However, this phone call took her by total surprise, and with curiosity but foremost cautiousness, she was going to handle it very prudently. Rightfully so, since after listening to him for only a few minutes, she knew that her caution was more than appropriate—she couldn't believe what he dared ask her!

"So, you're saying that my little girl, Ivy—my one and only—is the last chance for Julie?"

"Yes, and she wants to do it. She's a brave girl."

"Don't you ever tell me what my girl is or isn't, you

understand? Never. You have no rights regarding her."

"Crystal, please stay calm. We don't have much time. Ivy is healthy and young. She can do it. She'll be fine. They starting preparation this evening, and the transplant is scheduled first thing in the morning."

Now he emptied his glass in one gulp. Ivy was his only hope, and legally they didn't even need her mother's approval. But he had to tell her, didn't he? Going ahead with the transplant without her being in the loop was too low—even for him.

"Did you tell her, I mean, the truth about who her father is?"

She was cooking, and she flipped through her calendar to see if she could switch appointments and clear her schedule for the next couple of days.

"No, of course not, and there is no need to. She doesn't have to know, unrelated people can be donors for a kidney transplant. However, the success rate is much higher if they are closely related."

He sighed, relieved. The worst was over—so he thought.

"Henrik, I forbid you to further pressure Ivy to undergo this surgery. In fact, I don't want you to talk to her at all until I get down there."

"You're coming?"

"Yes, I'm flying down to Rio today. Don't bother picking me up at the airport, I'll take a cab."

She knew she had to go to Rio, even though she hated flying alone. She wished Roger were there to join her, but he was in

North Carolina, working on some real estate business.

Perhaps it was best that he hadn't been here to avoid being involved in this whole story—at least at the moment. Of course, he knew that Ivy was not his biological daughter—they met a couple of months after her birth.

And of course he knew the whole story about her father, a man Crystal had once trusted with her whole life. She was so young, so naïve, she didn't know any better, and Henrik was *the* man to fall in love with.

She was a summer intern at the club where he worked as the head pro. All the other girls went crazy over him, but she'd kept her cool, until one day, he came over and asked her if she would like to come with him to the driving range.

Soon she was pregnant and hoping that he would commit himself to her and the baby. Instead, he told her that he was happily married and had a daughter.

It was so embarrassing—at first she didn't know what to do. He'd told her he knew of somebody who would take care of the pregnancy, and he offered her money.

There was this buzzing in her head and a nagging pain in her heart, so she never really realized what he was up to. All she could do was get away, get home, and never, ever let anybody hurt her again.

All Crystal remembered was that, when she got home and told her mom her story, the most wonderful response came in overwhelming joy for the new baby.

Both of her parents were thrilled with the idea of a grandchild. And no word was given to question her irresponsible behavior.

But now Henrik was back in her life with a serious threat for her little girl. She scanned online travel agencies for a good connection to Rio. Of course she would go—she had to. Yes, this was a good flight—Tampa to Miami to Rio. Departure tonight, arrival early in the morning. Booked!

In the meantime, her brother would have to make sure that nothing happened to Ivy. She sent off a text message to Brad with her itinerary.

Clearing her calendar was not very complicated. Only one appointment stood out—the annual charity event of the local business women's association was scheduled for tonight, and she was the current president.

I'll give Eileen a call, she thought. As vice president, Eileen had a lot on her shoulders, and often didn't get credit for it. Crystal had no doubt that she would be delighted to take over the spotlight tonight.

Then the phone rang—the display showed *Eileen*.

"Hello, Eileen? What a coincidence—I was just about to call you!"

"Hi hon, did Mr. Dickerson give you a call? I told him not to, since I figured you're pretty busy today." Eileen's high-pitched voice sounded even more shrill than usual.

"No, actually he didn't!"

Crystal pulled up the agenda for tonight's event in front of her. Mr. Dickerson was the chairman of the charity her organization was supporting that night.

"Yes, that's him, and he just gave me a ring to ask a special favor. I know it will be hard on you, because you probably have already prepared everything in detail. However, he would like to take advantage of tonight's event to deliver his inaugural speech.

Problem is, that wouldn't allow any time for you to speak. Now, before you refuse—I know, it's a lot to ask—in return, we can use his beautiful facilities down at the beach for our monthly meetings. Isn't that wonderful? What do you think?"

Then a pause followed, which was very unlike Eileen, who could talk nonstop for hours.

"Crystal?"

Crystal crossed herself and said silently, "Thank you!" She was already one step closer to Rio.

"Yes, I'm here. I think this is a great idea. Eileen, why don't you call him back right away and give him the green light? And he shouldn't worry about me—as a matter of fact, I'm going to take a rain check on tonight's event and give you the chance to introduce him to our audience. How about that?"

"Wait a minute, what? Roger is in Boston and you . . . I mean, you aren't having a secret affair, are you?"

"Eileen! That's ridiculous, you know me better than that." With Eileen, it was always better to stop stupid rumors right away.

"But what could be so important that you would cancel an event like this? I know you, Mrs. President, so tell me what's so urgent?"

"It's about what matters most in my life—Ivy. She's down in Rio and now she really needs me. Sorry, Eileen, but I don't have time to explain now. I need to catch the red-eye to Rio tonight. But I promise I'll catch up with you as soon as I'm back."

"Rio de Janeiro? You're telling me you're flying tonight to Brazil? Alone? What's Ivy doing down there? Oh wait, I think I remember, you talked about this at our Thanksgiving dinner at Brad's."

"Yes. Please excuse me, Eileen—Ivy and Brad need me, and I've got to pack. I wish you a wonderful event tonight, and I'll see you soon."

"Wait, wait! Brad's in Rio as well?" Eileen's eyes lit up.

"You know what, Crystal, I think it's not good for you to travel alone—what do you think of me coming with you?"

Eileen was already texting her first secretary about taking over the introduction of the chairman tonight, and got an instant reply—*love to :-))*.

"Eileen," Crystal continued, "I truly would love to go with you, but I think tonight is too important for our organization—there's no way to cancel last minute. So I'm really counting on you to take over."

"No, you don't! I just got the perfect replacement. Our first secretary will take over. Give her the chance, please. And no more protesting. Let's pack and catch a taxi to the airport. Are you booking the tickets or would you like me to do it? Crystal, I'm so excited! I haven't been in Rio since the Millennium Party!"

Harry Butcher was exhausted. Again and again, he mumbled, "Thank you for your understanding," into his smartphone, truly hoping for their ongoing support and fulfillment of their contract.

Ever since the news got out that Julie Ferguson was in critical condition, his phone hadn't stopped vibrating for five seconds in a row. Tour officials and sponsors all over the world wanted to know how serious the situation was.

Sweating, he got up, and instead of his preferred choice,

bourbon on the rocks, he selected a club soda from the minibar. He dropped extra ice into a glass and watched the soda flowing over it.

A clear mind was of utmost importance over the next hours. Too much was at stake here. So far, he had everything under control. Then he looked into the mirror and marveled at the wrinkles under his eyes.

Today was one of those days where he not only felt his age, but also, to his despair, he could actually see it. This needed fixing as soon as the heat over the kidnapping and the condition of his show horse had cooled down.

He looked up a number on his smartphone as a knock on the door interrupted his thirty-second break.

"What is it? I'm real busy here."

"Sir, I'm sorry to interrupt, but I have an overnight delivery for you that we just received at the front desk."

He opened the door, collected an oversized envelope and handed the hotel attendant a generous tip.

As he closed the door, he turned the envelope over—no return address. *URGENT AND CONFIDENTIAL* was written in bold letters on the front.

Just holding the envelope in his hands, he knew the worst was not over yet. He walked back to his desk to open it. His club soda didn't appeal to him anymore. He needed something stronger. He went for Tennessee Bourbon at last.

Quickly he cut the envelope open and pulled out a single page:

Gunman is dead.
You're next, unless you stop Ferguson from talking.

Do not underestimate our organization. We're watching you closely.
FOG_Friends of Golf

Dammit, he thought, the room was probably bugged and so was Henrik's.

He had to warn him. No, a warning wasn't enough—this moron was so out of control over his daughter's illness that he was unpredictable—a real threat.

Harry flipped through his contact list. Yes, there it was, the name he was looking for.

Eased slightly, he raised the glass to his lips, enjoyed a swig of his bourbon. With a smile, he thought how good it was to have old friends and a good memory, so that, once in a while, he could collect some open dues—plus interest.

"Excellent!" Brad tipped the bellboy, who handed him the keys for his new rental. A Ford SVT Raptor SuperCrew, an epic off-road sport truck with enough room for him and his two beloved ladies. He was going to pick them up right now.

Personally, he would have preferred to keep the Mercedes, however, this afternoon, he was on a mission, and to accomplish something special, sometimes a little finesse would do the trick. He'd promised Crystal that much.

After the cooler with beverages and picnic supplies were loaded, he got into the driver seat and drove slowly off.

His first stop would be at the hospital to pick up Laura. They'd confirmed that she was well enough for an afternoon at the beach, and he would make sure that Ivy would join them as well.

After he had spent the last hour with Crystal on the phone, he knew he had to take action. Crystal and Eileen were coming down—they'd boarded their international flight in Miami—and he expected them to arrive at the hotel at dawn.

This left him the remaining hours of the afternoon to have a serious discussion with Ivy about her forthcoming organ donation before she had to get ready for it, provided she was still willing to go for it.

He understood only too well that this wasn't an easy call. Hadn't he lost his wife, Regine, because a matching donor couldn't be found in time?

However, Ivy was very young, and she was still recovering from her accident and the fatal loss of her fiancé.

She was so stiff about it ever since the blood test was done and the doctor informed her that she was a potential donor. Of course, everybody had pushed her toward it—the doctor, Dustin and Henrik—without even giving her a chance to really think it through.

Brad was convinced that they'd stopped the search for another potential donor. It was just so easy and convenient to rely on Ivy's kidney.

So without disclosure to anybody, he had started a worldwide search for an alternative donor. He was certain that a matching donor would be found within the next few hours and the kidney could be shipped here by tomorrow morning.

Someone honked a horn impatiently behind him—yes, yes, I know, but I have to make a left turn. Now he was stuck in traffic. He quickly texted Laura to wait for him at the main entrance so he wouldn't need to find a parking space for his monster car.

Personally, he would have left it to Ivy to come to a decision alone, but with his sister being overconcerned, nervous and hectic —normally, she was such a calm and longsighted person—he wanted to be there for her to facilitate and mediate the decision-making process.

This four-wheel fun car was a first step to break the ice, and then he would drive them down to Barra da Tijuca, the largest beach in Rio, where they could picnic and watch surfers and beachcombers while enjoying the crystal green waters and great waves.

Later, he had another surprise for them. He smiled as he turned into the driveway of the hospital where Laura and Ivy were waiting.

With a chuckle, he noticed that the ladies didn't recognize him behind the wheel of his fully loaded off-roader. They would certainly never have expected him to show up like a gasoline-driven motorhead in a luxury hotel driveway.

"Brad, I can't believe you're driving such a macho car as this," Ivy giggled and jumped instantly onto the backseat, while Brad opened the passenger door for Laura.

She held onto his arm as she climbed into the power truck. She looked a little pale, but a couple of hours on a sunny beach, picnicking with their best friends would change that, so he hoped, and he was delighted to see her wearing the beautiful ring.

"It looks like a lot of fun. So where are we going?" Laura

inquired. She loved getting away from that hospital, and even though she was still a bit shaky, she knew it was far better to be out for an adventure than to feel bored in a starched hospital bed.

"Wait and see! It's a surprise," Brad kept them in suspense, "and I hope you are both hungry, since we have an overloaded picnic basket and a cooler full of beverages, including some fine wines."

Slowly, the bully car rolled out of the check-in zone, the deep roaring sound of the engine echoed in perfect harmony with the driving samba rhythms on the radio.

"Come on, Uncle Brad, what's going on, and what is this big secret about where we going?"

"Okay, okay! Now that we're on the road and you have no chance to escape, I am free to tell."

He laughed. He could already see that the ice shield Ivy had built up around herself was starting to melt down. He hoped that she would soon be open again to reconsider her heroic intentions.

"First of all, Laura and I have to announce some wonderful news."

"Oh, that's old news! I know about your engagement, I saw the ring. It's beautiful, where did you buy it? In Naples, right? It looks so special, like customized for her. Did you smuggle it into the country?" Ivy was bending forward, not to be missing anything of the conversation in the front row.

"All right, old news." He squeezed Laura's hand and gave her a warm smile before she could deny anything. "Then let's get to the latest news—we are going to drive to Barra da Tijuca."

"No, not to that jungle again, Brad, I'm really fed up with it. Although, it's actually quite beautiful, especially by daylight."

"Laura, of course not! No, Barra da Tijuca is a master-designed neighborhood in Rio, and it is well known for its beaches, lakes and rivers and its upscale lifestyle. And it is home to the largest shopping mall in South America!"

"No kidding?" Ivy locked eyes with Laura, if she weren't having this surgery tomorrow morning, she would have loved to take Laura there to shop for some nice wedding presents.

"They also assigned an eighty-eight-foot-high replica of the Statue of Liberty and other replicas of international architectural icons, like the Leaning Tower of Pisa, the Tower Bridge of London, and the Eiffel Tower of Paris." He continued cruising along the beaches.

"Wait a minute, isn't that where the Olympic Games in 2016 will mostly be held? In Barra Olympic Park—I've read about it."

"Yes, spot on, Ivy!"

"What a brilliant idea. I should have thought about it myself."

Laura looked at him, turned to Ivy, and smiled widely and brightly. They all belonged together, she knew that now. For every minute she spent time with him, she got to know him better, and she loved him more and more.

The minute she'd heard about Ivy's decision to donate one of her kidneys, she'd taken the blood test herself. Unfortunately, she was not a match. Still, she was hoping that there was another solution.

Ivy's condition was not as good as everybody thought it was. She had just recovered from her deep-seated depression, and she was still weak and undernourished. That's why Laura had encouraged Brad to attempt to talk her out of it.

"Laura, look over there at that kite surfer. I want to try that some day. Brad, can we stop here and eat?"

"Almost there, ladies, we are almost there!" Brad made a right turn onto a dirt road, and the four-wheel drive offroader finally had the chance to show what it was built for.

They passed gently rolling hills covered with lush green grass—an almost bucolic setting, if it weren't for the sprinklers hard at work under the glooming afternoon sun. It was the construction site of a nearly completed golf course.

Brad stopped the car at a small covered picnic area overlooking the west end of the preserve, the beach and the Atlantic ocean—a magnificent sight.

"It's the Olympic golf course, isn't it?"

"Yes, Ivy, it is."

"Oh it's so beautiful! Look at the cranes, and the fairways, all in the middle of this nature preserve." Ivy couldn't contain her excitement. She unbuckled her seatbelt and jumped right out of the car before Brad even had a chance to stop the engine.

Laura nodded silently in agreement to him. That was the best idea. To bring Ivy down here, to show her what it would look like, feel like, to play golf here, to represent her country and to win gold next summer.

"Look at the power of man. Yes, it is beautiful, but it is also a little over the top—they probably needed it to mark golf's triumphant return to the Olympics after more than a hundred years of absence."

"I like it."

"Ivy, do you know who won the last gold medal in golf and where?" He was half joking, knowing she knew. But he wanted to stress one point here—getting her back to golf.

"Sure, 1904, St. Louis, George Lyon from Canada, gold as individual, but the U.S. team won gold too."

"Correct. But who was the first woman who won gold?"

"That's a tough one, I didn't even know if there was a ladies' golf discipline at the Olympics in 1904," Ivy said while she unloaded the cooler and helped Laura setting the table. The high tea-style sandwiches, scones and fruit platters looked delicious.

"See, you are right that there was no women's golf competition in 1904. However, four years earlier, the Olympic Summer Games in Paris were the very first games to feature woman competitions in an eclectic mix of events that included tennis, archery, angling, horse riding and, of course, golf."

Now Laura began to wonder.

"Uh-huh, it seems you know it all, don't you? Or you're just well prepared for today. If you continue lecturing in that way, I may just return this ring, so be careful!" Laura laughed and bit hungrily into one of the cucumber sandwiches.

"No, Brad, please continue—I want to know who won."

"It was Margaret Ives Abbott. She was the first golden girl, as she won the women's golf tournament, consisting of nine holes, with a score of 47. With this, she became the first-ever female Olympic champion from the U.S."

"Ives. Ivy, her middle name's very similar to yours—isn't that a good omen?" Laura slung her arms around Ivy and whispered in her ear: "I know you're gonna do it, because you'd like to know how it feels. I'm so excited and I'm going to coach you."

Laura squeezed Ivy tightly and kissed her forehead, and Ivy knew she could do it, too.

"Brad, thank you for this wonderful afternoon!"

And for the first time, she kissed him in front of Ivy.

❧

Ivy got back just in time for her appointment with Dr. Spencer. Quickly, she jumped out of the car and waved goodbye as Brad and Laura drove back to the hotel.

With a deep sigh, she walked through the entrance doors of the hospital and asked at the reception desk where she could find Dr. Spencer.

What a wonderful afternoon that was, she thought, and how clever it was of her uncle to show her the Olympic site and the golf course. She was very well aware of his attention, his mission, and she loved him for that.

Laura was a little different. She also wanted only the best for her, and she definitely wanted her to join the Olympic team and play the golf tournament as one of the sixty best golfers in the world. However, Laura wanted her to make the decision herself, and she loved her for that, too.

She wondered if both of them knew what a perfectly fit they were.

As she was waiting for the doctor to call her in, she saw Dustin crossing the hallway. How fragile, pale and sad he looked, she noticed, and waved over to him. When he saw her, he immediately changed his direction toward her.

"Hey Ivy, where've you been? I was looking for you earlier this afternoon, shouldn't you be preparing for the surgery in the morning? Have you changed your mind?" He nervously rubbed his hands.

"Dustin, no! I haven't changed my mind. I'm going along with the transplant, I made the decision as soon as I knew I was a potential donor. And they've been telling me that I'm a very good match—the likelihood that Julie's body will accept my kidney is over seventy-five percent." She took his hands in hers to assure him.

"Please, you have to believe me. I'm not going to change my mind, no matter what. And I'm here at Dr. Spencer's office so he can start with the preparation. He said he wanted to talk to me first and then they will provide a room for me.

As far as I know, they've scheduled surgery for 8:00 a.m. in the morning." Encouraging, she squeezed his hands and looked up as the door of Dr. Spencer's office opened and his assistant waved her in.

"Don't worry. And tell Henrik he shouldn't be worried either. I'm sticking to the plan. Big promise!"

Confident, Ivy walked into the doctor's office where he was sitting relaxed behind his desk. To her surprise, he was not wearing his white coat, just white slacks and a Navy polo shirt on top. He looked much younger and very handsome.

"Good evening, Ivy. I'm glad you're here. Please take a seat." He directed her to the pop art plastic chairs across his desk.

"First, I would like to inform you about the procedure, the preparation and of course the risks involved. And then I need you to sign some papers, the formalities. Do you have any questions for me at this point?"

"Well, I'm not sure if this is the right moment to ask that question, but it's the only one I have. Will I be able to continue playing professional golf after the donation of one of my kidneys?

Please be honest with me. Will I be able to practice ten hours a day, to run for twelve miles in a row and to do weightlifting afterwards until I collapse?"

She looked straight at him, and she already saw the truth in his eyes. Then he looked down as if he were collecting himself before speaking.

"Ivy, I know you want the truth, and I want to be honest to you. The truth is I do not know. I have a lot of experience with kidney transplants, but I have never had a professional golfer or any other active athlete donate a kidney. This afternoon I took the time to research more, and I could not find any article either supporting or denying it. During your recovery time, you certainly have to take it slow, but then it is really up to you to increase your activities."

When his warm brown eyes met hers, she had a hard time choking back her concerns.

"Of course, the final decision to go ahead is up to you, and I cannot give you any guarantees. However, what you are doing for Julie is a once-in-a-lifetime opportunity, giving something of such high value to another person. And I have seen it before, with many of my patients, that the unconditional giving of an organ brings more joy than anything else. Especially if it is for a consanguineous patient as in your case."

". . . consanguineous?"

"Oh, excuse me. It's a medical term that means blood-related."

"Ah, but—"

"What you are doing for your sister will forever forge you two together and will give both of you incredible meaning to your life!"

"What are you talking about? Julie is not my sister!" Ivy sat straight up and waited impatiently for his apology. It didn't come.

"Hmm, let me take a look," he said and flipped through a blue manila folder.

"Yes, you are right—half-sister—my mistake! Of course, she is your half-sister."

"Half-sister? You mean my mother is not my mother?"

"Oh, I am sorry, I thought you knew. But it is my duty to inform you of it. Julie and you are agnate siblings, or in other words paternal half-sisters, meaning you have the same father but different mothers."

Ivy didn't know. That was obvious to Dr. Spencer now. Why hadn't anybody told him that she didn't know, especially Henrik Ferguson? He could have been much more careful with how he phrased it.

Nevertheless, she needed to know the truth before the operation.

"Doctor, I think you should retest my blood. It can't be possibly true. Henrik Ferguson could never be my father. He doesn't even know my mom!"

Ivy got up, walked to the window and peered into the sky. Her eyes welled up with tears.

"Your blood couldn't have been interchanged, since you where the only one at that time being tested for a match. However, we will begin preparation for the surgery in about two hours, and part of the procedure is more detailed tests anyway. But I need you to sign those papers first."

He quickly highlighted the places on the forms where she needed to sign and initial.

"I'm not going to sign anything. I'm sorry. I gotta go and call my mom."

EIGHTEEN

Two American ladies stood outside the international airport in Rio and waited for the cab driver to load their luggage. It was still dark during those early morning hours, yet the world megalopolis was frantically alive, mostly with people busy to get to work.

Horns were sounding as drivers cut quickly through the jammed traffic without paying much attention to the traffic lights or street signs.

Crystal was absorbed by the messages she had received from Ivy, while Eileen kept busy refreshing her makeup.

"Huh, Crystal, do you think the driver knows where he's going? Did he get the name of the hotel right?"

"Sorry Eileen, I'm a little distracted. Ivy has left me a couple of messages, and if I understand them correctly, she knows who her father is." Crystal's worst nightmare had came true, and this was not the way she wanted her daughter to find out the truth.

Roger and she had discussed it many times, over and over again, to decide how and when to tell her. However, the time never seemed to be right. Now it was too late.

"See, I told you so! She needed to hear the truth a long time ago. I remember when you told me about it. When was that? Right after you had your miscarriage with your second child and no hopes for another one, right?" Eileen applied more red lipstick, careful not to smudge it in the movement of the traffic.

Yes, and that was a mistake too, Crystal thought as they rushed by window lights and dressings, some streetwalkers, and more traffic. She should never have told Eileen.

"I think I'll go directly to the hospital. I need to talk to her. Should I drop you off at the hotel first?"

"Yes, please. Oh, I think it's right here, isn't it?" Eileen pointed out of the window as they drove into the circular drive of the Grand Palace Hotel. "I need a couple of hours of beauty sleep before I try to catch up with Brad. Be careful, will you? You are a wonderful mother, you always have been. And you did the best you could. She'll understand, I'm sure of it. Give Ivy my regards, and I'll see you later."

The driver unloaded Eileen's luggage and continued the drive to the hospital.

"Where can I find my daughter, Ivy Brooks?" Crystal was at the front desk, asking the tired-looking security officer at the end of his midnight shift. He couldn't find her in any of the wards.

Had Ivy changed her mind, and was she waiting at the hotel?

She pulled out her phone to give Eileen a quick call. Just then, Henrik Ferguson stepped out of the elevator.

"Crystal! I'm glad you're here! I was waiting for you, and I just saw you stepping out of the taxi. It's so good to see you. You look wonderful, you haven't changed a bit. Those beautiful blue eyes are still sparkling with life!"

Henrik moved in to hug her, but she stepped back.

"Henrik, save your flattery for your next vixen. Where is my daughter? What did you tell her?"

"I don't know where she is. And I didn't tell her anything. It was the doctor, he was explaining the surgery. We need to find her—soon. There isn't much time."

"Oh, there's all the time in the world to find her and to get her back with me. You're only concerned about Julie. See, I'm not.

Ivy's all I have, and I'll find her, talk to her and bring her back to the States."

"All of us—the hospital staff, Dustin and I—have been searching all night. Brad and Laura, too. We can't find her, and we're all concerned."

"Did you check the roof? That's where she would normally go to hide out."

"No, we haven't. Let's get up there quickly, come with me." He guided her towards the elevator and waved over to the security guy to have him come along. A few minutes later, they arrived at the roof top—and there she was, sleeping like a baby in the moonlight under the open sky.

"Ivy, my baby, Ivy, my little girl!" Crystal rushed over and sat down next to her.

Slowly Ivy awoke. "Mama . . . it's not true, tell me that it isn't true!" Ivy was weak and shaking despite the warm humid air. Thunder started growling in the distance. She looked up to her mom, who gathered her in her arms.

"Oh my baby, my little girl. I wish I could tell you otherwise, but Henrik is really your father. I'll explain everything to you, but first come down with me, so we can get you a hot cup of tea, and then we'll talk, the three of us."

Ivy jumped up. "No, I'm not going anywhere!" She was furious and exhausted, which was not a good combination for smalltalk.

The lightning and thunder intensified. Ivy didn't mind. She would sit here in rain, thunder and lightning until she learned the whole truth.

"Henrik, please, tell her the truth. I want it to come from you because then maybe I will understand too why you left us. And maybe we will get some knowledge of why you never called, wrote or gave a damn shit about us! Until now, when you want something from us."

The first raindrops began to fall, and streaks of lightning appeared across the early morning sky. Henrik sat down next to Crystal and waived Ivy back to join them.

"Come here, Ivy, please. I don't know if I will ever be able to make up for the past. But before I even start trying to be a father to you, to be worth it, I have to tell you more, both of you. The whole truth."

He sighed, looked up into the sky as a sharp lightning bolt crossed the sky, and deep thunder rumbled louder.

With tears running freely over his cheeks, he spoke. "I am a monster. I don't know how to phrase it any better. And I'm asking for forgiveness, even though I probably will never forgive myself for what I've done."

He told them openly about how he pushed Julie mercilessly to her limits to become the best and how he had betrayed not only his wife but also the Golf Association, their sponsors, fans and friends. He admitted to having written flattering fan letters to psych up Julie and letters full of hate to Ivy to discourage her.

Crystal and Ivy listened, speechless. Shattered, they watched this poignant scene as if it were a bad dream. Henrik Ferguson gave a full confession about how he approached and pressured —even blackmailed—Harry Butcher to promote Julie wherever he could to their benefit. He continued, coming close to a mental breakdown as he finally admitted to the craven attack on Ivy's life.

Not able to look them in the eyes anymore, his face collapsed into his hands, hysterically sobbing.

"I'm sorry, I really am. I'm so terribly sorry. Ivy, please, can you ever forgive me?"

Ivy looked sharply at him.

"This is unbelievable. I don't know what to say."

"I'm going to talk to the police, today, I promise. I'll turn myself in."

"Henrik, how in the world could you—"

"Crystal, I'm so sorry."

Henrik Ferguson turned to Ivy and continued. "Now that you know the truth, I feel a huge burden lifted from my shoulders. I can clearly see what I've done wrong. But most of all, I see and feel now how much I care about you. How much I admire your strength, and how much I always respected you as a golfer. You are the best golfer in the world."

Ivy stood up and looked toward the horizon, the thunderstorm had rolled by, and the rain had stopped. Soon, the rising sun would triumph over the scattered clouds, and Christ the Redeemer would watch over a new day.

"I'm totally wiped out. Far too much has happened today. I mean, out of the blue, I have a sister, then my real father pops up, and if this weren't enough, he's behind the criminal madman who tried to kill me. How weird is that?"

"Ivy, I'm so terribly sorry."

"Henrik, you're a piece of crap!" Crystal intervened, disgusted.

Ivy took a deep breath and stood straight.

"I cannot forgive you. But I've suffered enough. I cannot change what happened, and I cannot bring Jason back to life. But I can shape the future, and the first thing I'll do is get ready for the transplant. Julie's life is at stake here—I mean, she's my sister, and I'm not letting her down!"

She sighed and turned to her mom, who smiled at her and nodded.

"Will you do this for Julie?" Henrik lifted his head, his watery eyes met hers.

"Yes, I will."

And to Crystal's biggest surprise, Ivy walked over to her father, bent down and gently touched his hair. She kissed him on his forehead—and there was only love and salvation.

Crystal uttered a deep sigh of relief.

She was intensely dismayed over the malicious methods Henrik Ferguson had used to lure people under his influence, but she also knew that the truth could always be a new beginning. Over time, they would work it out.

And then she escorted her daughter back to the elevator.

"You idiot, what the heck's going on in your tiny mind?"

All of a sudden, Harry Butcher was towered in front of him, kicking him hard with his boot toe. As he looked up, Henrik could see that Harry wasn't alone. Some dirty runt was standing next to him, like a bullterrier waiting for his master's command.

I'd better face them standing, he thought, and got up.

"Harry, listen, Ivy's my daughter, and she's the only hope for Julie. I had to tell her the truth in order for her to go through with her donation. You've to understand this. It's good for you too—you must have a vested interest in Julie's recovery to top form."

"What are you saying? That's nonsense—Julie will never play professional golf again. And for me—hah!—this whole story is over. There won't be one sponsor left on the planet to take Julie under contract, and as a matter of fact, the same holds true for Ivy if she goes through with this donation!" His face was red hot.

"That's your fault. And now you're saying you're going to the police and talk. I don't think my boss likes to hear that, and neither do I, my friend."

Harry snapped his fingers and the goon came closer, punching Henrik, first slightly, then harder. He knew he had no chance against both of them, so he tried to move slowly back inside towards the elevator. Suddenly, he felt a strong push from behind, he stumbled and was pushed again, harder, and closer to the rim.

"Harry, you wouldn't kill me, would you?" he said, before he went over the edge.

❧

Two hours later Crystal, Brad and Laura sat in front of the OR. A few minutes earlier, Ivy had been rolled in, and they had time for words of quick encouragement. Soon she would be under anesthesia for at least a couple of hours.

"Anybody care for some coffee?" Laura asked as she got up from the white plastic chair. Everything seemed very sterile, bright white and clean in this waiting area.

"Yes dear, I will take one. Straight black, please. Do you need change?" Brad said and offered her a couple of bills.

"I've got some, but I never reject money. It's not good business." She smiled and looked over to a silent and distant Crystal and decided to pick up a coffee for her also.

She pocketed the change and pressed the automatic door opener. As the door opened, she ran right into Inspector Corelli.

"Oops! Good morning Inspector, I'm getting coffee, do you want one?"

"Morning, I'd love one, but I need to speak with you for a moment."

He desperately needed coffee, since he had been called in at 7:00 a.m. this morning. However, he'd rather get the news out earlier than later.

"This sounds serious, Inspector. Did you arrest the kidnapper?"

Brad walked up and stood behind Laura in support. One look at her was enough to tell him that she was about to have another attack and could pass out.

At first, he didn't believe her about her visions, but he was beginning to realize that, somehow, her remote viewings were real. Over the last couple of days, being so close with her, he realized now that she was almost constantly tangled between the here and now and something beyond.

Brad resolved to himself that, as soon as they were safely back in Naples, he would urge her to undergo tests with a specialist, but for now, he was curious to hear what the Inspector had to say.

"Yes, sir, I'm afraid so. In the early morning hours we found Henrik Ferguson dead in front of the hospital."

"No! That's not possible," Crystal yelped, "he can't be dead, not now."

All her life, she had wished the worst for him, but with Julie and Ivy in surgery right now, she needed him more than ever. She needed him to be there for his daughters, and she needed him for Ivy, to get her to know her father.

"I'm sorry, ma'am?"

"Crystal Brooks, Ivy's mother," Brad replied shortly. Shocked, he held both women in his arms.

"Are you really sure it's him?"

"Well, we've got his papers, he carried them in his jacket. But of course we need somebody who knew him personally to identify him in the morgue. I was hoping to find Harry Butcher here, who was a close acquaintance of him, so I was told."

"How did he die?"

Brad sounded concerned.

"Apparently it was a suicide. He jumped from the roof."

Inspector Corelli was uneasy with how much information he could release to them, because the circumstances of Mr. Ferguson's death weren't clear yet.

They'd found evidence of several people being at the rooftop this morning. He came here to check their alibis and questioned them about how and when they last saw him.

"I can do it. I can identify him." Crystal got up and wiped her face with a tissue. "He is Ivy's father, and I have to know if it's truly him before Ivy . . . before Ivy and Julie wake up. Laura, will you come with me?"

"Of course I'll come with you." Laura looked at Brad, who nodded in agreement.

"Inspector, let's go. I need to be back when my daughter awakes. And Brad, please could you go back to the hotel and see if you can find Harry Butcher? I know this man, he is mean and I think he is capable of anything. Inspector, maybe one of your men should join him."

She held Laura's hand and pushed through the door. She wasn't at all convinced that this was a suicide. Sure, Henrik was in a bad state when they left him this morning, but they'd all been hopeful that it would come to a good end.

And she wouldn't have said anything about Harry Butcher if it weren't for Laura, who had told her about her vision.

Bewildered and perplexed, she had quietly listened in as Laura described to her the scene at the roof and his fall.

She hadn't believed it then—over an hour ago—but she did now.

❧

The heat was burning brutally in the late afternoon hours as Crystal and Laura finally returned to the hotel. Exhausted to their bones, they entered the inviting air-conditioned lobby of the Grand Palace Hotel and moved straight to the cocktail bar. Piano music was playing in the background, and they selected their seats under a wide paddle fan.

"I'm always relieved when I'm back in safe haven, so to speak."

Laura made herself comfortable in one of the lounge chairs and enjoyed their luxurious, elegant and most convenient environment. The atmosphere was debonair and charming, money was old here and only visible to those who took a closer look at jewelry and watches, shoes and dresses, hairstyles and body language.

This was a world Laura was more acquainted with than Crystal.

"James and I used to travel a lot, mostly on business, but we always enjoyed a couple of extra days if the location was worth it."

Crystal smiled at Laura, knowing they came from different worlds. "What a day. My head is still spinning. The flight, than Henrik's confession, his death and, above all, Ivy's surgery."

She sank into the chair next to Laura and ordered a double espresso and a brandy. Laura topped the order with a large bottle of mineral water and selected a dry Chardonnay for herself.

"Crystal, Henrik is dead, and that's a pity. But you did great in the morgue. With your testimony, it will not be easy for Harry Butcher to justify his actions, and he'll eventually have to bear the consequences. The police are looking for him, and I'm sure they'll find him soon."

She thanked the waitress and took a sip of her cold mineral

water.

"Best of all, Ivy is well and, so far, the transplant was a success on both sides. The doctor said he expects Julie to awaken soon. Isn't that great news? Finally, this nightmare will come to an end."

"Laura, I'm so grateful to you. What would I have done without you today? And yes, Ivy and Julie will be well, I can feel it. Here, I just got this text message from Roger. He's coming down as well, and he'll be here in the morning." She texted him back—*I love you!*

❧

"I just wonder where Eileen's gone to, I haven't seen her all day. Oh—speak of the devil!"

Crystal waved with both hands over to the blonde sitting in the deep-seated sofa at the other end of the lounge. Before she could shout out loud, Laura touched Crystal's knee and hissed, "What is *she* doing here? And isn't that Brad, sitting next to her?"

"Hey, yes, you're right, that's him. It looks like they're back together. Let's go tell them the good news. We'll have dinner together, the four of us. "

Crystal did not notice the dramatic color change in Laura's face, and of course, she did not know about Laura and Brad at all, she was so excited to see her brother, and especially in a romantic setting, with his ex-girlfriend.

"Crystal, why don't you go over there and join them for dinner. I'm really tired. The last couple of days were tough on me, and I'm thinking of flying back home tomorrow."

Laura stood up.

"You know, I can't deny the fact anymore that I lost my family, and I can't delay my new start any longer. I've had a good distraction, but this is not my story."

Trying to hold back her tears, she stared over to Brad.

"I finally feel like I'm ready for my new life. And my brokerage account is already waiting for me."

She was more talking to herself than to Crystal, and tears were welling up fast in her eyes as she watched Brad kiss Eileen on the cheek.

She quickly looked down at her ring, trying to hide it from Crystal, but she wouldn't see the difference from the ring she had been wearing at Thanksgiving anyway.

However, she realized that she was just one more romantic encounter for Brad to make Eileen jealous enough to follow him to Rio.

Not her story.

She'd lost her personal history two weeks ago. And now it was time to start over. She hugged Crystal goodbye and crossed the lobby towards the elevators.

Brad noticed Laura walking quickly across the lobby. He shot up and jogged over to catch up with her, "Laura, hey, wait for me!"

But the elevator doors closed behind her, and he had no choice but to wait for the next one.

❧

Crystal hollered, "Brad, let her go, she said she's really tired and needs some rest. Give her some time. And I have very good news—the surgery went very well. Ivy is already awake and she is laughing and making jokes."

Crystal was excited. "Her only concern was that she may not be eligible to play at the Olympics because she lost a whole year. However, there is a slight chance that the Olympic committee will allow her to compete in a short shoot out to regain one of the top positions."

Since Brad still stood at the elevator, she got up and walked over to him.

"Oh my God, I'm so happy for you and Eileen—let's have dinner together. I asked Laura too, but she said she was flying home tomorrow. I think she's right, she has to go on with her own life and go out on her own for a while."

"What are you talking about—me and Eileen?" He pushed her softly but determinedly back, still waiting for the next elevator as Eileen joined them. She took Brad's other arm.

"Darling, I think it's a wonderful idea, let's celebrate Ivy's proud exploit."

"Ladies, I am terribly sorry to disappoint you, but I cannot join you for dinner. Please feel free to celebrate, and put the check on my account."

He then disappeared into the now-open elevator and pressed the button to close the doors before he selected the floor. Shaken, he paced the floor, hoping he could prevent any more damage to his relationship with Laura and that she would still trust his word.

NINETEEN

A white stretch limousine waited outside as they stepped out on the red carpet, walking hand in hand. Laura was so beautiful.

Her smoldering purple dress billowed at her waist and draped in folds down to her slim shins while pointy pumps in a slightly varying shade of amethyst adorned her feet.

She wore her golden blond hair loose and wavy, letting the whole length of it tumble down her back. Her eyes bore the mark of black liner and dark shadow while her cheeks blushed with rouge and her lips hinted of neutral lip gloss.

He looked delightfully handsome too, but he never took his eyes off his young lady. Heads turned as they stepped into the limo.

Everybody could tell that they were in love.

Only two hours ago, she was lying in her bed, screaming and punching her pillow and wishing Eileen to hell—no, not Eileen, Brad—for using her weakness, her vulnerably and her trust to gain a couple of hours of extra fun.

But then he had knocked at her door. Of course, she didn't

open it, why would she?

But he kept knocking until she realized he would not stop. He was a man with ambition, unlike James, who'd always chosen the most convenient way.

She finally opened the door and let him in, expecting another load of teddy bears, balloons, cakes and champagne.

But not this time.

He walked in, looking pale and sad, and sat down. Without even trying to touch her, he started talking. For the first time ever, he really let his guard down, and spoke until all was said.

He explained how he had been involved with Eileen after his wife's death, how he'd broken it off after only a couple of months, leaving her sad and venomous.

She'd always had a way of making him feel guilty about it, and he wanted to clear the air. When he saw her this afternoon, he thought it would be the right time to resolve their issues between them, totally unaware of her still-intensive feelings for him.

Laura was dazzled. He dazzled her. He wasn't just sexy, smart and rich. He was also handsome and caring. And so different from James—right here, she fell in love with him again.

And then he started talking about Laura's relationship with James. Brad told her that he couldn't get her out of his mind from the moment he saw her walking through the door to James' place. How he knew back then that she was the one. And how he had to keep it a secret since both of them were not free.

Then he told her about the recent letter from James.

Up to this point, she had let him talk without interrupting, but now, she demanded to see the letter right away. He pulled it right out of his jacket and gave it to her. He'd carried the letter with him all that time, waiting for the right moment.

After she had read it, she leaned back and let out a low, liberating laugh.

"I'm free. Free for you—and I feel awesome about it."

She reached out her hands for him. "I love you, Brad, let's forget about the past. Let's move on, and if you still want me, I'm here for you."

"Oh, Laura, darling, I want you with all of my heart!"

He took her hands and kissed her all over.

"Will you marry me?"

"Yes, I will!"

"I love you! Let's celebrate tonight, let's have a night out in Rio, a wonderful, magnificent night. With dinner at a fine old-world restaurant, samba dancing 'til morning, and then I'll take you home—back to our home in Naples!"

They didn't quite dance the whole night, since at one point they were eager to get back to the Grand Palace Hotel, where they continued their celebration under the silky sheets.

Bright, warm sunlight woke her, and although she was still tired, Laura untangled herself from Brad's arms and got up. She gazed back at him and felt butterflies fluttering around in her stomach.

He looked like an angel, peaceful and so innocent, yet omnipotent and powerful. When she was close to him, when he embraced her, she felt one with him, one with all.

Was this love? Pure love? She'd never felt it before, certainly not with James.

Silently, she tiptoed into the bathroom and started her morning routine. Today was the first day of her new life, and she prepared a mental list of things she would do differently and with more care, more meaning, in the future.

Life had given her a second chance, and she felt full gratitude for it.

✌

She thought about her list again as she sat with Julie and Ivy in their hospital room.

Life gave them a second chance, too.

Julie had awoken in the early-morning hours and was in good condition. The news about her father had given her a slight setback, which was minimized by heavy medication. Still, it hurt.

Roger had joined Crystal in the hospital, and he'd insisted on telling Julie the truth, and only the truth, immediately. Tears flowed freely, but it seemed that a heavy burden had been lifted off her shoulders.

At that point, Dustin stepped in, took Julie's hands, and officially announced their engagement and his resolve to take care of her for the rest of his life. The touching moment affected everyone in the room.

Julie tried to rise up to kiss him but groaned in pain and slid back into her pillow. He bent over and gave her a long, intimate kiss.

They look so happy together, Laura thought.

All that time, Julie held on tightly to Ivy's hand, not letting her sister go. And now, she beamed over at her.

"You saved my life. How can I ever thank you for this? And of course, I'll withdraw my qualification for the Olympics so you can play. You're the better player of the two of us, anyway," Julie mumbled, still a little drugged and dizzy.

"Oh Julie, it wasn't your fault, none of this was. And I've gotten an older sister, which is so great. Do you know how much I wished to have an older sister while I was growing up? I always felt as if you were part of my life, and now you are, and you even have a part of me—take good care of it!"

Ivy laughed. She felt great. Besides the small surgical wound, she felt as if the whole ordeal had left no lasting injury.

"And don't worry about the Olympics."

With her free hand, she held up a piece of paper, a fax print. "This arrived about an hour ago, from Lausanne, Switzerland. It's from the International Golf Federation, saying that the top sixty world-ranked players will be eligible for the Games, regardless of the number of players from a given country. So we're both in! We'll compete at the 2016 Olympics, here in Rio de Janeiro. Isn't that wonderful?"

Ivy squeezed Julie's hand and beamed.

Laura walked over to the girls and touched them slightly on their shoulders, "Ivy, Julie, I'm so happy for you both, and Brad is, too."

She looked back at him, smiling.

"We have to go, our plane is waiting. But we'll see each other soon, at the latest at our wedding on Christmas Day. You will look beautiful together as my bridesmaids." With a twinkle in her eye, she continued, "And then, in January, after our honeymoon, I'll coach you both to become medal winners!"

She kissed them goodbye, turned around and took Brad's outstretched hand.

❧

He poured two flutes of champagne and put the Dom Pérignon back into the ice cooler before handing her the glass.

"To us!"

He clinked his glass to hers. A little off-balance, she took a sip and sat hurriedly down. The turbulence at their cruising altitude increased slightly.

The cockpit door opened and the copilot appeared.

"Sir, do you have a minute?"

"What is it?"

"It's rather urgent. We have a direct call from Washington D.C."

"Good, I take it in the private room."

Laura looked up and noticed with surprise the change in his face.

"I am sorry, darling, but I have to take this phone call. It won't be long. Perhaps it is better if you sit down and buckle up in this turbulence."

He put his glass down on the table and disappeared in the small master bedroom at the front of the plane.

"Coleman here, three—zero—zero—five—eight—seven."

He listened carefully to the voice on the other end.

"Yes, I understand. I took the Boeing, and I am on my way back to the States."

He glanced out of the window.

"That is fine," he said, "We just left Venezuela and are entering the Caribbean Sea. Shortly, we should be flying over Aruba."

The *Fasten Your Seatbelt* light flashed as the private jet started shaking as it passed a group of dark clouds.

"And by the way, I want no more turbulent weather conditions for the remainder of my flight—over and out."

EPILOGUE

Julie Ferguson married Dustin Cooper, and a year later, they became proud parents of twin baby girls. She gave up professional golf but managed and coached her sister, Ivy.

Ivy Brooks made a very successful comeback and won gold for the USA at the 2016 Olympic Games in Rio de Janeiro.

Harry Butcher planned to leave the country and nothing was heard of him again. His escape route on a maritime freighter was meticulously arranged by one Manuel Gustavo Rodrigues, by recommendation from a high profile contact in Switzerland.

Laura and Brad are happily married. Laura founded The Research Institute of Clairvoyance (RIC), while Brad decided at the last minute to enter the presidential election campaign for the 2016 U.S. presidency. He became the first independent President of the United States of America.

Weather control is now widely accepted, even though some countries, including Germany and France, have strict limitations in place to minimize certain unwanted spatio-temporal side effects.

ABOUT THE AUTHOR

Emma Gordon, PhD, has had a passion for writing since her childhood. She has published several newsletters, short stories and scientific research papers.

She lives with her family in Naples, FL.

Coming soon:

SEA CREST

by Emma Gordon

This new page-turner by Emma Gordon is a romance murder mystery set in upscale California.

Jill Forsythe, a young and successful private hedge fund manager based in Naples, Florida, returns to the West Coast to learn more about her late mother, a famous Hollywood actress.

After a life-changing event in the heat of the Mexican desert, a plethora of new dangers awaits her and Tucker, her beloved Golden Retriever, in beautiful Carmel Valley.

Determined to sort out the mysteries of the past and to make Sea Crest, a splendid mansion overlooking the rough cliffs of the Californian coast, her new home, Jill must first discover the dangerous secrets that Sea Crest holds.

Uncertain whom she can trust, she turns to Tom Neuheuser, a stranded wealthy Austrian, who always seems to be there for her.

Yet the growing romance between them might turn out to be a costly mistake. Jill ignores the threats and warning signs, desperate to find out the truth about her mother's death.

A dangerous move—with her beloved Tucker gone, a dead body found on her grounds, and herself named a prime murder suspect, more shocking news is revealed.

Enjoy your free preview of

SEA CREST

by Emma Gordon

Big Sur, Central California

Jill could hear the roaring sound of the ocean as her red Porsche approached the cliffs of Big Sur. It was a chilly mid-August morning, and the sun brushed the splendid landscape with a warm golden tone. The air was filled with fresh ocean fragrance.

After riding for a couple of hours through the glorious ocean cliffs, charming villages and moments of joyful expectations, Jill made a quick stop to put down the top and take a deep breath of fresh cool air.

This is gorgeous, she thought. It was invigorating to feel the cold wind while she continued her journey. After years of dreaming about moving back to California, now it seemed her dream might be about to come true—even though a little different from what she'd envisioned.

Having come a long way from Naples, Florida, where she and Peter had lived for the last seven years, Jill was about to arrive on the West Coast for good. Her final destination was Carmel, south of San Francisco. There was no rush—she had enough time to enjoy the last leg of her road trip, so as she passed a sign pointing to a State Park, she decided to take a break.

Coastal morning fog filled the air as she stopped her car in the parking lot. She let Tucker, her Golden Retriever, out and walked over to the visitor center, longing for a fresh cup of coffee.

"Good morning! How are ya?" a deep voice greeted her as she entered the store. Jill spotted a heavy bearded man in his mid-fifties in ranger uniform and a white Stetson who was filling a coffee maker with fresh beans. The store was neat and clean, and at this early morning hour, the inviting smell of French roast and the crackling wood in the huge fireplace transformed the place into a cozy hideout.

"I'm fine, how are you?" Jill answered, beginning to relax after the long night drive. She had stayed a couple of days in San Diego and wanted to spend another night there but a bad dream had left her restless and eager to move on. This recurring dream had been haunting her since she was a little child. While she is asleep in her baby crib, a woman, dressed elegantly in a small black cocktail dress, bends over her and kisses her forehead. Was it a memory? Who was it? Was it her mother saying good-bye? She would never find out. Would never know. The only person who could tell the truth was dead. Died one month ago. She had thought her whole life that her mother had died while giving birth to her, but since yesterday, everything had changed.

"Nice car you've got there! How fast can it go?"

"Faster than allowed by law, but today, I really want to enjoy the beautiful scenic drive."

Her powerful Porsche 911 Turbo Cabriolet came fully loaded with a 3.8 liter twin turbo six-cylinder engine producing 540 hp. Jill loved that car—it was like a companion who shared some of the most memorable moments of her life.

After the first sip of freshly brewed coffee, she had felt

comfortable and refreshed. It was like coming home, and she loved it. She looked at Tucker and smiled. He just had come back to her after he had sniffed through the whole store and was now ready to continue his inspection outside.

"Looks like you gotta go, Ma'am?"

"Yes, Tucker seems to be ready to leave. See you!"

"Peace!"

Jill finished her coffee and stepped outside. She took a deep breath of fresh air and a final look over the stunning cliffs. Did she just see a gray whale migrating? Sometimes, they could be spotted throughout the summer months. It reminded her of San Diego, where she grew up. How long ago was it? She wondered while walking back to her car. Were all her happy childhood memories built on lies? Thoughtful, she went to her car and looked for Tucker.

"Tucker, where are you? We need to get going!"

Then she saw him rushing down the cliffs chasing a small cottontail.

"Tucker, hey, not now! Come here!"

But it was already too late. He detected prey and off he went—deep in the scrubs. Jill waited, since usually, Tucker would come back quickly, and he never caught anything anyway, especially not here in this thick undergrowth.

Then she heard his whimper. She was concerned he might have fallen down, after all, the cliffs were steep and unstable.

She followed his path. "Tucker, stay where you are, I'm coming." She was literally jumping downhill through scrubs and rocks, since there was no trail.

"Ouch!" She lost her balance, and after a small slide down, she landed next to a Golden Retriever who was happy to see her and started licking her face.

"So, what should we do now, old boy?" she asked him.

"I can't carry you up those rocks, you're too heavy. So, let's see if we can find a path down here that leads back to the parking area."

Jill got up and brushed off the dirt. Luckily, she had nothing more than a few scratches and the dog seemed fine too. She looked up but couldn't see anything. Her eyes were dazzled by the first rays of sunshine streaming through the mountain peaks. Was there a person standing on top of the hill? Jill used her hands to block the sun to see more clearly.

"Hello sir? Please, can you lend us a hand? We're down here," she shouted, but the man was already gone.

Half blinded by the sun, as Jill turned back to Tucker, a memory flashed through her mind. Bright sunshine, glazing heat over the Mexican desert. Peter was there. Yes. Shouting at her. What did he say? She couldn't remember.

A slight touch on her left shoulder made her scream. Tucker barked aggressively, and she felt a panic attack coming on.

"Take my hand. Let me help you up!"

"Peter? Is that you?"

"Here, take my hand!"

"No! No, please don't. Hold me, don't let go!" Jill was in shock. She grabbed that hand, not knowing who it belonged to. Cold pearls of sweat appeared on her forehead, and her face was pale as snow.

"Ma'am, please calm down. It's all right—I have you tight. Just two more steps and you are on a safe trail. Here, over this rock.

All right!" He let her go.

Jill was still shaking from her panic reaction. Not now, she thought, stay calm! Jill felt Tucker close to her, his warm coat pressed against her body. He was still barking, but not so angry anymore.

She looked around to thank the man. But there was nobody. Strange. Where was he? Just gone? Did she dream all this? Was it real? Tucker's barking was. Maybe he vanished once they were on safe ground because he was afraid that her screaming would attract people who might draw the wrong conclusion.

"Oh well, we're okay, aren't we, Tucker?" A short bow-wow confirmed it. "All right then, let's go up to the car and get out of here!"

She dusted the dirt off her clothes and removed a couple of thistles from Tucker's paws before they returned to the parking lot. She was happy to see her Porsche Turbo still parked there, now surrounded by other cars, mostly SUVs belonging to early hikers.

She let Tucker jump in the back and got into the driver seat. Once she was rolling, the solid sound of the powerful engine helped calm her mind. Jill quickly checked the rear view mirror and saw a manila envelope on the back seat. "What the heck?" she said aloud while merging onto Highway 1—but she decided to ignore it for now.

PUBLISHED BY

The Old Bookstore

Copyright © 2015 Emma Gordon.
All rights reserved.

www.ingramcontent.com/pod-product-compliance
Lightning Source LLC
Chambersburg PA
CBHW031248170626
46807CB00001B/46